THE PUNISHINGS

THE PUNISHINGS

A NOVEL

Quillamaio Press

H.R. BELLICOSA

2021 Quillamaio Press paperback edition

Library of Congress Control Number: 2021919899

ISBN 979-8-9850293-1-4

Book design by Jessika Hazelton, The Troy Book Makers, Troy, NY

To Bryce…for showing me how motherhood can knock you down, leave you breathless, absolutely annihilate you.

I

THE FIRST SWISH OF THE WHIP whistles through the silence. I'm not ready for it, even though I know it's coming. Neither is the girl. Her torso arcs as the switch slashes across her creamy back, tattooing her in an instant with a long, jagged gash, the first of what will become a tangled latticework of scars. Her body, stunned for a moment, freezes. Then a rivulet of blood seeps from the wound and trickles down her skin, weeping. Wrapped in the all-consuming agony of that one blow, she forgets to brace for the next one, and when it comes, crisscrossing a second leaking wound over the first, her toes, suspended an inch off the ground, flex and twitch. There will be twenty-eight more, I know, subconsciously counting the snapping lashes. Will there be enough flesh left? Her back is so small.

Her wrists hang from the top of the wooden tripod; the Trinity, as they like to call it. Bound together, her hands dangle from a small hook near the top of the pole. No doubt it's meant to look like a shepherd's hook. The girl's feet swing as the snarling whip strikes her for the third time. A noise escapes then, the first she utters. Keening, I think one might say.

The crowd, riled and rabid mere moments before, stands in silence, savoring the cracks that smack across her body. Number four. Number five. I will the girl to faint.

Her white dress, the top half bunched down at her waist, is already stained with so much blood. Oh, how they had relished tearing it from her, making sure everyone in the crowd got a long look at her breasts so that her Punishment began laden with hot shame. I cannot see her face but I know she's somewhere beyond crying, her features contorted with the disbelief of such a shocking sensation.

Her back is a mass of shredded ribbons. She strains and drips and spills over. Number ten tears at her, or is it eleven? She writhes and twists, her entire body laboring, though no birth will follow.

Her head tips forward with the next lash and her body stills. Don't get the bucket, I beg inside my own head. Please.

They get the bucket.

She sputters as cold water sloshes over her. Someone in the crowd laughs but everyone else is silent, hypnotized by the swaying, battered girl. I look for Emilie but don't see her. Maybe she's behind me but I don't turn around. A strange sort of paralysis has taken hold of me.

Only a few minutes have passed since the Punishment began, but the shadows on the ground already look longer. The sky is filled with silver-bellied clouds and the air is hazy with diffused light. On the Trinity, blood runs down the girl's spine like rain streaming down a window.

One of the Officers reaches up and cuts her loose with a switch of his blade. As her bindings fall from the top of the tripod, her dress slips from her narrow hips and falls to the ground the moment before she does. Crumpled at the base of the Trinity, curled into herself, the girl looks younger than her fourteen years.

Someone, her mother perhaps, is allowed to collect her, and as she is placed face down onto a stretcher an Officer tosses the bloodied dress over her naked body. This is not done to cover her, but as one last scarlet marking of her transgression.

The righteous and riotous crowd erupts. They cross themselves and pump their fists in the air. Flags unfurl; the red and black of the Southerly State flapping under pregnant gunmetal clouds. Female voices, from the back, begin to sing a hymn. Of course they do. Divine and conquer, I think to myself.

A word rumbles from deeper, angrier throats, until it envelops and engulfs the hymn completely. The angel voices singing God's word abandon their melody and take up the cry as well. It rolls over the crowd, that one word, the word the girl is forever branded with: *Sanguidam. Sanguidam. Sanguidam.*

I want to turn and run, but I know better than to move just yet. I put down my head and stare at my black boots. Anyone watching me might think I'm praying for the girl's soul, or maybe my own. There's a squeeze on my arm. Emilie.

We stand there a long time. Her hand grips the flesh of my arm. When a new hymn rises up against the rallying cry, I finally look at her. She nods and we turn around to push through the crowd, but a bullish man stands in our path. I've seen the mocking leer on his face many times; they all look the same.

I know what he wants. Emilie's hand tightens around my arm but I shake her off. I look up at the flag in his hand, the bold colors of the Southerly State hanging over me. I catch a furtive glimpse of the bulge under his jacket and recognize the outline of his gun. I touch my right hand to my heart and make the sign of the cross. I raise my three middle fingers to my lips and kiss them, then touch the tip of the flag. Emilie does the same.

The man nods at us, pleased with our allegiance. He touches his own heart and crosses himself. I bow my head, trying to look as demure as possible, and sidestep around him as he raises his three fingers. Emilie's hand returns to my arm, holding me tighter than before.

We walk out of the square, our steps quickening as we near the outer fringe of the crowd. Our boots tap the concrete in perfect synchronization.

"Was she yours?" Emilie whispers, not daring to look at me.

"No. I don't know her," I answer, trying to keep my lips still.

But they are all mine in a way. She might as well have been under my care.

We don't speak another word on the street. Our footsteps grow louder as we walk farther from the square. I concentrate on each echoing step, but they aren't loud enough to drown out the dying strains of the *Sanguidam* chant that flicker in the bruised light of the evening, following us all the way home.

II

I SHOULDN'T HAVE GONE to the Punishment last night, but something pulled me there, just as it always does. It's as if the rope from the Trinity is tethered to me somehow, drawing me into Place d'Armes Square. Maybe I still barely believe that people are capable of such brutality, until I am reminded with every lash of the whip and every spreading stain of blood.

I used to love the square, surrounded on all sides by faded pastel two-story homes, their curling wrought iron balcony gates swirled through with rust. There was an ornate romanticism about the place. It used to be that if you stopped and listened, you could almost hear a rush of water pouring from the crusted nozzle of the faux marble fountain. If you strained your ear, you could just catch a spectral blue note crying out from an irreverent saxophone, the echo wrapping around the branches of perfumed magnolia trees. But that was before the Trinity was erected, placed only a few yards from the crumbling fountain. The little white cherubs that flutter over its large scalloped basin, streaked with age and grime, are now forced to bear witness to the Punishments along with the rest of us. The square has become a gathering place for the worst kind of convergence.

On my way to work this morning, instead of cutting through it, I skirt around the Place d'Armes. This adds a few minutes to my two mile walk, but I don't want to see the wooden tripod. They used to take it down immediately after a Punishment, but lately it has become a permanent fixture in the square. Even without seeing it, I feel it, waiting ever patiently like the crocodile waits in its swamp.

Xavier Orphanage is two miles from my house, but the early March morning is clean and clear and so I don't mind the walk. I dread the coming months though, knowing I will be slogging through sticky humidity, breathing in decaying leaves from the bayou and swatting hungry mosquitos from my skin. But this morning the only thing hanging in the air is a faint scent emanating from the cypresses, oddly reminiscent of sage. It's early, just after six, and the streets are wonderfully quiet.

The Orphanage clings to the vestiges of the university it once was. Many universities have closed, after years of dwindling enrollment. Education has not been valued here for quite some time. Brambles of choking ivy climb the brick façade and a white clock tower stands squat atop the main building, its hands moss-covered and rusted in place. The smaller buildings that once made up the center for higher learning are in a state of decrepitude now, and I stumble over fallen bricks and spreading tree roots as I make my way toward the entrance. I look down, making sure there are no snakes sliding under the leaves near my feet. Breathless, at the top of the steps, I realize I'm almost running, anxious to find Emilie so we can talk about yesterday. I won't be able to snatch a private moment with her for hours, since our jobs will consume us both. Had I not been running late, I would have met up with her as we both made our way into work. A fitful night of sleep has taken its toll on me.

It's dim inside the old building, and other than the muffled rustling of workers' skirts echoing in the long corridor, it's silent. The bare walls, completely devoid of colorful drawings or bright paintings, give no indication that children live here. Art that does not depict religious scenes or imagery relating to the Southerly State is forbidden. I'm thankful there's no room in our budget for such things. I'd rather have the girls stare at empty walls.

I follow a thin ribbon of sunlight creeping along the faded stone floor and make my way to my assigned room. Rows of narrow beds litter the sterile space. The girls are just rising as I walk in. A few blocks away, there's an identical orphanage filled with boys, probably going through the same routine. You'd think we would converge once in a while and have a joint activity with the two orphanages, but that is not allowed. A few of the girls look over at me with languid eyes. It's easy to attribute their reaction to the early hour and usual teenage moodiness, but I know it's so much more than that. These girls are stateless, homeless, and parentless. The years have made them weary.

They file by me and I reach out to brush Kamon's arm. She turns to me and I catch a faint smile but she knows she cannot stop walking and so she follows the girl in front of her and I watch them walk down the hall toward the cafeteria. I have an hour to clean and make sure their beds are properly made before they return from breakfast. After that I will supervise them while they do their lessons, but I can't possibly give them the attention they need, and the lessons are uninspired and mostly religious in nature. We are all just going through the motions, the girls and I. And we all know it, too.

My ten years at Xavier have depleted and defeated me. I feel older and more tired than I should at thirty years old. I have long since stopped begging Rachel, the headmistress, to allow me to foster one of the children. I can't listen to her tell me one more time that the Southerly State wants to maintain complete control of orphans and mandates that they are raised in institutions. These girls, along with girls and boys all across the Southerly State, from impoverished southern cities to open plains, and from deserts to the Badlands, were fought for tirelessly when they were Unborns. But now that they are here, this is the substandard care they are given.

The girls look more alert when they return from breakfast and dutifully reach under their beds for their lesson books. There are nearly thirty girls in this one room, but some stand out more than others. There is Mishael, still small for her age, though she looks remarkably healthy considering the fact that she spent the first year of her life recovering from the cocaine addiction she was born with. Calah is slow in both speech and cognitive abilities, and we are certain she was born from an incestuous relationship. Serah was born with an arm missing, but she has adapted well and moves around so deftly you don't even notice the missing limb unless you're looking for it. She was brought to Xavier two days after her birth, her mother wanting nothing to do with her one-armed baby. I don't think Serah misses her absent limb, or ever gives it a thought. Her arm simply never formed and therefore was never a part of her. I sometimes think about her parents, who can't possibly have any idea of the sweetness they gave away. I know they must have some measure of kindness about them, since they gave a substantial donation to Xavier to ensure that Serah would be admitted here. Without that, she would have been placed in an institution for disabled and deformed children, which is also where they place all children of color.

And there's Kamon, her lanky frame stretching underneath her bed and pulling out a workbook titled *Creationism*. On the cover is a drawing of a man and woman picking strawberries from a bush. The man is turned slightly, smiling at a docile stegosaurus munching on the leaves. I want to rip it out of Kamon's hands the way my grandmother once ripped a booklet like that away from me. But I know I can't, not now, and it just feels like one more failure heaped onto a never-ending pile of my personal defeats at Xavier.

The name Kamon isn't on any birth certificate. I don't think it's written down anywhere. As far as the State is concerned, this girl, with all her intelligence and inquisitiveness and sensitive sensibilities, is labeled SC0708. It's a cataloguing system using birth dates and months and if provided, part of the last name of a male relative. In most cases, that information is hard to come by. If no male relative is known, the serial number is registered beginning with the letters SC, for State-Controlled. Of course, we can't go around calling girls things like SC0708 all day. The system might not care about these girls, but the people around them do. Somewhere along the line, it became an unwritten rule that the head of each orphanage can assign nicknames to the children. At Xavier, we address the girls by Biblical names. It was either that or names of flowers, and I'm guessing the headmistress who opened Xavier wasn't taking any chances. While these names are allowed to be used informally, they aren't recognized in an official capacity. When the orphans age out of the system at eighteen, they are allowed to legally register the name they've been called all their lives, along with the last name of Xavier. That surname is a potent reminder that they were raised by the State and not a family.

"Hey," I whisper, coming up behind Kamon. She's hunched over the booklet, her chin propped on her hand. She rolls her eyes in response, but I know it's directed at the book and not me, and I think that maybe there's a scant bit of hope that the Southerly State won't ruin them all. I see the ridges of her spine through her threadbare shirt and I know none of the girls are getting quite enough to eat, but I heard that Xavier is one of the better orphanages so I hate to think about what children in other institutions look like. I touch her shoulder and she continues to stare at the ridiculous pictures on the page, but I feel her relax a bit and so I linger by her side.

She's the one I would have taken, all those years ago. She's the one I fought for and begged to foster. I fell in love with her as soon as I started working here. It was the way she wrapped her little fingers around my hand when she was just a three-year-old, her eyes wide with a curiosity that most of the orphans lacked and a vocabulary that belied her young age. There was an openness to her. It was as if she had been conceived by a miracle rather than a violent assault, born to a loving mother instead of a teenager ravaged by drugs and her abusive stepfather. How could Kamon have come from that? I felt that meant she needed to be given a better chance, and I truly believed I was meant to find her. But it was not allowed. It was vehemently not allowed. And so I have watched her grow up as another ward of the State. I have loved her as best as I can, but as I said, it is not enough. It is not enough for her, and it is not enough for me.

The girls do not have math or science lessons. There are only texts about Biblical verses today, an assignment in their Creationism booklets, and a fill-in-the-blank sheet about the Ten Commandments. I back away from Kamon and circle the room. How could a crowded room be so vacant? Vacant eyes, vacant stares. There is nothing but a collective hush in the vacuous space. The rooms with younger girls are just as silent. Children rarely cry here. They learn early on that their needs cannot be immediately met.

When Emilie and I meet for our half-hour lunch in an old office that serves as a makeshift breakroom, we aren't alone. Rachel, headmistress and our direct supervisor, is already there, spooning cold soup into her mouth, her bulky frame hunkered over her bowl. She is broad and wide, with dark blond hair pulled taut from her face in a bun. Everything about her is large except for her teeth. They look as though they haven't finished emerging from her gums, revealing a disturbing flash of pink when she peels her lips back in a smile, though that rarely ever happens anyway. Rachel is puritanical in mannerisms and speech, and that nature is enhanced with her white uniform and severe hairstyle. Her skirt pulls tight around spreading middle-aged hips and faint lines crease around her mouth like parentheses. She leads us in prayer before lunch each day, and I know she actually means the righteous words, unlike some of us who say them but do not feel them. She is a staunch believer in the rights of the Unborn, and I know it isn't just because she is safeguarding her job. On the day after a Punishment, we usually hear about how the girl was deserving of what befell her. That she got off easy, even. That what happened to her Unborn was a sin. I can't listen to it today, not again, not with the memory of the girl's crumpled body running through my head. She was just a year older than Kamon.

I hear myself prattle on about the girls in my room just to keep Rachel from spouting off about the Punishment. It works, though the effort is draining. Emilie, who has barely spoken, looks as defeated as I feel, even though she's five years younger than I and hasn't been at Xavier for nearly as long. But her assignment, caring for the babies, is even more draining than mine. Endless feedings and changings and staring into so many sets of unwanted eyes. There are stains of watered down formula on Emilie's starched uniform. The cloying scent of spit-up wafts off her clothing and her skin. Our half-hour always passes quickly but today I'm grateful for that. Rachel doesn't look up from her soup as I push back from the table. I meet Emilie's eyes and give her an imperceptible nod. Now it will be hours until we can finally speak in secrecy.

After they return from lunch the girls are allowed outside on this spring day, and my charges, most of them teenagers or just on the cusp of becoming one, don't play so much as they pair off and stroll around the grounds. I watch as Calah follows a brush-footed butterfly, its red stripes blurring as it flits by her again and again. She chases after it, blessedly cloaked in her own ignorance. No wonder she is usually the one easiest to smile.

Kamon comes up to me, catching me by surprise as her hand slips into my own. She hasn't done that in a long time. Her head tips until it leans against my shoulder.

"I wish you could stay tonight," she says, but I have to tilt my own head toward her to catch the words. She hasn't said that in a long while, either. She used to say it to me every day. Every single day, and some days I thought I would just violate my orders and scoop her up and take her home with me. It was tempting, until I reminded myself that I would be fired and then lose all contact with her for good. We were both stuck, and we still are. She understands that now, though of course, heartbreakingly, she did not understand until recently. I guess now we are both resigned to our relationship and all its limits.

"I know," I say, because that's what I always say. But her head feels heavier than usual today, and her hand grips my fingers, squeezing three times. I. Love. You. Our little signal. One squeeze for each word. I squeeze back four times in response. I. Love. You. Too. She sighs into my shoulder, and I don't know if it's some mild form of contentment or frustration. Her breath shudders at the end though, just for a beat, and I hear something else. Sadness. Or is it fear?

"It's a long time until night," I say. "Let's try to enjoy the afternoon, okay?"

Kamon lifts her head away from me and nods, though I'm sure she's swallowing words that she was moments from saying out loud. I want to ask her, to remind her that she can tell me anything, or ask me anything. But just then Calah trips, probably over a ruined chunk of building or an unruly vine, and she is wailing, her unabashed cry sounding more like that of a toddler than a girl of almost thirteen. I rush to console her, running my hands over her legs. I don't find any blood, but even still, she's slow to calm down. When I look back to where Kamon was standing a minute ago, she is gone, and I see the brush-foot floating among the fans of palmetto branches. Its wings, bearing the colors of the flag of the Southerly State, spread open in the warmth of the sun.

* * *

Kamon is sullen for the rest of the afternoon, but she gives me a hug that lingers for an extra beat as I say goodbye to the girls. Some of them give me a goodnight smile or squeeze. Calah wraps her arms around me and points to her scraped knees. As I do each evening, I tell them that I will see them in the morning. Only on Saturday night do I not utter that phrase, as I'm off duty most Sundays. While I need a respite from Xavier on those days, the girls never get one, and I'm glad now that we will all see one another tomorrow.

Emilie emerges from her room at the same time; Rachel runs her Institution on a well-choreographed schedule. The State, I'm sure, would be impressed. We fall in step together and push open the heavy front doors, nodding a greeting to two women who pass us on the steps, arriving for their night shift. It is another woman, one I only ever see in passing, who will tend to my girls at night. But does she know to shush Calah to sleep with murmured whispers so she isn't agitated? Does she chastise Mishael with the right amount of gentleness when she grows irritable and doesn't want to lie down? Will she brush Serah's hair as her only hand rests under her head? I know she won't squeeze Kamon's hand three times, but selfishly, I am glad of that.

In another minute we're on the street, the droning of the cicadas our only accompaniment. We have a mile or so to walk together, before Emilie veers off at the Place d'Armes and heads in one direction and I turn in another, toward the bayou.

"So what do you think?" Emilie whispers. "Doesn't it feel like the Punishments are increasing lately?"

"It doesn't just feel like it. They are."

"And it's like there's more…"

"Agitation."

"Yes. I can feel it."

I nod. The tension of late has been heavy, even more so than usual.

"But there's something else. This time, I heard the trial lasted only minutes." Emilie quickens her pace.

"Trial?" I snort. "There has never been a real trial, no matter the length."

"But they didn't even pretend this time," Emilie says. "No evidence. Just the word of one supposed witness against the girl." Emilie shudders and I can almost see the fear ripple through her. "This is never going to stop."

She's right. I know too well how young women and even younger girls fall pregnant through force and intimidation and brute male strength. The level of abuse is staggering. Men, angry with everything about their lives and situations, exert strength over creatures they believe are even more powerless than themselves. These men have near-complete immunity from their brutal actions. They stand in the crowd as their victims twist on the Trinity, bearing yet another abuse because, in desperation, they tried to cure themselves of what was inflicted upon them. They are punished for the Removal, yes, but they are also punished for simply being a temptation that could not be resisted.

"So they are basically done with fair trials now," Emilie says.

"Done with the pretense of them, I guess."

"You need to be careful," she says. "Please."

"I think the girl took care of things herself," I tell my friend. "Had she gotten assistance, nobody would likely have known. She probably would not have had any telling complications."

Our boots slap-tap the cracked pavement in sync. We pass the perimeter of Place d'Armes Square and I can sense the Trinity. Emilie stops walking and turns to me.

"Just be careful," she repeats. "Look at what's happening. It's getting worse. And you will not have it as easy as the girl did." She grasps my arm, turning me to her. "You…they will destroy you."

III

Alone in my creaky little house, or my grandmother's house, as I still think of it, I wait for Eliza Pritchard. The arrangements were made a week ago. I know she's walking through the darkened streets right now, her heart fluttering and leaden at the same time. I can feel her coming toward me. I didn't have much time to spare after getting home from Xavier. A few minutes to eat the leftover stew I made Sunday evening, the flakes of fish and chunks of onion floating in the tomato broth like little white lilies resting in a pond. I just have time for a shower. Then I sink down into the lumps of the couch and feel the streams of water from my wet hair run down my periwinkle buttoned shirt. I'm wearing my other uniform now.

I'm grateful that the rolling blackouts did not crest over my area tonight. Being fairly isolated and so close to the swamp, I'm one of the last ones to regain power, and the blackouts have increased lately. I snap on a light and resist the urge to turn on another one. Miles saunters over to me, happy that he has me home for the evening. According to him, his sole purpose is to nuzzle his nose inside my cupped hand and press his full weight against my legs. Miles is my safety and my family and friend. He barks and growls at anyone new, even the girls and young women who find their way to my door in the evenings, though he soon deems them acceptable and nuzzles into their hands as well. I let him lean into me now and give him a rubbing, watching as my fingers disappear into his coarse gray hair.

I wish my grandmother were here, but I always wish that, not just on a night like this one. I also wish, more than I like to admit, that the house she left me wasn't sitting right at the fringe of the bayou. She'd be surprised at how the water level has risen. The swamp inches ever closer to the house with every passing year. It emits heinous sounds at night, too: shrieks and croaks and hisses. I can sometimes hear the mud bubbling and gurgling around the mangroves, but maybe that's just my imagination. The sounds are less frightening than those made by man, my grandmother would chastise me, but sitting here listening to them all alone, I'm not so sure. Still, the cypress trees and threads of dangling Spanish moss provide a measure of privacy, and that is why I am still here. More than anything, I need privacy.

Eliza is late. I have no way to contact her, but I wouldn't do that even if I could. Miles looks up at me. He seems to know we are waiting for someone. I give him a satisfactory pat on his rump and cross the small room over to the bookshelf. My grandmother's books are on the shelves, wearing their innocuous jackets as a disguise. The pages inside are another story. They are filled with drawings and photographs of herbs and pressure points and archaic medical instruments. One book focuses on purgatives: pennyroyal, aloe, even turpentine. Another is filled with prints of advertisements from over 200 years ago. They tout things like, "Farrer's Catholic Pills," and "Madame Drunette's Lunar Pills." Things to cure 'womanly complaints'. One bottle, listing pennyroyal, tansy and birthwort as ingredients, displays a large label stating it may cause miscarriages, the 'warning' a clever guise, since it drew women to it for that exact purpose. There are pictures of bottles promising to "restore female regularity" or to "remove from the system every impurity." Genteel words surreptitiously promising to rid the body of an unwanted pregnancy. Other books list chemotherapy cocktails designed to kill multiplying cells. The drug misoprostol is mentioned again and again. These bits of information are useless to me, as I could never obtain such things here. The worst books describe arcane methods used by only the most desperate souls: a copper needle or spike, a controlled fall down the stairs, veterinary medicines.

A hundred years ago, people would have found the dated and antiquated pages nothing more than an interesting curiosity. Anyone who came across them back then would have shaken their head and marveled at how much society had advanced. But that was back when the United States was a huge country with one central government. That was before the Peaceable Separation, which left the Southerly State with jagged borders stretching from the narrow, sunken strip of land that used to be Florida up north to the territory of Virginia, and westward, encompassing the wide open Great Plains to the Rocky Mountain border. The misogynistic and authoritarian laws and decrees that have since come out of the Southerly State's Capital in Atlanta have made these old tomes modern once again, and even more secretive than when they were first printed. I remember my grandmother telling me how in the 1960's, women's rights activists studied and practiced and developed their own skills to safely rid women of unwanted pregnancies at a time when they could not legally do so. This was done to prevent bloody and ill-fated backstreet abortions, or self-induced ones. It was all very covert, of course, and rather than come out and actually ask where they might find a secret floating abortion clinic, a woman would call a protected phone number and ask for instructions on how to find 'Jane.'

That too, would have seemed antiquated a hundred years ago. But here we are now. Kissing flags and pledging sovereignty to the Bible and our Southerly State, those two things as intertwined as the snakes on the staff of Hermes. Now we whip young women in the streets for the removal of an Unborn, even if it was borne of a savage assault.

I don't have to pull a book from the shelf now to study how I will help Eliza, should she be able to break away tonight and make her way to me. I've done this often enough. Of course my exact method will depend on how long we have together. Usually, my time with a patient is too short, but I have my reasons for assisting them. And I know they need me. I think of the Trinity for just a moment, and hear Emilie's urgent warning from our walk home.

Suddenly Miles is on all fours as he hears Eliza's boots climb the three steps of my front porch. He growls until I shush him with a steady hand on his head, though his whole body is rigid as he stares at the front door. Once again, it's time for me to begin my other work. Moonlighting, one might say.

* * *

I have said a great deal already, but there is much more to tell. And yet I have not even spoken my name. I find it easier to be nearly anonymous. To trust almost nobody, to live quietly and plainly, to be a forgettable face. And yet, like the orphans, it's difficult to be utterly nameless. What if, for reasons that should be coming into focus quite clearly now, I refer to myself, quite simply, as Jane?

IV

Eliza Pritchard is breathless. I don't know if it's from the long walk or fear of the sheer enormity of what she is doing, but I offer her a steady hand. My other hand is busy with Miles' collar, struggling to keep his straining body beside my leg. He wants to smell this woman on our porch, and I know she can't deal with his nuzzling muzzle right now.

We do not know one another, Eliza and I, but of course we know of one another. Her visit has been arranged by a trusted party. That's how this all works. I see her staring at the flag jutting out from the rusted pole attached to a shingle beside my front door. She looks up at the two jagged black slashes splayed across the center of the flag like lightning bolts: two S's for Southerly State. They are nearly identical to the gashes that appeared on the Nazi SS flag, "but I'm sure that's entirely coincidental," my grandmother used to remark. She remembered things from her history books that were not covered in the books of my generation. The background of the Southerly State flag looks like the old Confederate flag, still revered around the State, with its red and blue colors and its smattering of stars. I'm sure Eliza is surprised to see the flag here, but of course I display one. I don't want to give anyone a reason to think I pledge anything less than undying fealty to our glorious Southerly State. She raises three trembling fingers to her mouth and goes through the motion of kissing them, but I notice that her fingertips never touch her lips. She raises them to the flag but they don't touch the material either. I do the same and then step back so she can come inside. Nobody is watching us, two women on the old porch of a ramshackle home on the fringe of the bayou, but it makes us both feel better anyway.

"I'm grateful your name come up, as I didn't know of anyone in the entire Parish," Eliza says to me in greeting. She glances at my sparse furnishings, but I imagine the place is palatial compared to her own home. I can still smell the fish stew and I'm sure she can as well. I should have saved her some. She sounds younger than the eighteen or nineteen years I peg her at. Her voice is one part Cajun and two parts poverty, like so many folks living in the territory of Louisiana.

"I reckon I need to explain myself," Eliza says, her fingers twisting the front of her skirt. "You see, ma'am, I had…" her voice catches and she stops for a moment, "I done had a situation happen to me."

She doesn't need to explain herself to me. That's not why we are here. This place is not a confessional, and I offer neither absolution nor judgement, but almost every woman who crosses my threshold is looking for the former and expecting the latter.

"You came to me for help," I say. "That's all I need to know. I'm glad you were directed here."

"It were Margaret who told me," she blurts out. I know it was Margaret, obviously, since she warned me Eliza would be coming, after clearing the day and time with me. Margaret was here for her own treatment once. That's how a situation like mine works. A chain of women, who have been in their own predicament, telling other women where to go for help. They only ever tell a soul who's in the same desperate, hopeless situation they were once in. That's my insurance policy, though I hate to think of it like that. No patient of mine would waggle a loose tongue: to do so would be as harmful as tying themselves to the Trinity in Place d'Armes Square.

"You have nothing to explain," I say. "Okay?"

She nods but her fingers keep twisting. Miles lays down at her feet, having decided that this young woman with her sweet-tea drawl poses no threat to either of us.

"Will your absence tonight be missed?" I ask.

"Not for a little while. My Mama knows where I'm at. Not where, exactly, but she knows what's doing. My Daddy thinks I'm meeting up with a friend."

"So, you can't stay the night." I say it as a statement of fact. I like to begin the administration of my remedy and then watch over the patient for a while if I can.

"No, I need to be back at my house soon." Her forehead folds into a crease. "Is that all right?"

"Yes, we'll make do. Come and sit with me and I'll explain everything and tell you what you can expect," I say. "Does that sound okay?"

She nods and sits on the couch, her eyes glancing over the books on the shelf across the room. She has no idea what's behind those covers. She doesn't know how they have helped so many women, and how they will help her.

I talk for a few minutes about the packet of herbs I will send her away with, explaining that ideally I would administer them here and watch over her for at least a few hours, but that's not possible tonight. Eliza slips off her black boot and rubs Miles' back with her stockinged foot as I talk. I worry that she isn't really listening to me, but I understand. She doesn't want to know *how* I'm going to help her. Relief has settled over her because I *will*.

I decide against pennyroyal. It can be too potent, poisoning the woman along with accomplishing its other deed. That's not something I can send her off with unmonitored. The same goes for birthwort, an herb my grandmother was always hesitant to use. I leave Eliza sitting there, her foot resting on Miles, and go into my bedroom. Under the bed, among the dust and dog hair, are tea tins. They aren't labeled, of course, but I know exactly what they are. I make up a paper packet for Eliza to carry home: tansy and scotch broom and yarrow being the main ingredients. She will need to make a tea with my mixture and drink a dose every few hours, and I will have to make sure she understands not to use too much at once.

I remember sitting in this room with my grandmother, back when this was her bedroom and I slept in a room down the hall, no bigger than a closet. One night, when I was an early teenager and just starting to really wonder why we had so many hushed female visitors in the evenings, I sat on her bed and watched my grandmother with her herbs and tins and made some off-hand remark about how she looked like a witch.

"Malleus Maleficarum," she muttered, and that was all she said. I loved the mystical sound of the phrase, and it played over and over in my head like a potent spell. Days later I looked up the words on her computer, in a rare instance when the Internet was working. I spelled them horribly wrong but somehow the search engine deciphered my meaning. I stumbled across a disconcerting definition. "Translated as 'The Hammer of Witches,' a 1487 publication from Germany, accusing midwives who performed abortions of witchcraft." And after that, without her ever saying the words out loud, I knew exactly what Ophelia Dupre, my genteel grandmother, really was.

V

I CAN'T STOP THINKING ABOUT ELIZA PRITCHARD. All through the morning, inspecting the rows of beds and monitoring the girls during their morning work, I keep thinking about her, somewhere out in the Parish, no doubt in one of the most impoverished sections, filled with squalor and despair. I worry that she has taken too much of my herbal tea at once. I worry that she hasn't taken enough and will resort to drastic matters in a fit of desperation. I worry that she is all alone. I worry that she is not.

This always happens, not just this time. The women and girls are strangers when they come to me, and yet we share deeply personal and intimate moments together. There is an unspoken trust between us from the start, and that is our bond. I will likely never see Eliza again, at least I hope not, but I will never forget her.

And let's be honest…I'm not being completely selfless either. I know that if Eliza had a complication that she could not hide, heavy bleeding for instance, she would be the victim of an investigation. An interrogation. Even natural miscarriages are investigated by Officers of the State. I know what a blood test would show. After a mock trial, she would be strung on the Trinity in mere days. Would they be able to trace her back to me? Would she give me up willingly? I have not yet had a patient with severe complications, but I feel like I'm on borrowed time. My stomach turns and I have a bitter taste in my mouth, as if maybe I've ingested pennyroyal myself.

I wish, for the millionth time, that I could be more proactive in my assistance. Since unmarried women are not permitted to get birth control from their doctors or medical clinics, I wish I could covertly offer my own herbal concoctions as contraception. Ophelia told me that smartweed and Queen Anne's lace have been known to prevent pregnancy. But how would I go about offering such illicit things without arousing suspicion? That would bring too many women to my door. And it would be yet another illegal act. It is enough, I tell myself, to just keep doing what I am doing. Providing birth control must be someone else's burden. I don't think anyone else has taken up the cause yet, though. If they had, our orphanages wouldn't be so full. Women like Eliza would not need to slink to my house at night.

I have to force Eliza from my mind, because I feel myself going into a dark place of fear and paranoia. Plus, I'm not being fair to the girls if I'm not present with them in the moment. They don't get enough attention from me as it is. They're busy scribbling in their notebooks. There's one old computer in the corner, but it rarely connects to the outside world via the Internet, and I tell the girls not to even bother trying to use it to look up definitions. Kamon is sitting on her bed, absently shading in the stegosaurus's plates on the cover of her book. I should tell her to open it and get busy, but I don't want her to read the words inside, so I don't say anything. Her face is paler than usual, accentuating the freckles that pepper her nose. She looks exhausted.

"How'd you sleep?" I ask, lowering myself on the edge of her bed. Kamon tosses her pencil down and narrows her eyes for a second.

"I wish you could have stayed," she says in answer.

"So we could've pored over your Creationism book all night?" I nudge her playfully but she doesn't smile. Usually we could share a conspiratorial whisper over such things. I might not have been allowed to foster Kamon and take her home with me, but she feels like mine in so many ways. I would never allow my own child to be numbed by the fodder of the Southerly

State. My Mamie Ophelia made sure I learned what was taught to her as a child, back when religion did not color every aspect of life. She took great pains to quietly correct the lessons I brought home from my State-run school. "You don't say what I'm telling you out loud in that place, *Sha*," she would whisper into my ear, using her favorite endearment for me. It was a Cajun twist on the French *Mon Cher*, and when Ophelia said it, *Sha*, she pulled those three little letters out into a long, lilted drawl. "But you just keep the knowledge inside of you. Maybe one day the truth will be important once again around here. And if you can get out of this place, you will be armed with the truths that people in other places already know."

Ophelia grew up in a very different time, and she often said she would be damned if I grew up any less educated than she was, even if she had to teach me in secret. I never fully appreciated how much it must have galled her to send me off to that State-mandated institution to listen to teachers talk about how Darwin was marred with psychosis and the Earth was just around two thousand years old until I watched Kamon open her first booklet on Creationism as a five-year-old. And then I felt a searing anger course through me. Kamon deserved to hear other theories, those rooted in fact and science. I couldn't do this for all the girls, even though I wanted to, but I could do it for her.

But this morning she doesn't share in my joke. Instead she sits up straight until she's eye-level with me and slips her hand into mine. Three squeezes, each one a hair longer than the last.

"It's not the same here when you go," she says. "The new lady doesn't even leave a nightlight on. And she barely makes sure everyone is laying down before she goes down the hall to go to sleep. Calah cries herself to sleep every night. This lady doesn't know how to calm her down like you do."

I struggle to think of the woman's name. I know she replaced Savannah Lacroix a month ago, but her name escapes me now.

I should know this, I think. She's on the nightshift for my girls. How do I not remember her name? But we just brush by one another on the steps as we change shifts, and Headmistress Rachel informed me that she would brief the new woman on the girls so I didn't need to stay late on her first evening to provide any information. I should have insisted. Nobody knows these girls better than I do. I wonder if perhaps I was running home that particular evening, expecting someone.

"She'll learn," I tell Kamon. "You can help her, too. You're one of the oldest in the room."

Kamon shakes her head. "I tried to get in bed with Calah the other night, but I wasn't allowed." Kamon wants to say more, I know she does, but she presses her lips together. "Do you think maybe you could stay tonight?"

I know I can't. Rachel won't allow it. I can already hear her telling me not to get any ideas in my head, the girls are fine, I can't get too attached. All things she's said before, over and over.

"I can't, Kay. I'm sorry."

And I know that she understands, even though she's so young. She knows it isn't because I don't want to. But I don't expect the silent tears that balance on her lower lids, waiting for a slow blink to set them free. She turns her head away. I don't want the other girls to notice, because if Kamon is upset, they will be upset too. And so I don't pull her into me, even though it goes against every instinct I have.

"It's hard to take," she says, her back to me. She swipes at her face and I imagine she's trying to hide her tears. She knows as well as I that the other girls shouldn't see her cry.

"I know," I say to the back of her head. But another drop of pennyroyal poison stirs in my stomach, and I begin to wonder if maybe I don't really know after all, and that nighttime in Xavier is much worse than I think.

* * *

The blackout comes without so much as a flicker for warning. Miles whines, sensing a shift in the air. It's already inky black outside, and not even a firefly lights up the edge of the bayou. I have candles ready, of course, and a flashlight. There's an old phone in a drawer somewhere but the battery is long dead and with cellular service so unreliable, it doesn't make sense to pay for a new one. I'm grateful Eliza came last night instead of tonight. I would be less lonely in the dark, yes, but it's difficult to deal with an already distraught woman when the lights go out.

Just as Emilie pointed out that the Punishments are increasing, so too are the blackouts. Of course they are. The main power grids are in the North, and those the Southerly State erected have always been shoddy. The summer will be especially brutal when the power cuts out even more with old air conditioning units straining and sputtering in windows. The storms are sure to come then as well, swelling and expanding the swamps and the Mississippi River and causing days on end filled with floods and darkness. But we suffer from more than just seasonal flooding. Many fear that one day we will be underwater just like what happened to Florida and New Orleans. What used to be Louisiana's most lovely city has been overtaken by water, the Gulf of Mexico drowning buildings and coursing down streets. It's part ghost town, part Atlantis now; an uninhabitable grouping of islands. I sleep at Xavier when our floods come, as do we all, because otherwise what would happen to the girls? Miles will join me, which will make the girls so happy. I wonder if Kamon is anxiously awaiting the hurricanes and floods, knowing I will have to spend the night during a bad storm.

I sit in the dark, a candle illuminating the State-mandated newspaper. There's an article about the Punishment that took place the other day, and other articles about Punishments that took place in nearby Parishes. Luckily no photo accompanies our local girl's story. *Sanguidam Punished,* the headline reads. I trace over the words. I can almost hear Ophelia's scoffing laugh. "*Sanguidam,*" she would say. "High-falutin' word for a bunch of uneducated fools." But they are well-versed in the language of religion, I want to remind her now. I don't know who it was who first melded two Latin words together: *sanguis* for blood, and *gravidam* for pregnant. The word feels exotic, rolling around the mouth like a deep red wine.

The article says her name is Isabel. Fourteen years old. Punished with thirty lashes for the Removal of an Unborn. There was no Remover to punish; Isabel did it herself. I wonder if she used a curling iron or a tapered candle or even a knife. I know those things have all been used in desperation before. Her mother brought her to the hospital when she suffered severe complications and heavy bleeding, and the nurses there knew immediately what transpired. I'm sure her mother was aware of what would happen when she took her for help, but she surely would have died otherwise. I wish this young Isabel had heard somehow, through a network of whispers, about how to seek a Jane. Maybe she would have found me. Surely all of this could have been prevented. As I do at the orphanage, I feel the weight of my failings. I did not even know of her, and yet I have somehow failed her.

I wonder how the girl is. I hope she is being treated kindly at whatever clinic she was taken to. I know some of the nurses like to dress the wounds with stinging medications and tend roughly to the lashes, believing they are administering an additional layer of well-deserved punishment. I think of the girl's mother, horrified at seeing her daughter savagely beaten. She will be shamed for raising a *Sanguidam*. The whole family is marred now, and the scars of that are even more lasting than the lumpen flesh that will streak across the girl's back for the rest of her life. Her mother's boyfriend, the father of the Unborn, is requesting further punishment for Isabel because she murdered his child. He wanted parental rights, the article states, and she took those away from him.

He is referred to as the Unborn's father in the article. Not a rapist or an attacker. A father. Isabel is not labeled as his victim. Murderess, they call her. *Sanguidam.* But she is not murderous. She is fourteen and she is indeed a victim. I want to take my candle and carry it outside and throw it on the dry sawgrass, watching the entire wretched Southerly State spark and ignite and flutter down in a papery heap of ash.

VI

I DON'T LIKE THE LOOK on Rachel's face when she pokes her head into my room and tells me in clipped words to please step into the hallway. I try not to sigh too loudly as her head retreats from the doorframe like a box turtle pulling into its shell. Mishael suppresses a snorted little giggle. It does feel like I've gotten called out by the headmistress to be given a stern talking to. Mishael must be glad that it's me, not her, that Rachel is looking for.

"We were just about to start our lessons," I tell Rachel in the hallway. That's not quite true. The girls were relaxing and chatting in small groups and I had no immediate plans to call them to order, even though Rachel likes us to keep to a strict schedule.

"I'm glad I caught you before you started, then," she says. She holds something out to me. Sitting in her arms is a stack of booklets. A thick band of words adorn the top cover: The History of the Southerly State.

"We already have history books." I use the term loosely. I'm fairly certain the booklets we have are a conglomeration of fantasy and fiction, peppered with propaganda. "History changes based on who's telling it," Ophelia liked to remind me when I was in school. And our books were all written by the Southerly State.

"These are a revised edition," Rachel tells me. Her lips purse together and I know she's waiting for me to give her an argument. She thrusts the pile of booklets at me but I don't take them.

"Our curriculum is not up for debate," she says, leaning into me, the booklets pressed between us.

"Nothing is ever up for debate," I say. I peek into my room to make sure the girls are behaving without supervision. They are, even Mishael. I pluck the top booklet off the pile and rifle through it. This revised edition contains more illustrations than our current copies. Everything is in black and white. It's much cheaper to print that way. I imagine in other places, schools use personal computers to teach the children. Aside from the fact that our computers are old and unreliable, it's much easier to control the flow of information when you only pass out photocopied booklets.

Fanning through the pages, I give it a quick skim and catch glimpses of images I've been inundated with all my life: Christian crosses and guns and the flag of the Southerly State. The drawings are crude and almost childlike, with thick bold strokes scratched across the pages. I find the drawing I'm looking for near the front of the booklet. Filling the entire page, it depicts a cathedral with swirls of black smoke pouring out its broken windows. The destruction of this church was the catalyst of the Peaceable Separation.

"Rachel..."

She holds up a hand to stop me.

"Have you read this?" I ask.

"I don't have time to read it; I barely have time to pass it out. And I definitely don't have time to argue with a staff member over it."

"On a quiet summer morning in New York City," I read aloud, "a bomb ripped through St. Patrick's Cathedral. The church was filled with locals and tourists, busloads of children visiting from day camps, and elderly people making a pilgrimage to one of the most famous places of worship in the country. Thousands were killed. A shocked nation watched in horror on live television as injured survivors fled onto the streets covered in blood."

"You don't have to read it to me," Rachel says. "Just hand them out to the girls."

Ophelia always spoke about the violence that had been building throughout the nation in the years leading up to the massacre in the church. Assaults on facts happened with increasing frequency. Patriotic hymns became a mandatory part of all gatherings at churches and rallies. She said you could feel the shift in the air: the intolerance, the hard bend to the conservative right, the methodical chipping away of the rights of others. Something was coming, Ophelia said. Everyone knew it.

I keep reading—*aloud*—in spite of the fact I can sense Rachel's impatience with me. "The attack on the church was an attack on the entire United States of America. Our Christian nation was under siege by radical Muslim terrorists who wanted to launch a 'great war on infidels.' Thus began the forced registration of Muslims throughout the country. Many were interred, many more were deported. With that, the God-fearing people who loved their country began to bring it back to its true Christian roots, and that is the foundation of the Southerly State we live in today."

I fan through the rest of the pages. Patriotism and religion are everywhere. Unsurprisingly, specific details about the Separation and what followed appear to be scant. I slap the pamphlet against my leg.

"This is bullshit," I say to Rachel. I'm being insubordinate and she's probably going to write me up, but I don't care. "I'm not giving this to my girls." I feel like I'm at a breaking point of some sort. Maybe I'm splintering apart because, despite my bravado, I know I will indeed hand out these booklets. It's that or get fired and be away from the girls entirely. I know it, and Rachel knows it. That's probably why she indulges me for a moment.

"We've talked about this before," she says, not unkindly. But she does sound tired. "It's the mandated curriculum."

"But it's not true."

"That's not up to us to decide. We just implement."

"I'm tired of implementing."

She pushes the stack toward me, and I don't have a choice. It's so heavy in my arms.

"I'll excuse your tardiness with lessons this morning," she says. "But you'll need to begin now." She's already moving away from me.

"Why don't they say anything about how hatred of immigrants and non-Christians was glorified well before the attack?" I call after her, but she doesn't turn around. It was true though. Ophelia told me that radical Christian leaders had been waiting for some tipping point, something they could blame on their chosen enemy. They had a president in power who pandered to them. Conditions were ripe. When the church was bombed, they were ready. It's exactly what they'd been waiting for. It was the call to return to a Christian nation, they said. They swore it was what God ordained.

They were wrong.

Rachel disappears into her office. I'm standing alone in the hall. Mishael peeks her head out. "I heard yelling," she says. She doesn't look concerned, only interested. I steer her back inside the room. Against everything I believe in, I call the girls around me and pass out the booklets. There are the usual groans. It's their natural reaction to yet another photocopied book that looks identical to the ones they already have. There is no joy in learning here. I'm sure the girls sense my reticence, but they take the packets to their beds and begin the first awful lesson.

* * *

I make my way around the room before heading out for the evening. It's been hours since the history booklets were tucked under beds. I'm sure the girls have long forgotten about them. Me, I've thought of nothing else.

When Kamon sidles up to me for her evening hug, I pull her close. I only have a minute or two before another girl will press into me, so I hold her tight and whisper to her.

"It isn't always as it seems," I say. I hope she knows what I mean. She looks up at me, and I know she doesn't understand.

"Your lesson today. Not everything is as it seems." I should stop talking. I don't.

"History changes depending on who tells it," I quote.

"I know." She nods. It's not the first time she's heard this.

"The church exploded. It was terrible. But it wasn't radical Islamic terrorists who hurled a bomb into the cathedral." Kamon is shaking her head. I'm completely contradicting what I personally handed her to read only hours ago. "Just listen a minute, okay?" She nods. "It was planted there by a group of militant white terrorists from the state of Kentucky, Kay. They did it to punish the 'educated elite' they'd been taught to hate so much. They chose New York City because it was considered to be a melting pot of the country's immigrants. They hated immigrants even more than the elite. But by the time the truth came out, it was too late. The registration and deportation campaign against Muslims was already in full effect."

Kamon doesn't say anything. I know she trusts me, but I can tell she's thinking through this new information.

"Your Mamie told you?" she asks. Ophelia frequently comes up in our conversations.

"Mmhmm. She remembered it firsthand. She watched it on TV. The true story, about the guys from Kentucky, came out on the news after a few weeks. But there were other newscasters and radio hosts who said it wasn't true. It was hard to know what to believe."

"Like now," Kamon says.

"You can believe me," I say. "I promise."

I know why she feels this way. When you're constantly inundated with one-sided information, it's difficult to believe anything else. I used to push back on Ophelia's secret teachings when I was Kamon's age. There were times I told her she was just plain wrong. She would give me a half-smile, allow me to argue with her, and then patiently continue explaining her side of the debate. She always had first-hand facts to share with me—she had witnessed events unfolding around her, after all. Over time, I began to understand how to separate fact-based evidence from the Southerly State's propaganda. Many people of her generation passed down those same facts to their loved ones, but we are powerless to speak against the authoritarian regime under which we live. We are left with nothing but a tacit understanding of the truth.

Kamon nods, agreeing with me for now. I can only hope she continues to do so as she gets older. You never can tell. I want to keep talking, but Serah comes up to us before I can say anything more. Her one arm curls around me.

"What do you promise?" she asks. She's getting so tall; she'll be my height soon. They all will be.

I shake my head and kiss her cheek. Kamon squeezes my hand three times. I squeeze back four. I wink at her. We will finish this talk tomorrow.

* * *

All morning, Kamon looks tired. I keep waiting for her to approach me and ask if I will finish my history lesson from yesterday, but she doesn't. She doesn't say much of anything, really. When we go outside after lunch, I notice that she veers off by herself and sits underneath the shade of a sycamore tree. It's my chance to speak with her. I hate leaving things half-finished.

"Hi," I say, sitting down beside her. I lean my back against the rough bark. Nothing about this position is comfortable. "You okay?"

"Tired," she says. "I didn't sleep well."

"Relax when we go back inside." She nods and rests the back of her head against the tree. Her eyes are closed. I can just see the faintest birthmark on the bridge of her nose. I used to tell her it was there so I'd know just where to kiss her.

"Want me to finish what I was telling you yesterday?" She opens her eyes and rolls her head in my direction. There are dark circles under her eyes. She shouldn't have trouble sleeping. She should be in a home, in her own room, in a comfortable bed. She should be in my home.

"I get it," she says. "I get that they made it up, about the Muslims. I just don't get *why.*"

"I think there were a lot of people in the southern part of the United States who wanted things to change. They thought people were losing their way. They thought God was angry with them. If they blamed a religious group very different than their own, it would rally people back toward Christianity. In their minds."

"And the people in the north didn't agree with that?"

"There's a lot they didn't agree with."

"But not *all* the people in the North would have felt like that. Not, like, every single person."

"No. Not every single person. But the majority. Same as here. Not every single person here feels the same either."

"You maybe shouldn't say that," Kamon says.

"Probably not." It's sad that she already knows this.

"They make it sound like the Peaceable Separation was a good thing, though."

"It was. For the people in charge. I guess it was a good thing for the Northerly State as well. You know they were the ones who broke off from the country. It wasn't really the other way around."

Kamon shakes her head and looks off into the distance. Her eyes follow a group of girls running by. They're laughing. They sound genuinely happy. I don't hear that as often as I should.

"You always thought it was the Southerly State that separated, right?"

"Well, yeah. It seemed that way."

"It was the North. I don't think they wanted to break up the country. But they didn't like the very conservative rules being put in place. Elections hadn't been going their way for a while. After the implementation of the Muslim registration, the states in the North tried different legal strategies to slow down the country's new laws. But nothing worked. Human rights groups couldn't break legal barriers the South put up. They were no longer playing by the same set of rules. Of course, a lot of people in the South loved the new laws. A lot of the middle of the country did, too. That's why the Southerly State is so big. There was a lot of fighting. The separation wasn't as peaceable as the name implies. But finally, the Northerly State broke away. The Westerly State did too. They would have joined with the North but they were just too geographically separated." I lower my voice. "They kept moving forward, and left us behind."

"But most people got what they wanted," Kamon says.

"Yes. Unless you're someone in the North who doesn't agree with their forward progress. I imagine there're people like that. I'm sure they are unhappy."

"And if you live here and you don't like their laws, then you're unhappy, too," she whispers.

"Right."

I want to tell Kamon so much more, but she's already resting her head against the tree trunk. It's a lot to handle all at once, at her age. It's a lot for anyone, really. I decide to wait for another day to tell her what Ophelia told me: that once the Separation was complete, lawyers in the Southerly State didn't stand up for people's rights, they stood only for the rights of the rulers. I want Kamon to understand that courts were filled with judges appointed by evangelicals in political positions. She should know how so many people of color were wrongly incarcerated. I wonder if she's ever given thought to the fact that all the faces at Xavier are white. And then I remember that she's never even seen a Black person, because she doesn't leave the orphanage. She doesn't yet know about the State's vile, antiquated system of segregation.

I need to make sure she understands that the printed history of this place was rewritten, keeping some facts, but twisting and omitting so many others. There are hints and whispers at the truth, passed down by those who remember, but those will fade one day, unless we keep passing the secrets down to the next generation.

It makes me sick every time I think about what happened. How did I get trapped here, on this side of everything? In this strange place, where people who once rose up a great battle cry of freedom now swear that they got exactly what they wanted? The same people who pumped their fists in the air and vowed to defend freedom for all don't even hold elections anymore. Now they have a Marshall who dictates laws and Officers of the State who enforce them. They screamed cries of liberty, but bent toward authoritarianism when it suited their needs. It turns out, Ophelia said, they didn't want freedom for all. They just wanted to get their way. And sadly, they have.

VII

I HATE SUNDAYS. There's no Punishment today, thank goodness, but I'm meeting Emilie at church and that's my least favorite hour and a half of the week. There's a skeleton crew at Xavier on Sundays, but Rachel never puts me in the rotation. I do need the break from it though, from the slog there and back and from the draining nature of the job, but I know the girls miss me, and I miss them.

Emilie is already there when I arrive. When I think of the word "church" I remember photos my grandmother showed me of Gothic cathedrals in Europe filled with stone and protruding gargoyles and massive organ pipes. Kaleidoscopic stained glass bouncing off stone walls and spires jutting into the sky like needles. But I have never been inside a church like that. This church, *Word of Our Father*, is a sparse open space with enough seating for everyone in the Parish, and it's usually filled to capacity. Hundreds of folding bleachers fill the room. The walls are stark and white, clinical. There's a particle board partition running down the length of the center aisle. Men sit on one side, women on the other. Women are not to tempt men while they are worshipping God. A quote from Ephesians is painted in red on the women's side of the partition. "Wives, submit to your own husbands, as to the Lord." I don't know what's written on the other side. There are metal boxes for weekly tithes, and of course the envelope with your offering must be labeled with your name and address. Miss two weeks in a row and expect to be called on by someone from the church office, "just to be sure you're all right."

Emilie's sister, Bella, is beside her and I nod to them both as I slide down the row. They are only about three rows from the pulpit, way too close for me. When I give Emilie a look, she whispers, "Bella just sat here and I didn't want to make her move." I roll my eyes and she pretends not to notice. Bella is studying the weekly prayer sheet, paying no attention to either of us.

"How's your mama an' them?" I ask, slipping for a moment into the Cajun that Ophelia disdained, even though it used to slip out of her every so often, too. Emilie was about to answer when the lights dimmed and then only the pulpit remained in a spot of white light. *Word of Our Father* church does not have to concern itself with rolling blackouts. Our tithes have provided the very best generators.

Preacher Pote approaches the pulpit and stands in silence for a moment. It's enough time for his followers to take in the black jacket he has draped over a black button-down shirt and his black denim pants that disappear into black snakeskin boots. His hat of the same color sits in one hand; he would never wear it inside God's house but he rarely puts it down, either. Pote has pale skin with day-old ashy stubble on his cheeks. His hair is platinum, and far too short for what I think it should look like. Someone of his character should have long hair that straggles down over his ears. His eyes are the color of a heron's feather.

When he speaks, his voice pierces the air with staccato notes that skitter over the austere walls and chipped paint of the bleachers. He starts with his usual favorite.

"My brothers and sisters in Christ," he says, his voice strident through the microphone, "Raise up your hands and your hearts with me. Let us pray for the lost souls who have turned to homosexuality. They anger God, and we, the Righteous, know that an angry God is a vengeful God. Are we going to allow them to make Him turn His wrath on us anymore?"

"No," the crowd agrees. I can't see the men, but I hear them. It's a much larger group than the one in Place d'Armes last Sunday, watching Isabel bleed. Those folks are here, of course, but they are joined by so many others as well. I know that a good deal of these people feel like I do, though we are powerless to say anything. I know there are many ambivalent people as well, people just trying to get by with their own lives and their own kin. They are not passionate about the cause of homosexuality or abortifacients or anything else, but the ones in power are, and so they go along with it. Aren't we all complicit of that?

I'm not sure why Preacher Pote still rages against homosexuals. It must be a warning more than anything else. They were the second group forced to register, preceded only by the Muslims. Christian leaders said that the rampant homosexuality in the country was making God angry and that's why He allowed the swell of wrath from Muslim terrorists. Gays were made to register with the government under the guise of monitoring STD's. They were no longer allowed to adopt children or to marry. There was an actual group called the War on Gay America that raised funds for the evangelical groups railing against homosexuals. Transgender people were murdered in the streets. Understandably, there is nobody openly gay in this Parish, or any of the other 63 parishes in our territory of Louisiana. There are no open homosexuals in the entirety of the Southerly State. They have not gone away but they have certainly gone underground. The Trinity waits for them, as well.

Pote prays for the Officers of the Southerly State in Louisiana and the other territories, and gesticulates wildly at the flag that hangs behind him, grandly kissing his fingers and touching them to the edge of the material. This is where I think long hair would be so fitting; a toss of the head so it flares out dramatically as he stares up at the flag. My thoughts are ridiculous but my whole body wants to get up and walk away and I have to do something to keep myself in place. Soon we are all singing hymns and Preacher Pote is leading us in our pledge to "Guns, God, and Freedom." Faith is highly politicized these days. We aren't really free, but I know at least half the people in the room believe we are. Pote pulls his jacket aside and displays his own gun for us to marvel over.

"Before we part, my brothers and sisters in Christ, let us bow our heads to pray for the Unborn," he says, and I pray too, though I'm not quite certain to whom I'm praying. I don't want those little groups of cells to come into being only to be Removed. Who would want that? I only know that they will be removed, whether or not I assist, and it's less dangerous for the mother if I'm involved. I'm grateful that my head is bowed. I feel Emilie stiffen next to me. She does not give my hand a squeeze or make any outward motion toward me at all. She wouldn't dare.

"There is something I want you to see," Pote says, breaking his congregation's silence. He sets his hat down atop the pulpit and reaches down behind it, pulling up a metal box slightly larger than the tithing boxes. This one is labeled in red lettering but I can't make out the word.

"Don't worry, now," he booms. "It's not another tithing box." He waits for the obligatory laughter and then continues. "My friends, I give you the Tamburo." There's a long pause. Preacher Pote seems to expect the lack of enthusiasm. After all nobody, myself included, knows what a Tamburo is. My stomach flutters because I'm certain it's nothing good. The preacher relishes in the collective and anticipatory silence. I know his body is tingling under the glare of his followers' eyes. You can just tell. He lives for it.

"The Tamburo," he finally continues, "has been around for centuries. The people of Florence, ungodly as they were, had enough sense to place these boxes in the back of their churches hundreds of years ago. An anonymous person could slip a piece of paper inside, tipping the officers of the law to any, shall we say, hedonistic acts. They knew, my good people, that homosexuals went against God, and with boxes such as these, thousands of sodomites were arrested and punished." He allows this new information to sink in. I wonder how many people in the crowd know that he's referring to Italy, a place my grandmother had the good fortune to visit when she was a child and everything was, as she used to remember it, damn near perfect. She showed me photos of sculptures and a cathedral with a dome the color of the rising sun that stood over the city of Florence. I am immediately saddened to think that even there, in a place filled with beauty and learning, they were as close-minded as we are.

For a moment I wonder if Preacher Pote is making it up. It would not be the first time. It's incredibly difficult to decipher what is true and what isn't. If Pote wants this to be true, if he wants to add an element of romance or intrigue to his story, there is scant little to stop him. The followers who want to believe him will do so with complete conviction, and the ones who don't will not have any recourse other than to silently accept Pote's words as fact, in some form or another.

But I choose to believe him this time. Something about it sounds just plausible enough. Human nature has not changed much, I don't think. If we seek people out and punish them now, certainly the idea to do so was not original.

"It's true that we have very little problem with homosexuals in the Southerly State anymore," he continues. "We have good, God-fearing people among us. But there is an even worse evil that continues to blacken the soul of this great place. Our prayers have not been enough. God needs our help, my Christian brothers and sisters. As mighty as He is, the scourge is great. He is calling us. We must help Him to seek out and destroy those who commit crimes against the Unborn. You good people must be vigilant. When you hear the whispers, when you see the evidence, you will have no reason to be afraid of making a claim against the sinner. Nobody will ever know that you are the accuser."

I know what the Tamburo is then. A receptacle for anonymous notes slipped inside, naming *Sanguidam.* I wonder how many men back in Renaissance Florence were falsely accused as a manner of revenge or a simple mistake. What proof will be needed to accompany these notes? None. Seeing the names in ink will be enough for Pote. His position gives him a great deal of power. The State allows men of religion to bestow Punishments. If Pote believes someone to be guilty, they are finished. I can't help it, I reach out and grab Emilie's hand. She pulls away before her sister can see, and the three of us sit there, stunned. Many surely feel the rush of Christian warrior blood rush through them as Pote delivers this instrument to help them serve God. They have been waiting for this. Others likely feel uncomfortable but powerless. And then there are those feeling exactly as I am in this moment. Terrified.

VIII

Bella gives us both a quick hug as we say goodbye. She promises to give her parents my best. I'm glad to have Emilie for the day. It's a rare treat.

"I promise I'll have her walk home in the light," I tell Bella as we part. The days are longer now so I'll still have plenty of time with my friend.

I saw Margaret in the congestion on our way out, but I didn't acknowledge her. Eliza Pritchard was there too, being led by the elbow by a ruddy-faced older man with a bulbous drinker's nose that could only have come from too many years of absinthe or gin. I was relieved to see she was all right, though her father's grip on her made me wonder if he was perhaps her baby's father, or if he would have beaten her to a pulp if he found out what she'd had to do.

I don't tell Emilie any of this as we walk under ribbons of Spanish moss and brush by groups of burnt sienna trumpet creepers and sprays of Queen Anne's lace. It feels good to inhale the air that's been washed and cleansed in morning dew. I appreciate the silence. My whole body is vibrating with Preacher Pote's words.

As the tops of the cypresses come into view, Emilie finally says what I know she's been thinking.

"I think you should stop."

There's no good reply, so I don't say anything.

"I mean it," she says. "I knew it was getting worse, but things have definitely escalated."

"I'm not sure I'm in any more danger than someone who has never actually done anything wrong. An anonymous system? Anyone can say anything. It will be one person's word against another. Am I in more danger than anyone else?"

Emilie shakes her head. "You've been fortunate so far, but I think it's time."

"I'm helping these women, Em. You know that even without me, they would still terminate their pregnancies. I'm just ensuring their safety as best I can."

"I told you last week, you'll pay even more dearly than they do. You aren't listening to me." Her voice is raspy. I know she's scared for me and I hope she knows how much I appreciate it. But she knows I can't stop. I promised Ophelia Dupre I would continue the work she so truly believed in. And I made my own promises along the way. To take care of desperate women, because so many of them would die by their own hand otherwise. For some it would be a tragic misstep as they were administering their own treatment, and for others, it would be their only way out of a hopeless situation. She knows all of this, but she's more worried about my safety than anything else.

I want to remind her what Ophelia taught me; the statistics are staggering. I want to remind her about the women who have gone to church and come home with a stolen Roman candle to initiate their own Removal. I want to tell her about the women who have accidentally poisoned themselves with strange concoctions they had no business mixing, and about how they have scalded themselves sitting over pots of hot steam. I want to remind her that right up until 1989, almost ninety years ago, nine thousand women died in Romania due to the strict laws against Removals. Ophelia used to wonder if the government there finally changed the law because of the women who lost their lives or because they couldn't handle the overflowing orphanages, filled with listless and unloved children who were starving and covered in their own filth.

But I've told her all this before. She doesn't want to hear it again, and I don't want to think about it—let alone repeat it—not after everything else I've seen and heard this morning. We are at my porch now, the blasted flag snapping and twisting on its pole. An egret casts a blurred shadow on the steps as it flies by and I can smell the stagnant algae that coats the nearby water in a scummy film. I don't kiss my fingers but Emilie does.

"There's nobody watching," I say, hoping to reassure her.

"It feels like there's always somebody watching," she says, and raises onto her tiptoes to place her kiss upon the flag.

* * *

We cook together all afternoon, stirring up a huge pot of gumbo. I chop a mountain of vegetables for the base that folks here call the Holy Trinity: onions, peppers and celery. The irony of the name does not escape me. We boil up crawfish and sit on the porch pinching their tails and sucking their heads as the afternoon wanes.

Full and content, Preacher Pote's words seem far less potent out here. Emilie is more relaxed now, too. Her lips are slick with the juices of our meal. There's enough left in the pot for lunch for the whole week. I wish Kamon could sit and eat a bowl with me, but of course that isn't allowed. And suddenly I'm thinking of her and a whole new set of worries thrums through me.

"You haven't heard anything about Xavier, right?" I ask Emilie. Her head is tilted up to catch the last of the sun. She'll have to start walking home soon before her family worries.

"What do you mean? Nothing out of the ordinary, no."

"I don't know… Kamon seemed upset the past few days. She doesn't want me to leave at night."

"She's at that age," Emilie says, offering the answer for every ailment afflicting a teenager. Emilie's charges can't even speak, so my questions are silly. Of course she wouldn't have heard anything.

"Do you remember the name of the new woman who takes the night shift in my room?" I ask. But Emilie is already pulling herself up from the step and brushing off her skirt. She's not wearing the watch she usually wears to work, but the purple streaks in the sky alerted us both to the late hour.

"Belinda, I think," she says. "Why?"

"I was just thinking I need to meet her. It's not right that we haven't spoken. Nobody knows those girls better than I do."

"I'm sure Rachel doesn't agree," Emilie rolls her eyes. "If you speak with Belinda, Rachel gives up some measure of control, and you know how she feels about that."

I don't want Emilie to leave, but I don't want her walking home in the dark any more than her parents and Bella do. I give her a hug and her parting words to me are, "Just think about what I said." Then she's gone and I'm alone in the bayou, listening to the cries and calls of my own little corner of the Southerly State.

* * *

Miles curls against my feet as I lay down in my grandmother's old bed. It's already too humid for a sheet but I can't sleep without its weight covering me. With Emilie gone and the spicy scent of the gumbo dissipated, my mind turns to the Tamburo and the orphanage and Preacher Pote and the increasing Punishments. I feel like I'm drowning under the muck of it all. And I'm thinking of Emilie, too. I wasn't angry at her earlier; I was appreciative of her concern. But in the quiet of this old place, laying directly over the tins of Ophelia Dupre, I am angry with my closest friend. She knows why I do what I do. I should not have to explain it to her, and she should never ask me to stop, no matter her good intentions. She knows I am doing this to save lives. She knows, because I once saved hers.

IX

I DIDN'T SAY A WORD to Emilie for her first three weeks at Xavier. This wasn't deliberate, but I only ever saw her in passing, and there was little time to say anything. She was working with much older girls then, and I was with children barely able to read. We didn't eat lunch at the same time. I like to think I smiled warmly at her when we passed in the hall, but I'm sure we exchanged a few harried glances at best, until the morning I saw her standing in front of a hallway window, her skirt translucent in the sunlight, vomiting daintily into a paper bag. It was little more than a choking gasp, but I saw her back spasm with the retch and heard a little plop as stomach juices hit the bottom of the bag. I figured it was a virus, but there was a strict rule about not coming to work sick and infecting the girls. She would be terminated if found out. Emilie's head snapped toward me as she heard my boots tap on the worn stone. Her paper bag was already hanging at her side.

"You need to go home if you're sick," I said. I'm sure I didn't remind her of my name, and I know I didn't remember hers.

"I'm not sick," she said. It was the way she looked at me then. Imploring. Like she was saying, *please don't tell my secret.* I looked at the fingers on her left hand and saw no wedding band.

"You are sick in the mornings, though?" I said. We Janes are masters at doublespeak. I can say a great deal by saying very little.

"Yes," Emilie said, and that was it. There was an understanding between us then. She stepped out of the sunbeam and her legs disappeared under an opaque white skirt. She knew I would keep her secret. I didn't plan on ever bringing it up again, as her situation didn't concern me. I don't know if I even said anything else after that, maybe just nodded and turned back to my room. I'm sure she did the same. That was the only exchange we had, until a few weeks later when I exited the orphanage a minute after she did and found myself walking home behind her. I didn't know if I should quicken my pace and come up beside her or hang back and give her more room. Either way felt awkward, and we were the only two on the street. When she glanced back to see who was behind her, I waved and sped up. She stopped to wait for me.

I'm sure we exchanged the usual pleasantries. I remember a giggly formal introduction, both of us apologizing for not remembering the other's name. And I remember several stretches of silence that felt comfortable, neither of us feeling the need to fill the empty space with meaningless words. With Emilie, everything felt just right, right away.

We didn't speak about her morning sickness that first evening. I figured she had plenty of opportunity if she wanted to talk about it, but she didn't say anything. She didn't look pregnant. If I hadn't seen her with the paper bag, I wouldn't suspect a thing. She didn't say anything the next night or the next one or the next one. But after around a week of walking together, right as the sky turned ochre over the magnolia trees, she blurted out, "I can't tell my parents about this baby." I led her all the way to my house and sat her on the couch where she sobbed into her hands. She told me about how her parents would disown her immediately since she wasn't married. She told me how the man she was in love with dropped her the moment she told him her news, because, he shamefully admitted to her, he was already married. You would think, I remember telling her, that very religious people like her parents would welcome a baby as a gift from God and rejoice in the fact that their daughter chose to give it life. But no, she said. There would be no joy in such shame.

I trusted her. She trusted me. And so I told her I could help her. I told her to go home so her parents didn't worry, and to tell them that she'd be spending the following evening with her new friend from work. She came home with me the next night. I explained my concoction as I blended it. I told her what would happen. We waited together. We cried together. I covered for her the next morning, telling Rachel that she was suffering from a migraine. When I returned home that evening, she was sitting up in my bed, pale but serene. Relieved.

"How do you feel?" I asked.

"Thank you," she said in response. There was a look of pure relief on her face, and that answered my question perfectly. I remember making her a cup of chamomile tea and bringing it to her. She was asleep when I returned, her hair fanned out on my pillow.

"You'll be okay," I whispered.

The next morning, she walked to work with me. It was very quiet between us, in that same comfortable way. I waited for her to fill the silences but she didn't. It felt like there was an invisible rope between us, linking us together. It was spun from our shared secrets, and it has been tethered to us ever since.

* * *

I'm still thinking about Emilie and those early days of our friendship on my morning walk to Xavier. The air is swollen with thick humidity today. That's the thing with the bayou; the wet heat drops from the sky one morning and then settles over you for months on end. Even the air is overbearing and burdensome here.

There's a trickle of sweat tracing the line of my spine and droplets of perspiration dot my upper lip. "You taste like a boiled peanut," I remember Ophelia teasing me as a child, on those many nights when the blackouts came rolling through and we lay prostrate on her floor, both of us sticky. I used to say the same thing to Kamon when she was younger and would let me kiss the back of her damp little neck. I am grateful that Rachel permits us to stay in our same rooms as the girls grow. I wonder if Emilie will be relieved as her babies get bigger and the incoming infants are placed with a worker whose girls have just aged out of the system. I dread the day when my girls begin to age out. Not only do I not think I'll have the energy to be handed a roomful of newborns by then, but I can't stand the thought of the girls I have raised for so long being thrown out into the world with their meager separation money from the Southerly State and only their Xavier education to go on. How will they take care of themselves? Women are not allowed to handle finances professionally, so they cannot obtain a job relating to business in any way. Most are destined to clean houses or perhaps babysit for wealthier people. Even a job in an orphanage is difficult to come by.

Suddenly these worries are weighing me down as much as the heat of the morning. I'm barely aware that Emilie is calling to me as I cross the street by the Place d'Armes Square. I don't want to cut through the square and pass the Trinity but I'm already so hot I want to make the walk as short as possible. I wish I could fill my grandmother's old Chevrolet with gas, but a tank of gas costs more than a week's salary and how can I really waste so much money? Best to save it for the misery of the summer when it's completely unbearable, so long as there are no floods that could sweep away the rusted car with me still in it.

I wave to Emilie and wait for her, trying to push aside my morose thoughts. Of course then I remember her lack of support from last night and I'm annoyed all over again. Clearly Emilie doesn't pick up on my agitation. She's perky after the day off yesterday and looks fresh and relaxed with a newly washed uniform. I know her mother washed and ironed it for her, and I wonder if she knows how fortunate she is to have help like that. I gesture to the bag swinging from my arm.

"I brought you a container of the gumbo. I hope the whole blasted thing isn't spoiled by now."

"You packed it in ice?"

"Yes, but it must be melted already."

"I'm sure it's fine. Let's walk fast and we'll get it into the fridge."

I feel sloppy beside her. I can't remember the last time I ironed my uniforms, and I don't even wash them as often as I should. Then again, I don't have spit-up on mine.

"That was nice yesterday," she says.

"Starting right after church, yes."

"Bella enjoys it," Emilie says.

"I was surprised your parents weren't there."

"I brought their envelope for them."

I nod. That is as good as being there, for all Pote is concerned. The congregation is too large for individual absences to be noticed on Sunday morning. It is the tithes that are missed.

"I should have you bring mine," I laugh. I can't really be angry with her. It feels good when we pair up like this. Emilie is the only person in the world who knows everything about me. Many women know one part or another, but Emilie knows all the parts. You need to have a person like that. The only other person I ever had that with was Ophelia, and I will never get over the missing of that woman.

"I'd rather have you sitting there beside me," Emilie says. I look past her and realize that we are already through the square. We walked by the Trinity and I didn't even notice. I'm grateful my friend didn't point to it and reiterate her pleas to me.

When we walk through the doors of Xavier I reach into my cloth bag and hand her a glass container of gumbo. It nearly slips through my fingers, there's so much condensation on it. It is still cool enough.

"See you for lunch," I tell her. She smiles at me and walks off to her room full of babies. Not one of them is crying.

* * *

"I am thrilled, personally," Rachel says in the breakroom, between tiny mouthfuls of her sandwich. I wish she wouldn't insist on eating here with us. We can never fully relax around her, although maybe that's the point.

"I don't know," Veronica says. She's the nurse in our infirmary and usually doesn't eat lunch with us. When she does, she rarely says more than a pleasantry here or there. I'm surprised she's stating her opinion to Rachel. "I mean, can't anyone accuse anyone else now, without proof?"

"I don't know how much the State was relying on proof before," I say. The gumbo tastes so much different than it did last night. Hot spices shoot through it, burning my tongue and throat as I swallow.

"It's for the best," Rachel says. I try not to focus on her stubby teeth as she eats. "I know Preacher Pote said it originated as a way to report homosexuality, but using it in a way that helps to deter Removals is a good thing."

"Of course," Veronica says. "We wouldn't be here otherwise."

Rachel stops eating and snaps her head in Veronica's direction.

"Not that I mean to say that the only reason to pray for the end of all Removals is because we'd be out of a job," Veronica adds quickly. "Of course not."

"We know what you meant," I tell her, certain that she will never again speak freely. "But this new Tamburo, as Preacher Pote insists on calling it, sounds like a very frightening thing. I shudder to think how many people will write something on a paper with nothing more than a hunch or an assumption, and a girl will be flogged for it, or worse."

"The people in charge aren't worried because it isn't the men who will be falsely accused," Veronica continues. I've never heard her say so much. I look over at Emilie but she's concentrating on her food, stirring bits of onion and crawfish around inside the container.

"I don't think Pote insists on calling it anything," Rachel says to me. "He calls it that because that is what it is called, and it apparently has been called that for many years." She turns back to

Veronica. "And a *Sanguidam* deserves punishment because they *kill*, Veronica. I don't think God can be more clear about that."

Emilie looks up for the first time. "I think what they are saying is, what if someone isn't really a *Sanguidam*? What if they are just falsely accused of being one, because for some reason or another, an enemy or a stranger lies about them?"

"How many enemies can a young girl have?" Rachel asks. "If she's accused of such a serious thing, surely there is a reason. This Tamburo will root out evil, and I say it's about time. We shouldn't stop until every Unborn has an honest chance at life."

I want to ask her what chance at life our girls really have. We all know many will wind up on drugs or in abusive relationships or homeless or some combination of all of those things. If only the State was as concerned with them now that they are out in the world as they were before they were born. But I keep those dark thoughts to myself. I know Emilie would not forgive me if I voiced any sort of dissent.

Rachel wraps the crust of her sandwich neatly in the paper it came in and slips it into her pocket. I wonder if she's saving the crumbs for later. As she turns to leave, I call to her.

"I'd like to speak with Belinda this evening," I say. I worry that I got the night worker's name wrong as Rachel gives me a blank look. Then she narrows her eyes and her lips press together in a tight line.

"There is nothing you can say to her that hasn't already been said. And I can't pay you any extra to have you stay beyond your regular hours."

"You don't have to worry; I'm not looking for extra pay."

"I do have to worry about that, because that's my job," she says to me. "I'm sorry you don't feel that I've done a good enough job of keeping my own workers informed. But you can't stay later. We are responsible for having you on the grounds until 6:00 p.m. and that's it. But thank you for your concern."

I feel like throwing the remains of my blood red lunch across her starched white skirt. Rachel spins around and walks out the door, and I know she'll be standing on the front steps at 6:00 sharp this evening, certain to bid us all a good evening as she greets the incoming night shift.

When I return to my room, the girls are getting ready for their afternoon outside, though none of them want to leave the shelter of the building. The air-conditioner isn't running yet but there is mild relief from the blazing sun and the very worst of the soupy heat in here. But they have no choice, so they saunter outside looking for the leafiest trees to sit under. I try to talk to Kamon but she takes Serah's only hand and sits beside her, reading a chapter of *Little Women* aloud. After a few sentences she has nearly all the girls inching closer to her, soaking up her words about Jo and Beth and Meg. I want to sit and listen too, but Calah finds me and grabs my hand and soon the two of us are chasing a little white butterfly and when Calah leans in to wrap her arms around me, I bury my face in her neck. I want to tell her that she tastes like a boiled peanut but I don't think she will understand, and so I just let her hold me for a minute, despite the heat and her pungent skin. None of them would be here, I tell myself, if their mothers had been *Sanguidam*. Some thoughts are so big and hard to wrap your mind around, they leave you breathless. No wonder some people take comfort in prayer. I wonder if they think maybe God will sort it all out, since they certainly can't.

X

THE NEXT MORNING, I'm just about to plait Serah's hair when the rusted bell hanging inside the entryway of Xavier begins to ring. Serah turns to me, her wide eyes meeting mine; it's been several months since we've heard the three clangs. I look at her open, expectant face, and see something akin to joy.

"A baby," she whispers to me. Her fingers snake their way into my hand as she pulls me toward the door. I know this is not at all ideal, and will be an incredible strain on Emilie and the baby room, but Serah's enthusiasm is contagious, and I laugh, tugging her back.

"We'll all go together," I say. I start to tell the other girls to form a line, but they're already doing so. There are excited whispers among them. Serah is still holding onto me, and I bring her to the front of the line, then turn and face the tittering girls.

"Remember ladies, it's best behavior in there." I give Mishael a pointed look. "And show your respect for Headmistress Rachel." Then I relax my face and smile at them. "But I know you will make me proud, as you always do."

I lead them down the hall, back to the dining area where they've just finished breakfast. Already the tables have been pushed aside by the maintenance crew. The oldest girls, led by a stout, red-faced woman named Hannah, stand in a row on the far side of the room. Some of them will be aging out of Xavier in just a few months. There is little joy on those days, when we say our goodbyes.

Rachel enters this crowded gathering space, holding a baby wrapped in a thin blanket. She is unsmiling. This unexpected arrival is a strain on her, and I know she must have started running numbers in her head the moment she discovered the infant in the Foundling Box. I always thought it should be called the Foundling Drawer, as it's built into the side of the building and slides open with a tug on the handle from the outside. Rachel checks the Foundling Box each morning as soon as she wakes, looking for babies anonymously left there in the night, but I imagine she does not expect to actually find a baby in it these days. Xavier recently hit full capacity. However, many other orphanages have as well, and though it has been well announced in the Parish that we're full, we are forbidden by the State from sealing the Box.

Rachel begins the morning's proceedings as we start everything at Xavier. We recite our Oath of Loyalty to the Southerly State and then we sing the mandated hymns. We cross ourselves and kiss our fingers and stretch our hands out to the flag that stands in the corner of the room. Then we sing our Xavier hymn, written years ago by the first headmistress. It's much less of a dirge than the Southerly State hymns, and the girls' voices fill the hall with strong, clear tones. We even hit the harmonies this morning. One girl hangs onto her note for a second too long, and there are a few muffled sniggers as her voice cuts out upon realizing it.

"Good morning, girls," Rachel says. "We find ourselves here unexpectedly, but a gift from God is always a blessing. And so we gather together around this new little life to welcome her to our Xavier family, and promise to raise her with love and tenderness." Rachel places her hand on the baby's head, nestled somewhere within the folds of the blanket.

"I have already filled out this little one's official paperwork and it will be sent to the Offices of the Southerly State by the end of the day. In accordance with State law, she shall be registered as SC0411. However, as always, we will call this new blessing by a special name. I think we will call her Damaris." Rachel looks down into the baby's face and then back up at her audience. "Welcome to Xavier, little Damaris. Here, you are wanted and loved."

* * *

Emilie pops into my room after lunch. My girls are working on their lessons, and I assume her babies are all sleeping, which is nothing short of miraculous. She curls a finger toward her chest, motioning me to follow her into the hallway. She's clearly been crying.

"She's so sweet," Emilie says as I open my mouth to ask what's wrong. I snap it shut in time. Clearly I know what's wrong. "But there's no room for her. I had to put her in a cradle with Ada for now. And I'm already watering down their formula so much, I don't know how much thinner I can make it." She shakes her head, and new tears slide down her cheeks.

"The new orphanage is coming, remember?" It's months behind schedule though, and the last I heard, renovations on the former art museum had completely stalled. The Southerly State will be hard pressed to find the necessary funds for the project, even though the new orphanage is indeed necessary.

Emilie nods, but she knows the reality. And the promise of a new facility, whenever it opens, does nothing to help her now.

Emilie swipes a tear from the side of her nose. "She's really sweet," she says again. And I know that little Damaris is lucky, despite her inauspicious start in life. I think Emilie has already fallen just a little bit in love with her newest charge, and it won't be long until her charge falls in love with her, as well.

XI

After the excitement of Damaris's arrival, the rest of the day was a blur, leaving me completely exhausted. Although it's only 8:30 p.m., I'm about to collapse for the night when there's a knock on the door. I'm not expecting a patient, but I assume it's a woman coming to me in some sort of emergency. I exchange a nervous look with Miles, who is on his feet, whining and pacing. When I open the door to see Preacher Pote standing on my porch, I nearly gasp out loud. Miles growls at him so much I have to hold onto his collar with two hands. I step out onto the porch, not wanting to allow him into my home. But he opens his hands wide and looks at me benignly, taking a step forward. Miles barks and tries to nip his ankles. The way Pote looks at the dog, I'm sure he wants to kick him aside. But he clears the look from his face and smiles down at me.

"Jane Dupre?" he says, only he doesn't really say 'Jane,' of course. He makes a show of pulling a folded piece of paper from the jacket pocket of his black pants and reading from a list of handwritten names. "Might I come in for just a spell?"

His words are more drawn out than they are at the *Word of Our Father* church and I wonder which one is his actual speaking voice. Ophelia would say he was putting on airs, one way or another.

His face takes on a look of feigned pleasantness. I don't know how to tell him he can't come inside. He is a respected member of the community and according to every rule of law in the Parish, Southerly State, and our church, I am subservient to him as both a parishioner and as a woman. Telling him no would be unheard of and would draw unwanted attention to myself, to say nothing of putting myself at the top of his list of people to remember. But I'm terrified at the thought of him coming inside my home and looking around. Might he open a book and see that the pages do not match the jacket? He wouldn't dare look under my bed, would he? The thought is preposterous. I'm being ridiculous.

Then it hits me that I'm alone out here and if he wants to push his way inside, he certainly can. Miles, for all his bravado, can be silenced easily enough with the sharp black tip of Pote's boot. I truly am at this man's mercy. I decide that being accommodating is my best bet, and I smile down at Miles, cooing at him. "It's okay boy. You can let Preacher Pote in. Good boy, good baby." I rub his ears and his growl turns into a low rumble. He wants to trust me but I know he is wary of this intruder, who looks and smells so much different than the visitors we usually get. Miles is completely unfamiliar with men.

"You know, Preacher, let me just get this guy settled for a minute. Come in. I'll be right back."

I drag Miles into the bedroom and close the door. His angry protest dwindles after a moment. He knows it will do no good. By putting Miles in there, I've also cordoned off the tins of herbs from Pote. I can't imagine he will want to open the door.

When I return to the living room, the preacher is standing in front of the bookshelf, his hat in his hands. I think my heart might burst with anxiety but he turns to me and says, "I didn't want to take the liberty of sitting down without you."

I sit on the single hardback chair and gesture to the couch. There's no way I'm sitting next to him. I can't believe how silent it is. Even the shrieks from the bayou would be welcome, but it's as if the creatures in the swamp have an ear cocked to my house, waiting quietly to see what will happen. Whatever he wants with me, he will have his way. There is a strange resignation in that singular thought.

"I'm on a bit of a community outreach visit, you might say. Visiting the worshippers in my Parish." He glances at his hat. "I thought

I might as well start out here in the bayou and work my way back. Not all in one evenin', of course." He looks at me intently. I have the strange sensation that his eyes should not be that pale blue color. They are unsettling in their intensity, but the color is almost pretty, which doesn't befit him. As he speaks, he drops the endings of some of his words, something he must take pains not to do from the pulpit.

"Did you drive here?" I ask, but then realize that of course he did. Our tithes would buy premium gasoline for him any day of the week.

He ignores my question. "I thought it was perhaps high time to pay a visit here," he says, only it sounds like "ha time to pay a vis-ut he-ah."

"To me, Sir?" I hate addressing him like this. I hate how my voice is soft and submissive and oozing with respect.

"Not only you, Ms. Dupre. You and all my followers."

"You mean God's followers?" It's out before I can stop it. I'm almost dizzy when I hear the words in my own ears. "Jesus H. Christ," Ophelia would say. "My word, you've stepped in it now, *Sha*."

But he doesn't get angry. His voice is almost a whisper when he speaks. "But of course, God's followers, Ms. Dupre. I only mean that I am the vessel through which they speak to Him."

There's a lot I can say to that, but my good sense has returned and I nod demurely.

"Of course, Preacher. I knew just what you meant. It was a silly joke, but I don't think it came out quite right."

"It came out just fine," he says. "My real reason for visiting the parishioners is to speak about the Tamburo. I know it's causing a bit of a stir."

I can't imagine that this actually concerns him. He is in charge, there's no election that could possibly oust him, and there are a good many people who are besotted with this new development.

"Do *you* have questions or concerns, Ms. Dupre?" he asks, leaning forward. I catch just a hint of leather and oaky moss and breath mints emanating from him. The scent isn't entirely unpleasant but I don't want to be close enough to him to smell it.

"I do not," I say. Of course I do, but I'd never voice any of them to him. I'm not that brave or that stupid.

"I confess I have been wanting to pay you a visit," he adds. He does not have the decency to look shy as he continues. "You've caught my eye once or twice sittin' in congregation. You never have any kin with you, do you? Your envelope is just for you. There are no other Dupres on my register." He doesn't wait for me to answer. "I admire the work you do with the girls at Xavier, you know," he continues.

I don't like that I've caught his eye. I really don't like that he clearly knows a great deal about me.

"How did you know where I work?" Maybe I shouldn't ask this but I'm too disconcerted not to.

Now he does look caught off guard, but only for a moment. "Your place of work is listed on the envelope, you'll recall, along with your address. It was easy enough to find you."

I wonder if he's spoken to Rachel about me. I can barely stand the thought of the two of them, her white uniform in striking contrast to his charcoal clothes.

"It's sad to me that someone like you is all alone in the world," he says, no trace of sympathy in his voice. "I do believe life would be safer for you if you had someone lookin' out for your best interest."

"That's very kind of you, Preacher, but I'm doing just fine."

"You are now," he says, tracing a slow finger along the brim of his hat. "But we wouldn't want that to change in the future."

I don't know what he's implying but I go from being uncomfortable to being afraid. He stands up and moves toward my chair and I wonder if he will try to overpower me. For one white-hot moment it seems as though he's contemplating doing exactly that. But then he tips his hat to me and places it on his head.

"I know you have an early mornin', Miss. I should be gettin' outta your way now." Then he remembers to finish the endings of his words. "Let's just call this a getting to know each other visit, shall we? I'd like to call on you again."

"To discuss any concerns I might have?"

"If we want to call it that, we most certainly can." I stand up, anxious to lead him to the door. He takes my hand and raises it to his lips. His skin is clammy but his lips are dry as they scrape across the top of my hand. I try to suppress a shudder but it courses through me, regardless. A sense of relief flushes through me that he hadn't come over here on a suspicion he had, or to follow a lead in an investigation about me. It would appear as though there was not a little slip of paper with my name on it in his Tamburo. But the thought that he seems to want to pursue me is only slightly less grotesque. The best approach is to ignore his advances for as long as possible without making him angry. I don't want to think about how long that might take.

Suddenly Pote's eyes slide down from mine and look at the floor, somewhere behind me and to my right.

"Well, I'll be…" he says, dropping my hand and striding across the floor, squatting down near the corner. Before I even spin fully around, he's standing again, holding something in his fist. With abject horror, the most primitive part of my brain screams 'snake' before the rest of my mind processes it. But it is; it's a twisting, writhing snake that was apparently sitting in the corner *of my house*. I have seen them often enough out in the swamp, but never in my home. I want to scream but I don't know how the preacher will react to that and my throat is seized up anyway. Pote has the snake just behind its head, the underside facing me, and its body ripples back and forth in the air as it desperately seeks purchase. I almost feel sorry for it, the snake and I both in the grasp of this man, but the slithering thing repulses me. No matter how many times I come across one in the bayou, the revulsion never dulls. And to think this made its way inside. I already know I won't sleep tonight.

"This here fella's a speckled king snake," the preacher says, but all I can do is watch the snake writhe. "Not poisonous, though I'm sure he would've given you quite a scare if you happened on him with bare feet."

"Get it out. Please."

"You don't want to see?" He takes a step toward me and I back away. "Harmless, Miss Dupre. Totally harmless."

"Please," I say again. I can't have him bring it closer.

He laughs then, the first time I've heard an actual laugh from him, and crosses the room in a few wide steps. He opens the door and walks onto the porch. I don't want to watch but I need to know the thing is really and truly gone. He throws it—far. I can't stand to see it jerking through the air but I can't look away. And then I'm biting back a sob. My entire body is shaking. How would I have gotten it out of here if he hadn't come by tonight?

I walk to the door before the preacher can come back in. I should thank him but the words don't come out. He seems to accept that, maybe even relish it a little bit.

"Glad I stopped over," he says, and he does not try to take my hand again. I shut the door before he's off the porch and I run to open the bedroom door for Miles. I want to collapse onto him and press my face into his fur and cry and cry, but he doesn't have time for that. Usually he senses when I need a cuddle. But now, he races straight to the corner where Pote stood a minute before. Miles sniffs the floor in a frenzy, turning repeatedly in a quick circle. He starts to whine again and looks at me as if to question my involvement. My knees almost buckle when the realization washes over me.

Miles would have sniffed out that snake in an instant. It couldn't have been in the house when he and I were relaxing before. It never would have escaped his nose. And so I think it must have been brought into my home by a man who wanted to appear to rescue me. Or was he giving me some sort of veiled warning?

I let the dog spin and sniff, his nails skittering on the floor as he tries to find the elusive intruder. But his antics don't make me smile like they usually do. Instead, I sink to the floor and hide my face in my hands. I know exactly how Kamon feels, not wanting to be without me at night. I would give anything for company right now. Tonight, I need more than a big goofy dog and the ghost of Ophelia Dupre.

XII

For a week, I don't see the preacher. I worry that perhaps he was investigating me after all, and his interest in me was nothing but a ruse. But when I don't hear from him or any Officers of the State, I begin to relax a bit. I do have trouble sleeping, and more than once I've woken with a start, dreaming of snakes slithering over me, their eyes the palest blue.

I don't think I should skip church on Sunday, but I enter just before the service starts and sit in the back. I see Emilie and Bella and their mother sitting in the same place we sat a week ago. Her father will be somewhere on the other side of the partition, alone. I steal a glimpse of the Tamburo, wondering how many names sit on incendiary bits of paper.

I slip outside at the end, not waiting for Emilie and her family. Today is for them. Maybe she will cook a meal with them and sit on her own porch and her mother will iron her uniforms and they will make sun tea to drink along with a steaming pot of jambalaya. I don't want to be jealous, but I have a whole day alone stretched out before me. Maybe if I lingered after the service, Emilie's mother would have invited me to their house for the afternoon. She has certainly done so on many occasions. But as much as I want the company, I don't feel up to an entire day of small talk and tedious politeness. It will be a long day, but it will be mine.

* * *

I'm actually relieved when Monday morning comes around, but as soon as I get to Xavier I see that Kamon hasn't gotten out of bed. The other girls make their way down to breakfast but she is curled into herself, her back curving like the scalloped top of a shell. I can see she's awake but she doesn't acknowledge me.

"Kay," I whisper, sitting on her bed and placing a palm on her forehead. She feels cool. "Are you sick?"

"No," she mutters. Her body shifts and she moves away from my touch.

"You aren't allowed to stay in bed, you know that. You need to get up and have your breakfast."

"Then I'm sick," she says.

"You're cool as a cucumber," I tell her, and I remember my grandmother saying that same thing to me so many times, so long ago.

"I got hurt."

"What do you mean you got hurt?" Already my hands are moving over her, trying to find an injury. She looks fine.

"It's my leg," she whispers. "Here." She rolls toward me, and I see a long, jagged gash snaking its way up her shin. I don't mean to alarm her but I can't help taking in a sharp breath. It looks deep, much worse than a superficial scratch. It must have happened in the night, because dried blood is caked inside the gash. Near the bottom of the cut, drops of fresh blood seep out of the wound. She rolls away from me again.

"Oh, Kay," I say, and I lean forward to rub her back. My fingers roll over the knobby bones of her shoulder. "What on earth happened to you?"

"I got up to go to the bathroom last night. I was half-asleep. I wasn't paying attention at the sink and I scraped my leg against a rusted pipe sticking out of the wall."

My frustration is immediate. Why don't things get taken care of around here? Why is a rusted pipe sticking out of the wall in the bathroom? Why don't the evening workers have to stay awake all night to make sure things like this don't happen? But I don't want Kamon to see that I'm angry. I just want to take care of her.

"We need to get you to the infirmary. That has to get cleaned out. Why didn't you go up there last night?"

"I was tired," she said.

I think of her hurting, curling up into herself and trying to go back to sleep in the middle of the night. Now that she's shifted on the bed, I notice blood stains on her sheet. It's not wash day today and I doubt there are spare sheets, but I can worry about that later.

"C'mon, let's get you up," I say. I grasp her elbow and tug on her. She sits up in the bed but winces and looks down at her leg.

Then she flops back down. "It hurts," she says, her voice uncharacteristically small.

"I'll tell the nurse to come down here then," I say. I have to hurry, because the girls will be back from breakfast in under an hour and I need Kamon to be taken care of by then, so I can tend to the rest of them. There's no phone in our room and so I'll have to go upstairs to tell Veronica that she needs to come down here with me.

"I'll be right back," I tell Kamon. She doesn't answer.

Veronica has three girls splayed out on cots in the infirmary, and the entire room smells like disinfectant and cherry-flavored medicine. She looks harried. "Sore throats," she says, nodding in the direction of the girls. When I tell Veronica about Kamon's leg, she tells me she can't leave the sick girls alone in the infirmary; they are all fairly young. With no other choice, I rush back downstairs and tell Kamon that we'll go slowly, but she needs to come with me.

"Hang onto my arm and we'll take it slow."

Kamon sits up, her shoulders slumped. She has dried blood on her fingertips.

"Here we go," I say. She gets up gingerly and leans against me. She's so light I can hold onto her easily and make sure she stays steady on her feet.

By the time we get back to the infirmary, Veronica has already set up a cot for Kamon. It's right under the only window in the room; branches of a magnolia tree scrape the glass. Kamon is visibly relieved to be able to sit. Veronica talks to her in soothing tones as she washes out the wound with warm soapy water and applies ointment. Kamon bites her lip a lot, but she doesn't cry. Veronica wraps Kamon's leg in a gauzy bandage.

"You can go back downstairs if you'd like, honey," Veronica says. "Or you can rest up here if you'd rather."

"I'll stay here," Kamon says, not even thinking about it. Veronica nods and smooths Kamon's hair away from her eyes. The poor girl probably needed the attention as much as the ointment. I wish she had more moments filled with motherly touches.

I know Kamon is being well cared for, so I give her hand three quick squeezes and she answers with four. I tell her I'll check on her during my lunch break.

* * *

"She doesn't have a fever," Veronica says when I come back to check on Kamon. "But she's really complaining about pain. Nothing looked infected to me, and her leg isn't warm, but I'll open the bandage and see if there's any pus. I usually don't like to do that. They never close properly after they're opened."

Veronica couldn't just give Kamon a new bandage. State-run institutions are not known for their abundance of supplies.

"I'd like to keep her up here tonight so we can keep an eye on her. Plus, she was telling me she didn't want to take the stairs again." Veronica looks at the row of cots filling her cramped room. There are two small cabinets attached to the wall and a counter with jars of cotton swabs and cotton balls and tissues. I wonder how often she runs out of supplies and how long she needs to wait until they're replenished. "She can stay so long as nobody else gets sick," she says, more to herself than to me. "Otherwise we'll be out of beds."

"Thanks for taking good care of her," I say. Veronica is fairly new here. I'm not sure she's even a registered nurse, those are so hard to come by. But I can see she does her job well, with what little she has.

"I'm just going to say goodbye to her," I say.

Kamon is sitting up in the cot, watching the magnolia branches scratch against the window. She smiles when she sees me. I love that smile.

"I feel a little better," she says. I know she doesn't want me to worry about her. "Am I sleeping here tonight?"

"Yes. Veronica wants someone to keep an eye on that leg of yours. Does it feel hot?"

She shakes her head. "It hurts a lot, though. I want to stay up here."

"I know. You can. The girls will sure miss you. You'll have a lot of *Little Women* to catch up on tomorrow."

"If I'm back down there by tomorrow."

"You will be, sweetie. You're okay."

She nods. "Is the nurse here all night?"

"Not Veronica. A night nurse."

"And she stays in here with us?"

"Yes."

Kamon's eyes close. "So we won't be alone," she whispers, relief rushing through the words with her breath of warm air.

* * *

At 6:00 p.m., I say goodnight to the girls in my room and then slip into the bathroom down the hall. It's a shared bathroom for my girls and the roomful of girls who are older. They keep it very tidy; they don't have a choice. There are no hygiene products in here other than rough bars of State-issued soap, used for both body and hair. I walk down the row of sinks, bending under each one and looking for a pipe jutting out from the grimy lime-green tiles. The wall beneath the sinks has plenty of chips and pockmarks and several holes where pipes must have been at one time. But I can't find anything sticking dangerously out of the wall.

When I get to the last sink in the row, I do find a jagged, protruding pipe, burnt orange with crusted rust, but it's barely an inch long. And it's directly underneath the sink, so there's no way Kamon could have scraped her leg on it, producing a gash the length of her shin. She must have used the other bathroom, farther from our room. I don't why she would have done that. My girls don't like to use the younger girls' bathroom. It's a matter of pride. Maybe she was too tired to think straight. I really need to start my walk home, and I know how Rachel feels about us staying late, but I don't want anyone else getting hurt, so I walk down the hall at a fast clip, hoping not to bump into anyone on my way to the other bathroom. It will be a long, lonely walk home for me tonight; Emilie has probably already left. As I pass by my own room, I remember that I never pulled Kamon's sheet off the bed, and I'm sure there's a stain on her mattress that matches the rusted pipe in the wall. For a moment, I consider leaving it until tomorrow. I don't want to walk back in there and have the girls see me, since I'm already supposed to be gone. But I want everything neat and clean for the morning. I slip into the room, trying to be quiet, though I do get a few boisterous greetings from the girls.

Belinda gives me a strange look when she sees me, and I know she doesn't want me in here, now that it's her turf, but I nod to her and walk over to Kamon's bed like I'm supposed to be here. I don't have a clean sheet to replace the stained one, but since wash day is several days away, and I don't want Kamon to sleep on a dirty sheet when she returns from the infirmary, I decide to take the sheet home with me to wash. It probably won't be dry by morning; the air is so humid that my drying line isn't of much use, but I can always bring one of my own sheets back for her tomorrow.

I pull off the sheet from the bed, the fitted corners so loose they were barely clinging to the bed at all, and ball it up in my arms. I lean into the bed frame to nudge it into alignment with the other beds in the room. As I do, the toe of my boot kicks something, and I hear it slide farther under the bed. It must be a pen, one used to fill out the endless worksheets the girls are given. I want to take my foot and kick it again, the thought of what it's used for makes me that angry. But I bend down to pick it up, because Kamon will be looking for it when she returns.

But it isn't a pen. It's a knife. It's one of the knives the older girls are allowed to use with dinner. Fairly dull; after all, it isn't like it's needed to cut a steak. But it's sharp enough to make a slice through flesh, especially the tender flesh of a young shin. Kamon's blood is still on it. I want to vomit. I stand up so fast that I'm dizzy. Belinda continues to watch me so I press the knife against my skirt, rendering it all but invisible.

Is Kamon so unhappy here that she's hurting herself? Is she depressed? She never seemed to be. Quiet and melancholy at times, yes. But to want to cut herself? Was this just practice for something worse? I want to throttle her and press her to me all at once.

Everything comes together then, in an awful instant. "I want to stay here," I remember her telling Veronica. And to me, with a relieved smile, "We won't be alone." She didn't want to hurt herself because she was unhappy. She wanted to hurt herself because… *why?* She wanted to be sent to the infirmary. She made sure to complain to Veronica about pain, and to tell her that she couldn't walk back downstairs. She didn't want to be alone at night. I've been thinking Kamon missed me when I went home in the evenings. I thought she wanted my company, since the two of us are so close. But I don't think it was me at all. She just doesn't want to be in her room. But *why*, I think, with a sudden nauseated feeling. What is she afraid of?

XIII

I FLY UP THE STEPS TO THE INFIRMARY, my long skirt bunched in my right hand so I won't trip. Veronica looks startled when I bump into her just outside the door.

"I'm on my way out," she says. "My replacement is inside, if you want to say good night to Kamon again." She starts to walk away and then turns back to me. "It's after six." She looks at me pointedly. "I don't think you want to stay late."

She remembers my conversation in the lunch room with Rachel, but I don't care; there's something I need to ask Kamon.

"Good night," is my only response to Veronica, and then I push through the doorway of the infirmary. One of the girls from earlier has gone back to her room. No new girls have arrived. Kamon is sitting up in bed, her pillow propped against the wall. She's eating spoonfuls of pudding. Veronica's replacement nods at me and takes the temperature of one of the smaller girls.

"Kamon," I say, and I hear the word catch in my throat.

"You came back?" She turns to me, her eyes lighting up. She's in a clean nightshirt.

"Did you really trip into a pipe?" I don't want the nurse to hear either of us so I lean right over her and smooth her covers.

"Yes," she says. There's a dot of pudding in the corner of her mouth. I dab at it with my finger. She looks away from me.

"You really got hurt? In the bathroom?"

"I was *bleeding,*" she says, and her voice sounds much stronger than it did this morning.

I press her again.

"You don't want to stay downstairs tonight, do you?"

She puts down the spoon in the empty bowl and I take it from her. She doesn't answer me for what feels like a really long time.

"I think your shift is over," the nurse says behind me, but I don't turn around.

"Kamon?"

Just one tear falls. I watch it slide by the side of her nose and come to rest on her upper lip, not far from where the pudding was a few moments ago. I don't touch it.

"I can't tell you," she says.

My stomach is filled with acid, and it's rising up into my throat. "You most certainly can." I try to keep my voice calm, even though I want to shake her to make the words fall out. "Kamon," I say, though the word sounds sterner than I mean it to.

"You really do need to go," the nurse says, and this time I turn around.

"I need a minute, please," I say. I've been here years longer than she has and I don't care if she reports me to Rachel, assuming Veronica hasn't already. Nothing she could say or do will make me leave just yet.

"What are you afraid of? You need to answer me, Kamon. Please."

The girl turns her head back to the window. The late spring evening has another hour of good daylight, and the branches of the magnolia tree paint long shadows on the bed.

Just when I am certain I won't be able to get her to say another word, she speaks. Her voice is so soft, I have to put my head right against hers to hear her when she says, "The janitor."

"Oh my God," I say into her hair. "Oh my fucking God."

* * *

Rachel is stunned to see me burst into her office without knocking. She looks up from her desk, her eyes round. She says something with that strange little mouth of hers, probably telling me to get the hell out, but I don't hear anything other than a rushing in my ears that sounds like the mighty roar of a hurricane. Each of Kamon's words that I drank in are droplets of moonshine, burning me up from the inside. After she named her attacker, the whole story came rushing out. When she was finished, she looked relieved at no longer having to carry such a terrible secret. I, however, am apoplectic. Rachel snaps her mouth shut.

"Who's the janitor on duty at night?" I ask. I feel hot tears sliding down my face. Rachel stands up and places her palms flat on her desk. There's hardly any paper on it. The room is as Puritan as she is. I wait for her to yell at me, to tell me to calm down, but she doesn't. Instead she draws in a deep breath and lets it out in a tiny stream.

"Benjamin Pierre. Why?"

But the way she's looking at me with an almost timid expression, I think she doesn't want to hear my response.

"Who decided it was a good idea to have a male janitor in an all-girls orphanage, Rachel? On what level did anyone think that was a good idea?"

"I don't make those hires," she says. "You know that."

"You hired me."

"I have some say over the workers in direct contact with the girls. The State sends over workers involved with maintenance and upkeep."

"Well it sounds like Benjamin is indeed in *direct contact* with the girls." I can barely speak, but somehow, I tell Rachel what has transpired between the janitor and one of the girls in her orphanage.

I want to blame Rachel for this, but her face takes on a pinched look and her mouth twists in on itself. I can tell she's angry. It isn't fair for me to blame her for this. She has only so much control over Xavier; it's State-run. Suddenly I realize that she must put up with a constant barrage of bullshit and her hands are usually tied.

They have all the real control. But now there's a thirteen-year-old girl who's been repeatedly assaulted inside their institution, and she can't be the only girl, and the moonshine words blend with the pennyroyal poison inside me and I know that if Benjamin Pierre was standing in front of me, I would literally kill him.

"Why don't you want me staying after my shift ends? Why don't you want me talking with Belinda? Are you covering this up?" But I know she isn't. I just have nobody else to attack.

"No. No! You know I would never want anything to happen to any of the girls. I care for them very much. And I know how you feel about Kamon."

"I never said anything about Kamon," I say. My head is buzzing.

"I know that's who you were just speaking with. Veronica mentioned it on her way out." Rachel softens her voice. "She told me you were just up there saying goodnight and would be down in a minute. I think she wanted to be sure you didn't get in trouble."

"Why would I get in trouble? What was the harm in staying late and speaking with one of my girls? And what would have been the harm in staying late one night to speak with Belinda?"

"There would be no harm." Rachel shakes her head. "I'm sorry. I try to run a tight ship. People need to respect their hours. Especially you. I thought if I allowed you to start staying late, you'd stay later and later and I can't pay you for that." She holds up her hand to stop me from interrupting. "I know you wouldn't want to get paid for it. But that's the rule. And you got so attached, especially to Kamon. I thought you might start trying to foster her again, and you can't."

"If I did that, she wouldn't have been…abused." I can't say the other word. Not yet, not out loud.

"I don't know what to do," Rachel says.

I have never seen her look quite so bewildered before. "You need to get rid of him. Immediately."

"I can't terminate him. I can only put in a request to the State. A formal complaint first, followed by my suggestion for termination."

"Are you kidding me?" I slam my hand on her desk. "That is ludicrous. You sleep here, Rachel. You've never had dealings with this guy?"

"Of course I have. He's always seemed pleasant. He's young, this is his first job. He completes the maintenance requests I give him. I've never had reason for concern." She pauses, then adds, "He passed a background check."

"And you get to sleep in a room upstairs with a lock on the door."

"He has a skeleton key. But I've never felt unsafe."

"I guess he likes younger blood." Rachel looks ill when I say this.

"I can't write him up for not doing his work. He keeps everything in very good condition. I can't say that he abused an orphan. You know what will happen. They'll say it's her word against his and she had a crush on him and wanted to punish him for not paying any attention to her. They'll say it's not fair to ruin the life of a good, honest man over the silly hysterics of one girl. They would allow him to stay. And then he'll just be pissed off."

"So you're saying we let a predator keep prowling around at night? Because unless you can lock up all the girls, that's unacceptable."

"I can request a transfer for him."

"That will take weeks."

"Months, probably."

"Is he here yet? I'll talk to him myself," I say, and my level of rage actually frightens me.

"You won't do anything but get yourself in trouble," Rachel says. "Sit down. You haven't even told me the details. We'll get Belinda in here and go through everything together."

"Ah, so Kamon gets raped and now I can finally talk to Belinda. Thank you." When the word comes out, it cracks the air in half.

"Let me get Belinda," Rachel says through gritted teeth.

I sit in her office and wait. I have to ball up my fist and press it to my mouth to keep from sobbing. The adrenaline running through me is waning and I feel like my whole body is going to crash. I see

Kamon's face, still filled with the roundness of childhood, and I hear her words over and over. How this man, this Benjamin Pierre, came to her late at night, pushing his hand over her mouth the first time so she wouldn't scream. How he whispered to her that if she was very good and very quiet, he wouldn't hurt any of the other girls in the room the way he was hurting her. And how the last time he came to her, just a few nights ago, he spoke into her ear about how if she fought him, he'd write down her name on a little slip of paper and put it in a metal box in his church, and a preacher would find her name in there and whip her for being a sinner.

"I don't know why he said that," Kamon whispered to me a few minutes ago. "I don't fight him anymore. It's easier that way."

I think about how vulnerable I felt in my own home when Preacher Pote showed up. I think about how I was completely at his mercy. I think about how scared and overpowered Kamon must have been, and I realize that we are all that speckled king snake, caught by the neck, twisting helplessly in the wind.

XIV

When Belinda follows Rachel back into the office, her eyes dart around and look everywhere but at me.

"You knew about this?" I'm out of my seat in a moment.

"No," Belinda says, and she looks so upset, I know she isn't lying.

"Of course you didn't. Because you aren't watching the girls all night."

Rachel intervenes. "It's policy that after lights-out, the evening workers ensure that the girls are all sleeping and then they're allowed to lie down and sleep for a bit themselves."

"That's absurd," I tell them both.

"It's State-mandated. They're paid half of the daytime workers' salaries. They aren't expected to stand guard all night."

"Then maybe the State shouldn't allow disgusting pigs onto the grounds of the orphanage. Clearly some policing at night is needed."

Belinda twists the material of her skirt. "I feel so awful," she says, and she begins to cry. But I still can't feel anything other than a lightning bolt of rage slicing through me.

"You never saw this man? This…Benjamin Pierre?" My throat seizes as his name slides over it.

"I have," Belinda nods. "He's always been nice to me. I would never have thought…"

"Isn't that always the way," Rachel says. She rubs the nape of her neck, right underneath where her bun rests.

"You've had this happen before?"

"No, not since I've been at Xavier. But you know…so often it's someone you don't expect."

"He can't stay, Rachel."

"I know. I need to think."

"And I'm staying here tonight. Send Belinda home."

Belinda shakes her head. "I need the money. I can't lose any wages."

"Then stay," I tell her. "And I'll stay too. I'll stay awake all night. I couldn't sleep if I tried." I look at Rachel. "Nobody ever has to know."

Rachel nods at me and tells Belinda to go back to her room. Before she leaves, Belinda extends her hand out to me.

"I'm sorry," she says, tears still pooled in her eyes. "And I'm sorry to officially meet you under these circumstances." I don't take her hand.

As she leaves, I turn back to my supervisor. "I'm staying in the infirmary tonight. I trust you will make sure someone is awake in my girls' room downstairs. For the entire night."

I don't wait for an answer. Somehow I've taken charge, at least for now, and Rachel has willingly ceded to me. As I walk upstairs, I think about the chance that this janitor, this vile piece of shit, was honest to Kamon about not hurting anyone else. What does the word of an abuser mean? Nothing. But I think he might have been telling the truth. Some of the younger girls would have probably shown outward signs of psychological trauma. Or physical signs. The bastard knew exactly what he was doing.

Walking into the infirmary, I see Kamon sitting on the edge of a smaller girl's cot. She's rubbing the girl's feet under the covers and telling her a story, one I used to tell her many years ago, about a beautiful Snow Queen who accidentally froze her entire village. The little girl's eyes are wide and she's hanging on Kamon's gossamer-spun words. Neither of them look over at me, but the night nurse nods in my direction.

"I'll be here for the evening," I say. I sit down on Kamon's narrow bed, planning to wrap my arms around her for the entire night. I worry about Miles for a moment, for how he'll be anxious about me and miss his evening meal and undoubtedly make a mess on the floor, but I can't go home to him. I have to stay right here. When Kamon joins me on the bed and snuggles into my arms, she looks calm and unafraid.

"You're still here," she says into my neck, and then she's asleep, and I feel myself drifting off too, the relief of holding her a very tangible thing. When I pull my eyes open in the morning, we are both still in the exact same position.

XV

IT WOUND UP BEING EASIER than I thought to get rid of Benjamin Pierre. At first I wanted him to pay dearly for what he'd done. I wanted him strung up on the Trinity and beaten until he was unrecognizable. But Rachel insisted that would never happen, and that our best course of action was to make sure he did not set foot inside our orphanage again. I almost agreed with her, right up until the point when I realized that he would still be free to step inside a different orphanage, filled with other defenseless girls. We would be horribly complicit if we sent him away from here just so he could go and prey on someone else.

I won't lie; I even thought about the herbs under my bed, and how I could make a lethal cocktail for him, stirred into a glass of sweet tea, or maybe even a nice brandy milk punch. I did not say that out loud to Rachel or even to Emilie. I scared myself for even thinking such a thing. And I'm glad to say I dismissed it as soon as it appeared in my mind, though I did relish in the brief reverie of handing him a glass and watching as the contents slid over his Adam's apple.

In the end, it was his own words that we turned against him.

Rachel was adamant that I was never to speak to him. I could not promise that, but I swore I wouldn't do it on the grounds of Xavier. In the end, the two of us came to a compromised solution.

After several days of trying to go about our normal routine, even though nothing felt normal to me, I ducked out of my room early, knowing Rachel would stand in for me until Belinda arrived. Emilie popped her head out as I walked by, cradling little Damaris, and mouthed the words, "Be careful." I simply nodded and she silently stepped back over the threshold and retreated into her room.

I stood just off the property of the old university. The air hung like a wet sheet. I wasn't nervous, though maybe I should have been. I wasn't sure which direction Benjamin would be coming from, and so I scanned back and forth until I saw a slight figure approaching. A young guy sauntered up the broken sidewalk, his hands stuffed in his pockets, his eyes on his scuffed shoes. Rachel and Belinda were right. He did not look like a rapist.

I wanted to shove him and catch him off balance. I wanted to kick him with the toe of my black boot, right at the top of his cheekbone or maybe the soft spot of his temple. I wanted to see his eyes look up at me in fear, just as Kamon's eyes must have looked at him. But I've never hit anyone in my life. He would have overtaken me in a second. You're the speckled king snake, I reminded myself. Only there was this one drop of venom I was hoping would do the trick.

"Benjamin," I said to him, stepping in his path. He looked up, showing no recognition of my face. I was glad of that.

"Evenin', ma'am," he said, clearly expecting me to move aside for him. I leaned forward, close enough to smell just a wisp of gin on his breath.

"Benjamin," I repeated. "I have a proposition for you."

I can't imagine what he thought I might propose, but it certainly was very far from the words that followed.

"I know what you did," I told him. "Everyone knows." His eyes narrowed and he sidestepped around me, but I sensed it coming and moved with him, two strangers in a lurid waltz.

"Everyone knows what you did to that girl. Everyone knows, but we won't turn you in for it. It won't do any good, now will it?"

He smiled a little, he actually *smiled,* and stared me down. He knew I was speaking the truth. He had nothing to worry about.

"But here's the thing," I said, breathing in the gin and arrogance emanating from him. "You know that metal box you were talking about the other day? The one with the names of 'sinners' inside? The Tamburo?" The slightest note of discomfort mingled with his other scents.

"I wonder what would happen if *your* name appeared in there? Oh, not as the disgusting rapist pig that you are. We all know that wouldn't hold much water. I don't think that's even a crime worthy of the Tamburo. But if you were a homosexual? Now that just might do it." He took a step back from me but I moved forward with him, and our dance continued.

"I mean, there are several witnesses to the, shall we say, sodomy, that we have caught you engaging in. With an unknown male, of course. I have three witnesses who can attest to your hedonistic behavior. Not that we really *need* witnesses at this point. I mean, the Tamburo is based on anonymity, after all. But they want to testify anyway. We all just can't wait to see you destroyed."

He looked truly afraid and I admit I enjoyed it more than I should have. It helped to know that Rachel and Emilie were peering out their windows, making sure I was all right.

He didn't look intelligent but I saw the flash in his eyes as he realized what I was talking about.

"You threatenin' me with a framing? Nobody'd believe ya'll for a half a minute."

"There's those pesky witnesses, though," I reminded him. "People who will corroborate my story. They will put your name in the box, too. Several accusations could appear on the same day, in fact, written by unfortunate people who are just shocked and appalled at the sodomy they unwittingly observed. I doubt you'd make it to trial. There hasn't been a charge of homosexuality in quite a while. I think everyone would be very pleased to deliver justice to you swiftly.

"Although," I continued, Benjamin finally looking exactly like the disgusting coward that he really was, "that's a lot of effort. There is one other option." I paused and he leaned toward me, looking like he wanted to listen to me and hit me at the same time.

"You filthy whore." He spat the words and then he really did spit, not on me but just to the side. It landed next to my boot in an angry splatter.

"Here's my proposition, Mr. Pierre. Get out of here and don't come back. I have a check for two week's wages right here." I waved a piece of paper at him. It disgusted me that he would actually get paid after what he had done, but Rachel said that was the easiest way, and I had to choose my battles. "Let's say you told Xavier verbally that you are resigning immediately. Consider the wages your severance pay. And you are not to apply to work at another orphanage or other facility with children. We'll be watching for you. If you do, your name goes in the box."

"Maybe I'll put your name in first, bitch." There was no hint of the feigned gentleness that Rachel and Belinda had seen in the orphanage. I was witness to exactly what Kamon had seen—a mean, hateful young man.

"There are too many people who can accuse you," I said, though the mention of my name in that metal box made me want to retch. He had no idea how accurate that accusation would be. "Even if you wanted to put in my name, though I doubt you even know my name, I'd say, 'Benjamin Pierre wrote down my name because he wants to get rid of me, after what I've seen him do. With another man.' The others will come forward as well."

He looked sick. I don't know if it was fear or the thought that people would actually think he was gay.

"You're getting off easy. Wages, no accusations. Go to the Offices of the State and apply for something else. Since you're already in their system, you'll be placed quickly." I held up two other pieces of paper. "A glowing recommendation and a letter thanking you for your service." I almost did battle over that one, but in the end, Rachel was correct. She was just following all the proper procedures.

Benjamin snatched the check from one hand and the letters from the other.

"That little bitch in there isn't worth the trouble," he said. In that moment, when he spoke of Kamon like that, I wished I had opted for the brandy milk punch after all.

For some reason, he seemed scared to turn his back to me, which was preposterous because what could I have physically done to him? "You're getting off easy," I repeated as he started to back away.

He did turn then, and was at a veritable run by the time he was halfway down the street. I turned around and saw Emilie standing in her window. She was too far away and too shaded by the trees for me to really see her face, but I wondered if her heart was pounding as fast as mine.

* * *

I'm thinking about Benjamin Pierre's face now as I help the girls get ready for bed. My confrontation with him was a week ago. For the first few days, I was scared he would show up at the orphanage brandishing a firearm, like so many angry and frustrated young men are wont to do. But as the days passed I began to realize that he must have decided it was easiest to take his wages, get a new job, and vanish from our lives. He was unscathed, unlike my Kamon, though she is bravely fighting the demons he brought upon her each and every day.

It's just after six in the evening. I'm ready to leave, but I know Rachel won't mind if I linger for a few minutes. She and I have come to an understanding over the past week and a half. I look over at Belinda, just settling in to begin her shift. Our room is dusty and the floors need a good scrubbing, but the new janitor only started last night and she's catching up the best she can. We didn't leave it too bad for her, trying to clean up as we went along.

I look over at Kamon. She's sitting on Mishael's bed, something Mishael usually does not allow. There are six or seven other girls crowded onto the bed with her, Mishael pressed right against her side. The remaining girls sit on the floor, their faces looking up as

Kamon reads from the tattered copy of *Little Women*. I know she's at the very last bit, and I don't want to go home until she's finished, even though Miles has only just forgiven me for my absence and I don't want to be too late.

I know this book well. It's my own copy Kamon is holding, and it was Ophelia's before that. It was my mother's in between. Ophelia filled in my mother's absence so well, I don't think of her nearly as much as I should, but now I wish she had gotten the chance to read it to me herself. The girls are all intent on the picnic Mrs. March is having with her daughters. I wonder if the girls are imagining what it would be like to have a mother to picnic with. I wonder if they would consider me an orphan, parentless though I was, since I had a grandmother to love me and raise me, and a home to call my own. Probably not.

Kamon glances up at me for just a moment, her words trailing off. She's pale, and her face is sunken. She looks completely drained from carrying a burden beyond her years. Pierre has stolen so much from her, but he's given much to her as well: sadness and fear and distrust. Still, she gives me a smile that can only be described as brave, and then looks down to read the last line. I listen to Mrs. March wishing her girls no greater happiness than they have in that moment, and then I silently slip out of the room and make my way toward the bayou and home.

XVI

I MUST HAVE LOOKED LIKE I NEEDED IT, because Rachel told me to take a day off, and I would have refused, but she told Emilie to do the same. I'm sure that was deliberate; she knew there was a greater chance that I'd take her advice and stay home if I could spend the day with my friend. I thought Emilie might want to stay at her own home instead of walking all the way out to my isolated place, but she actually suggested it.

The sun is behind a thick layer of gauzy clouds. You can almost wring them out, they're so heavy with moisture. It's hard to breathe today, with the humidity and the overwhelming scent of stagnant decay that floats through the mangroves of the swamp. Emilie sits across from me in the pirogue. She's facing me, an old wooden paddle gripped in her hands, but it hasn't touched the water yet. I navigate through the roots of cypress trees that disappear beneath the water like long fingers and keep an eye out for crocodiles and snakes, venomous or otherwise. Emilie jumps when a tangle of Spanish moss brushes her shoulder as we glide underneath it.

I love having company in the old wooden boat. It was my grandmother's, of course, like everything else I have. My grandfather built it for her. I never knew him, but I can imagine his hands sliding over the curved wood as he sanded and polished it for his wife. Did they ever push it out into the bayou simply to take a pleasure ride? I never have. I don't enjoy being on this water, where it's so murky you can't see what lurks beneath the surface. I don't like the green algae blanketing the top or the rotting stench that bubbles up from the bottom. This is the first time I have company on the boat, other than Ophelia. I'm not enjoying the water any more than I usually do, but I feel infinitely more comfortable having someone with me.

Emilie does not look comfortable. I don't blame her. Even for someone who has grown up here, as we both have, there's a level of wariness when you venture out and are not at the top of the food chain. And so we are not out on a pleasure craft today. I'm taking Emilie to my patch of herbs, hidden away on the bank of the swamp. I didn't plan it ahead of time, but a precious day off like this gives me the opportunity to tend to and collect them, and having unexpected company to do so is a bonus.

I tease Emilie as we float along. "You didn't know exactly what you were getting yourself into." I point to her paddle, still dry. "It works better in the water."

"I don't know what creature from the black lagoon might hitch a ride on it," she says, shaking her head, but she's smiling a little.

"I'm just teasing. You're making up for it in company."

"I figured maybe we would just…cook. Like last time."

"We still can. I have vegetables from the market. No crawfish today. A link of Andouille. We'll make do."

"You sure nobody will be out here?"

"It's rare." I have certainly seen boaters out here, but not too often. Usually not in the middle of a weekday. "If we see someone, we won't stop at my spot. We could easily just be out for a paddle."

Emilie shudders. "I don't know why anyone would do this for fun."

"I'm with you there," I tell her, gliding the boat into a narrow section of the swamp. It was cloudy to begin with, but in here, under the thick cover of trees, it almost looks like dusk. I know we both want me to be quick.

"How's Damaris?" I ask, trying to distract her.

"She's too tiny," Emilie says, and I'm instantly ashamed that I haven't asked about the baby sooner. "I'm feeding her as much as

I can, without having the other babies suffer. But I worry that it's not enough."

"It's never enough, for any of them," I say. Emilie looks down into the water and watches my paddle get entangled in a cluster of lily pad roots. I shake it free and am about to say something else about the baby, but we've arrived at the herbs and I'm anxious to do my job and get out of here.

I can't call this an herb garden, exactly, but my small patch of medicinal herbs grows on the shore of the bayou a mile from the house. It's most easily accessible by boat, because then I can avoid a long slog through muck up to my knees. I know that's not why my grandfather built the pirogue, because Ophelia didn't have anything to do with Removing while my grandfather was alive. I don't think he would have stopped her, though, not from the stories Ophelia told about him.

Nobody would recognize the herbs for what they are. They're mixed in among the thick cattails and reeds growing along the bank. I speed up my paddling stroke and ram the front of the boat against the mucky shore. It's only then that I realize Emilie doesn't have the proper footwear for the short walk to the patch of herbs. She's wearing her black boots that she wears to the orphanage every day, and since our feet will sink into the sludge up to our ankles, the boots will be ruined. I'm wearing Ophelia's old Wellies and so I tell Emilie to stay in the boat.

"Are you kidding? No way I'm sitting here by myself. I'll clean the boots later."

"Seriously, Em, not your work boots. They'll be a disaster. Trust me, I'll be in your sight the entire time. And I'll be back in the boat in about three minutes, tops. Most of the work gets done at home. I promise."

She nods but looks ready to leap out of the boat.

My own feet sink as I step out, the viscous mud slurping and sucking at them. I push through the cattails and find my hidden stash. The tansy is potted, but I've buried the pots in the ground, just as my grandmother always did. It's incredibly aggressive and will spread as a noxious weed if it's planted in the ground, choking off my other herbs and the natural vegetation. Sometimes I boil up a batch to make a natural insect repellent. The pots contain it well, and are almost completely concealed in the mud. An osprey circles overhead as I bend down and examine the pennyroyal. It should be ready to bloom in another month or so, producing tiny pale blue flowers. I pluck weeds away from the stems and make a note to return in six weeks to harvest the flowers. There are pots of ginger root and parsley, not strong enough by themselves but powerful in combination with other herbs. The deep purple flowers on the birthwort look ominous without even knowing anything about the herb. They curve open into a strange bell shape, reminding me of a French horn that's melted like one of Dali's clocks. Ophelia used to say it was a shame that Georgia O'Keeffe never painted birthwort. "It would have been right up her alley," she'd say, fingering a bloom.

"This one," Ophelia would continue, "is the tricky one. The poison is in the dose. Always remember that, *Sha*. The poison is in the dose."

There's one plant missing here. Cotton root bark. Ophelia refused to plant any, even though it grows in abundance in our area.

"I can't even look at it," she would say, pointing out a drawing of it in one of her books. "Enslaved women used it to rid themselves of pregnancies after they were raped by their masters. Forced to pick it by day, forced to ingest a tincture of it by night. I cannot think of a more tragic plant."

I call out to Emilie as I'm plucking flowers and leaves, just so she feels steady sitting on the boat alone. It's just a few minutes later that I'm squelching through the mud to return to the pirogue. She looks relieved by my quick return. I see her glance at the cloth bag I'm holding, filled with my herbal harvest.

"That's what you gave me?" she finally asks as I'm paddling us back toward home. She juts out her chin towards the open bag that rests in my lap.

"In a combination, yes." She has never spoken of this before. Our boat glides out from the densest section of the mangrove and a shaft of hazy sunlight falls over us. Emilie squints and looks down over the side of the boat.

"I didn't think they'd look like that," she says, not looking at them at all.

I'm not sure what to say, but she fills her own silence.

"They seem so…harmless. I wouldn't think poison could be so pretty."

There's a purple flower the color of an eggplant poking out the top of my bag. I don't tell her the name, or my Dali musings.

"The poison is in the dose," I say, not even meaning to echo Ophelia until the words are out. Emilie looks like she's swallowed a spoonful of poison herself. I think maybe I shouldn't have taken her. It's been several years since I tended to her, and we haven't spoken about it, ever. There was always that silent understanding. But now I think that maybe she needed to talk about it. Maybe she still does.

"I wonder if God forgives me," she says. I see my house in the distance, the flag of the Southerly State nothing but a blur of bold colors from here. I do not expect these words from her. Not at all.

"Em," I say. But I have nothing to follow it with. We have never felt the need to speak of God, not even right after leaving the *Word of Our Father* church on Sundays.

"I was so young," she says. "My parents would have killed me."

"He was married," I remind her. "And he abandoned you."

"I know. Only, it's hard sometimes. Being around all the babies. It was much easier on me when I was with the older girls."

"I can imagine," I say. But I really hadn't imagined it. She seemed okay to me, and there was that unspoken rule that we didn't bring up such things. But clearly I should have.

"It's just…you hear about it all the time. The prayers for the Unborn. Every time I hear it, I feel like I deserve to be Punished for what I did. And then I go to the orphanage the next day and I hold the babies and it's like God is reminding me."

"I'm so sorry. I didn't know you thought that."

She shakes her head. "I didn't used to. " I slow down the boat as we approach the shore. I don't want the ride to end, for fear she'll stop talking. But there's nowhere else to go.

"It's okay," she says, comforting me when I should be comforting her.

"God doesn't want you Punished, Emilie." I feel ridiculous saying this. How would I know what God wants? How do I know anything about God? But nobody would want to punish Emilie, ever. Of this, I am certain.

"I feel like every day with the babies is my own little reminder of what I've done," she says, glancing back and seeing the house. For the first time, she slips her paddle in the water and gives it a halfhearted backwards stroke.

"I'm sorry," I say again, because I'm so sorry that she feels like this and I didn't know. I'm sorry that she cuddles babies all day every day and I was too stupid to think of how painful that could be for her. And I don't want to admit it, even to myself, but I'm sorry because of my role in all of this. When all is said and done, am I not the one who gave her the poison in the dose?

XVII

We eat inside, our plates balanced on our laps, our legs tucked underneath us on the couch. I don't want to turn on the air conditioner, even though it's sweltering inside, because the more we draw from the weak power grids, the sooner the blackouts come. I hope everyone else in the Parish will be as mindful.

I ask Emilie, in between mouthfuls of sautéed peppers and onions and spicy sausage, if Preacher Pote is making visits to other members of his congregation. She doesn't think so, at least not to her parents' home or the home of anyone they know. Since I wasn't arrested or visited by any Officers of the State, I suppose I have to accept the fact that he was indeed interested in pursuing me. I'd been holding out hope that maybe there were others he went to see.

"It's a sign to stop," Emilie says. I wonder if she means a sign from God. "You are risking too much." Her voice is high and wheedling and I don't want to listen. For the first time ever, I regret confiding something in my friend. It just made her more consumed with worry, and I don't think she needs that on top of everything else she's apparently struggling with.

Instead, I turn the topic to Benjamin Pierre and Kamon. There's been precious little time for us to really go over everything.

"Kamon is doing all right?" Emilie asks, but she seems distant, like she's still staring down into the dark water of the bayou.

"She is, but Belinda said she wakes up with nightmares. Belinda's been staying in the room with the girls because otherwise Kamon will wake them all up." The familiar rage builds inside me. "He's out there probably already working another job, and has suffered no consequences whatsoever, and she's waking up in a cold sweat every night."

"It will haunt her forever," Emilie said. But then she spears a piece of sausage with her fork, chews deliberately, and says no more about it.

* * *

Miles whines at my feet while I stand over the sink in the kitchen, washing mud from the collected herbs. I'm sure he thinks I'm preparing food that he should be sampling. He pants pitifully but I still don't turn on the air conditioning.

"Take a drink, Miles," I say, nudging him toward his bowl with my foot. But he stays where he is, begging for a taste.

I can't stop reliving my afternoon with Emilie. I think about her married lover and how he left her, alone and pregnant, the moment he heard her news. I think about Benjamin Pierre, and how he stole Kamon's childhood and her peace. I think of Preacher Pote and his wan blue eyes, standing in my corner with his hand wrapped around a snake. And I do something I rarely do. I think of my father.

My father sculpted and molded me into what I am today, but not with gently guiding hands. Rather, he turned Ophelia into what she was, and I am a byproduct of that. Funny how things work out sometimes.

Ophelia Dupre was what the State refers to as a Remover of the Unborn. This is not a legal title; it's the label of a murderess. Ophelia was fortunate to never be arrested and therefore was never officially labeled as such. The Trinity did not exist in her day; that's only been resurrected from the bowels of history within the last few years, but she would have been publicly beaten had she been found out. And yet Ophelia always thought of herself as a midwife of sorts, a midwife concerned with the health and physical and mental well-being of women. I think she was a saint and a sage.

I like to think that my grandmother, a woman with raging Cajun blood living at the edge of the bayou, would have become a champion for women no matter what circumstances surrounded her own life, but I don't know if that's the case. Isn't it true that most times we aren't passionate about a cause unless we have been personally afflicted by it? And for Ophelia Dupre, nothing affected her as much as her daughter.

Ophelia told me how afraid my mother was when she found out she was pregnant with me. Fourteen years old, her hips no wider than an adolescent boy's, feeling something take root inside her. You wouldn't think Ophelia Dupre would allow this to happen to her daughter, but my mother was too scared to admit she was being abused by a neighbor until she could no longer hide her swelling belly.

She was terrified to give birth, right up until the morning I was born, when she clutched at her mother and begged her to do something, anything, to help her. And Ophelia could not do anything but take her daughter to the clinic and sit by her bed and rub her back for the hours and hours of hard labor that ensued. My mother almost died following an emergency Cesarean section, and the doctor told my grandmother that it would be dangerous for this fourteen-year-old to bear any more children. But a glance passed between them, my grandmother said, because they both knew how unlikely that was. And they were right.

Two years later, my mother was pregnant again, by the same man. From the moment I was born, her abuser owned her. She had birthed his child and therefore was mandated to bring me to visit him, though I don't remember those early interactions. And that meant the abuse continued.

I know my grandmother never wished that my mother had terminated her pregnancy with me. Ophelia loved me as much as she loved her own daughter. She was intelligent enough to separate my existence from the reason for my existence. But when it happened again, after her daughter was warned not to have any more children, my grandmother lost her mind.

She begged my mother to remove the pregnancy. "Take care of it," she said over and over. But my mother, scared and scarred and still so young, was terrified of being arrested and Punished. The Punishments were less frequent back then, maybe because more women just bore down, quite literally, and carried their pregnancies to term. They were terrified not to. To my mother, the risks of a Removal were even greater than childbirth. Would anyone believe she had been raped? By her daughter's own father? Would it matter? Despite all my grandmother's pleadings, she chose to have the baby. And as promised, it killed her, and the baby as well.

Ophelia thought if she had been able to help her daughter herself, with knowledge of herbs and illicit pills, she could have prevented her death. My father, her longtime tormentor, was never held responsible for the years of abuse or for my mother's death. How my grandmother did not murder him, I will never know. She used to say that she didn't know, either. Shortly after my mother was gone, he moved away and I never saw him again. I guess it was my mother that he wanted all along, to control and to own, and I had been the easy way to her.

Ophelia admitted that before I was born, she tried to convince my mother to send me to one of the many orphanages, but my mother did not want to give me away. The damage, I suppose, had already been done. Having me around would have been the least of it.

After her only daughter was gone, Ophelia made inquiries into how she could find a Jane. After some time, and after proving herself to be trustworthy, she made contact. But she did not require the usual services. Rather, she wanted to be taught how to help other women. She wanted to do for others what she could not for her daughter. And when I was old enough, she taught me everything she knew.

Ophelia gave me the education I was not provided at one of the few remaining universities. My learning happened in my grandmother's house, with her weathered tomes and her own experience as my guides.

She taught me that the Unborn are revered more than any living being, in a cult-like fashion, and that the State cares a great deal more about people before they are born than after. Women carrying a deformed child, due to incest or genetics, would need assistance desperately, but we have no way of knowing what the Unborn will be like. Sonograms, once used routinely for pregnancies, have been banned in the Southerly State. God should not be questioned, they say. Too many women tried to self-abort after learning their child would be born with a heart defect or missing appendages or a spinal deformity. And so now, women are not allowed to know what it is exactly that they are carrying.

Those women who are carrying an Unborn with a defect so great that they don't survive until birth are fortunate in that they don't have to watch a baby suffer or die in their arms. However, their natural miscarriages are reported by doctors and investigated as a crime. Most women are found innocent of wrongdoing, but the mental anguish stays with them. Many women choose to suffer a miscarriage at home in silence rather than go through an investigation. Sometimes, that does not end well, either.

The work my grandmother taught me to do is almost the exact opposite of caring for the girls at Xavier, but both are equally necessary. To some people, one half of me is an angel and the other half is the devil Herself. But those people don't see things that I have seen. It isn't nearly as black and white as they like to believe, even though the State-run news outlets are feeding them a constant barrage of incendiary, and false, information.

But preparing the herbs at my sink, thinking about my father and where I've come from, I need to remind myself that there are good men in this world, too. Because of my background and my own life history I haven't been blessed with a good man in my life, but I know they are there. Men like Emilie's father. Men like my grandfather. Decent men. I wish I could meet one, though with my nighttime endeavors, it would be difficult. I may never be able to unequivocally trust a man and allow one into all the parts of my life. And so I've probably relegated myself to this. There will likely be no babies for me, a strange midwife of sorts to other women, a strange mother of sorts to other children.

And so this Jane is like Janus, minus the Roman God part. I wear two faces. One face looks toward the children, nurturing and caring for those who are already here. But the other face looks toward the mothers above all else, fighting to keep them healthy and safe, no matter what.

XVIII

I HAVE TO REMIND MYSELF THAT IT'S THURSDAY. Since I had the day off yesterday, I keep thinking it's Monday. It has certainly felt like a Monday, since I've already spilled my homemade chamomile tea all over my kitchen table, which dripped onto the floor. I banged my head on the underside of the table as I tried to simultaneously swipe up the mess with one hand and push Miles away with the other. He was only too glad to lap up the tea. My head is still throbbing, and I think for the millionth time that I'd give almost anything for a cup of coffee.

I've never actually had a cup of coffee, but to hear Ophelia talk about it, I know I would love everything about it. She used to make it sound almost ritualistic: the rich, bitter aroma that filled the kitchen as it brewed and dripped into the pot, the way a ribbon of cream would swirl and fold into it from a chilled pitcher, how she used to cup her hands around it, warming them, and breathe in the coffee before taking her first sip. It gave her a boost for the day, she used to tell me, and centered her as she took that first purposeful sniff and swallow. That woman missed her morning coffee every single day until she died. Coffee beans are nearly impossible to come by in the Southerly State since the leading exporters refuse to do business with our government, and so my morning routine consists of pouring boiling water over freshly plucked chamomile flowers. They won't survive the humidity of the summer and so I won't even have that for much longer. I rub the forming lump on the back of my head and think that yes, this Thursday morning would have been perfect for a cup of coffee.

The girls shuffle into the room and break my train of thought. The scent of warm spices wafts into the room with them.

"Hi," Calah says, sidling up to me and curling her arm around my waist.

"Hi, yourself," I say. I stretch my arm across my stomach until my hand finds hers and grasps her fingers. She missed me, I know. I was only gone for a day, but she doesn't do well with a change in routine. Her body relaxes as she leans into me.

"How was breakfast?" I ask her. She's one of the more voracious eaters at Xavier and I always worry that she's hungry after a meager meal.

"Good!" She lifts her head away from me and nods, a smile on her face. "Really good. We had oatmeal with cinnamon." She pats her belly. "I liked it."

"I'm glad," I tell her. "I know cinnamon is your favorite."

"Mmhmm." She looks at me with a serious expression. "Much better than yesterday. Yesterday was scrambled eggs." She scrunches her nose at the word *eggs* and I have to bite back a laugh.

"Oh, I know how you feel about eggs," I say. "I'm glad today was better."

"I hate eggs," Calah says. "But Kamon hates them even more."

"Oh, really?" I don't remember her disliking eggs. Then again, Kamon has always been a fairly picky eater.

Calah's eyes grow wide and she looks at me with great seriousness. "She threw up," she says. Her nose wrinkles again.

"Kamon threw up at breakfast?" Already my head is swiveling around looking for her among the group of girls.

"She didn't like the eggs at all," Calah says. "They smelled so gross."

"I'm sorry, Honey. I'm glad today was better." I give her fingers a little squeeze and untangle from her arm. There are other hugs to be had, and other fingers to squeeze and locks of hair to caress, and I love them all but I'm anxious to see Kamon. I finally see the back of her head, her hair falling down to the middle of her back in thick waves. When I reach her, I put a hand on her shoulder and she turns in surprise. I think she actually jumped at the touch. I'm surprised for a moment but then I know why and I have to take a deep breath to try and cool the hot blood filling my veins.

"You feeling okay?" I ask. Kamon nods and turns her head from me.

"I'm fine," she says. Her voice lowers and she leans toward me. "You don't have to worry about me every minute."

I take a step back in surprise. She never speaks to me like that.

"I heard you got sick at breakfast yesterday, that's all," I say. "I was just checking."

"I made it to the bathroom," she says, rolling her eyes. I almost make a comment about how she's become a real teenager overnight, but then I tell myself that she's lightyears older than that, even. And she has the right to be angry all she wants, so I don't say anything about the eyeroll at all.

"I was just checking on you," I say again. "Glad you're okay."

"Well, the eggs were awful," she says. "Worse than usual."

"Okay. Sorry they made you sick." I hold out my hand but she doesn't take it. Instead she cocks her head and gives me a sad little smile.

"I haven't had an appetite in weeks anyway," she says, and the look in her eyes says so much more than words ever could.

* * *

The following morning, I walk in just after the girls headed to breakfast. I'd worry about my slight tardiness if this were a few months ago, but I can't imagine Rachel would pull me into her office and berate me. We understand one another a little better now, I think. Still, I didn't mean to take advantage of her. The morning just got away from me, with Miles being extra sweet and demanding a long belly rub. Then when I finally got onto the porch, I found the sunrise streaking across the sky in an ombre pattern of gold and rose and tangerine. The Louisiana swampland was utterly still, the long fingers of mangrove roots casting off a perfect reflection in the water. The scene made me catch my breath. I rarely get to enjoy this place, but I have to admit that there's a strange beauty here, when you take a moment to appreciate it.

Xavier, with its barren walls and sterile hallways, is in sharp contrast to what I saw this morning. If only I'd been given off today instead of the other day. I would have jumped into the pirogue and glided through the water, catching the last of the golden hour before the sky turned to haze, and turtles and snakes broke through the glassy surface of the water.

When the girls return, Kamon is not among them. I don't worry, because she can't have gone anywhere other than the bathroom. But when twenty minutes pass and she still doesn't join us, a nagging feeling grows in my stomach. We aren't complete unless she's accounted for. At least, I'm not.

Ten minutes later, I'm ready to bolt down the hall to start checking bathrooms. I can't leave the girls unattended though. I wish, yet again, that the room had a phone. It's absurd to leave one adult in each room and not give them a way to communicate with anyone else. Then again, that's one of the more minor issues here. I step into the hall and peek into Emilie's room, but she's bouncing a little one on her hip while trying to bottle-feed another in her crib with her free hand. I should help her but she doesn't see me and so I back away, too worried about Kamon to feel guilty.

I've already left my girls alone anyway, so I venture a few steps further and pop my head into the room with the oldest girls. Several of them are quick to volunteer to stay in my room for a few minutes, and I choose a lanky brunette who looks like she'll be aging out of the orphanage in a few months. She follows me back to my room and I'm already back into the hallway when I hear my girls rushing to surround her. I have to smile. They would have just seen her at breakfast, but this unexpected surprise will be the highlight of their day. I hear her laughing as I push open the bathroom door.

"Kamon?" I call. There's no answer and no feet sticking out from any of the stalls. She has to be in the other bathroom then, even though it's further from our room. If she's not there, I'll allow myself to panic. I'm incredibly relieved when I push into the other bathroom and find her.

I hear her before I see her crumpled shape on the floor, huddled over a toilet. She's retching and crying and I knock on the door but she calls for me to please go away, and so there's nothing else to do but crawl under the door and squeeze up against her. We barely fit in there and I have to slide my arm up against the door to unlatch it from the inside just to give us a few more inches of breathing room.

"Oh, Kay," I say into her hair. "What's going on?"

She turns to me, spittle in her hair. Her eyes are red-rimmed and there's a slick line of mucus connecting her left nostril to her upper lip. She's too sick to be angry with me.

"It's okay, it's all right," I say over and over, grabbing squares of rough brown toilet paper and blotting at her cheeks and nose. I push her hair behind her shoulders and rub her back.

"Oh sweetie," I say. "Maybe you caught a stomach bug."

"Nobody has the stomach bug to catch it from," she says. She turns away from me and her little body spasms, the bones of her shoulders jutting out like the skeleton of a bird. Nothing comes up but a dry heave. She props an elbow on the rim of the bowl and rests her head in her hand, spent.

"You've been feeling sick for a few days? Maybe it wasn't really the scrambled eggs the other day?"

"It wasn't the eggs," she says. Her voice drops to a whisper and the tiniest trace of a wispy lisp laces through her words, heralding back to her much younger years. I remember that tiny little voice. I'd forgotten how much I missed it. "I can't talk about it," she says.

"You know you can talk to me about anything," I tell her. It can't be worse than what she's already told me. I hope.

"I've just been getting these awful headaches," Kamon says. She looks at me sideways and puts her hand on her forehead. "Right above my eyes. And when they get really bad, it makes me sick."

"That sounds like something called a migraine," I say, relief flooding over me. We can handle headaches.

"Well, migraines suck," she says.

"So I've heard. Maybe Veronica has something you can take, at least to take the edge off. You've been under so much stress, kiddo. No wonder you're getting headaches. Stress can manifest into all sorts of physical ailments."

Kamon turns her head away from me and stares at the cracked tiles over the toilet and the blackened grout that runs between them.

"I don't think it's stress. I think I'm being punished," she says in a voice so soft I think I must have heard her wrong. But when I see the anguish on her face, even in profile, I know I heard correctly.

"Punished? By whom?"

"God."

"Oh, Kamon," I say.

"It's a sin to hate someone," she says. "And I *hate* him." For a split second I think she's telling me she hates God, but the twisted grimace on her face gives it away. She hates Benjamin Pierre and she thinks God is punishing her for the transgression.

"I hate him," she says, stronger now. "Every time I think about it, I hate him more. I hate him so much, it scares me."

"I know," I say. "Me too."

She swivels her head to look at me.

"Don't look surprised," I tell her. "I love you very much, and he hurt you so badly. I'm angry and I despise him so much it terrifies me."

Kamon nods and swallows.

"But you do not have one ounce of sin inside you, Kamon." I put one hand under her chin so she can't look away. "Do you understand me? You did nothing wrong, and God would never punish you."

"Yeah, well, he didn't protect me, either," she says, and for that, I simply do not have an answer.

XIX

A QUIET STILLNESS COMES OVER ME at the end of my shift. Kamon had a good day today. She said her head didn't hurt and she smiled a little more and even laughed once, when we were all outside and Calah put a fat, fuzzy caterpillar on her arm. She asked if I had any other good books she could read to the girls, and I promised to look through my bookcase.

I'm thinking of several choices as I push through the front doors alone. Emilie was finishing a feeding in her room and waved me on when I poked my head in. I decided I'd wait for her on the steps. But as soon as I walk outside, I see that someone is already waiting for me.

A black hat shades pale blue eyes. The backs of his hands, the only flesh exposed, are nearly translucent in the orange evening light, with faint blue veins spider-webbing underneath his skin. He rests one foot on the step above him, his pale interlocked fingers resting on his thigh. He's perfectly still, and I wonder how long he's been standing there. The doors bang shut behind me and I'm perfectly still now as well. We are both waiting.

He looks up at me and something like a smile starts to spread, but his eyes are cool. I know he's waiting for me to address him. As a man and as a leader of the Church, it's what's expected. I feel my head lowering with some innate sense of deference. This pleases him.

"Good evenin', ma'am," he says. He pulls his hands apart and stretches one up to me. I walk down the steps but I don't take his hand.

"Good evening, Preacher. You caught me just as I'm heading out."

"I thought we might walk together." He must have caught a look from me because he adds, "For a part of the way. Fine night for it."

I look back over my shoulder, I can't help it, but Emilie doesn't open the door. We don't walk together every evening but we often do, and if I could will her out the door now I would. But it's Veronica who breezes down the steps in another moment, waving to me and looking about to say something until she sees who I'm standing beside. Then she ducks her head at us both and walks away. We are alone.

"Are you visiting your parishioners at work now?" I probably shouldn't say things like this, especially not with the bite in it that my words have, but I don't like how he's shown up here like this, and I don't like that I have no choice but to acquiesce and walk with him.

"No I am not," he says. "It's you in particular I wanted to see. And how are you? I would have come sooner but the church has kept me tied up."

Counting all your money, I think, but I have the good sense to instead say, "I'm fine, thank you. Really, there was no need to check on me, though I do appreciate it."

"Well, the last time I visited you, you had that frightened look in your eyes, like you saw the Devil hisself. I couldn't get that vision of you out of my head."

"I couldn't get my own vision of that night out of my head," I say, and I realize that we're walking side by side down the cracked and crumbling sidewalk, and his hand is just barely touching the back of my arm. We must make a stark image: the clock tower rising up behind us, his black figure beside my white one, a lavender twilight painting everything it touches.

"Well, I'm just sorry we had to end on such a note. I thought I might catch you after church some morning, but you always scoot out right quick."

"I only have Sundays off," I say, "and there's always much to do."

"A girl like you shouldn't be out there by the swamp all alone, in my opinion. I can imagine the workload is tough for you."

"I manage. It was my grandmother's place and the only home I've ever known."

"We are indeed comfortable with what we know," he says. I'm relieved when he drops the subject.

As we walk, the houses grow closer together, adorned with curling wrought iron balconies. They were bright and colorful once, but they've all faded with the sun and with time, to faint pastels. Thick sycamore trees line the streets and a group of old men stand at a street corner, gesticulating with gnarled fingers as they argue a point. A palmetto bug, half the size of my hand, skitters across the sidewalk. From somewhere inside one of the houses, a child cries.

"God wanted us to meet," Pote says suddenly, and I almost stop short but somehow my legs keep going. "He works quietly sometimes, and mysteriously others, but this time, I heard his message clear as day. I looked out in the congregation and there you were, and I knew it. God put you right there, right where I could find you. I believe that with all my heart. I think he means for me to save you, Miss."

"I don't need saving, Preacher. Really, I'm doing just fine."

"I don't mean savin' your soul. I know you're a God-fearing woman; I can tell that. Of course you are. But I think you need someone to look out for you. That's the kind of savin' I mean. Those tithing envelopes, with only your name on them…that was a sign to me. God wanted me to find you."

"Thank you for your concern," I say, my tongue thick in my mouth. I can't have him walk me all the way home, and we're just a block away from the Place d'Armes already. The noises of this congested part of the Parish blend in with my words. The streets themselves are quiet, with hardly any cars ever driving by, but there are voices and the chug of air conditioning units and the chirping of nighttime insects as they rouse themselves for the evening ahead.

"Now listen, I understand you don't know me real well. But I am a man of God, I give you my word on that, and I'll give you time to get comfortable with me. I'll spend as much time walkin' beside you as you need."

"Sir, I'm not…I'm not looking for someone to take care of me."

"God knows what we need when we ourselves do not. You'll see soon enough." The preacher nods, and I glance at him long enough to catch his eyes. I think about how I sometimes wish I could trust a man and let him into my life. But it would never be this man. It would never be this man with his fiery words and his narrow beliefs. He is speaking kindly to me now, but I have heard him spew enough vitriol to know who he is. At the same time, I can't anger him. He's a powerful man in the Parish, if not the most powerful, even more so than the Officers of the State. And I, I am nothing. If it comes down to it, I have no doubt he will remind me of that.

His hand pulls at the back of my arm, just a touch. We are standing in the middle of the square. The faux marble cherubs on the fountain look at me gleefully, their white paint flaking. The basin is filled with insects and flecks of dried leaves. A pregnant mother walks a few paces behind her two small children, but other than that, we are alone. Standing stoically over everything is the Trinity.

The Preacher looks up at it, and now the smile on his face is genuine.

"Did you know," he whispers, "that there's to be another Punishment?"

I don't want to have this man breathing secrets into my ear. As he leans in, I catch the now-familiar scent of leather.

"It's gonna be a bit different this time. I won't say anything else about it, but I feel I can trust you. I'm not wrong about that, am I?"

"I won't tell." I turn my head away.

"I know," he says, touching my chin with the tips of his alabaster fingers and turning my face back to him. I take a step back.

I can't help it. His fingers fall away from my face but his smile remains. I mutter something about needing to get home to let out the dog, and I want to collapse with relief when he does not follow. The rest of my walk home, I keep seeing him standing there; his unsettling eyes sliding over me, his dry fingers on my face. And the Trinity, its wooden beams patiently waiting, rising up behind us.

XX

Pote was not lying about holding another Punishment. I hate that I knew about this before most anyone else. Emilie is not in the Place d'Armes Square with me. She went home directly after church this morning, and she told me to do the same. However, curiosity got the better of me, and I feel a strange pull to witness, first hand, that with which I flirt. Also, I need to see Pote here today, to remind myself again who he really is, lest his soft words whispered in a purple evening ever take hold of me, even for an instant.

I stand a few rows behind the preacher; I can just see the top of his hat. He looked back at me a moment ago and nodded. I almost expected him to offer me a place beside him, right in front of the Trinity for a good viewing spot, but he turned back around and did not look for me again. The Punisher stands in front of the crowd. Like the preacher, he too is wearing black, however, his head is covered with a hood so only his eyes are visible under thick eyebrows. A growing anticipation buzzes through the crowd.

The woman to be punished is brought out from the back of a gray van that has *Word of Our Father Church* painted on it in thick black letters. Two Officers lead her to the Trinity, one pulling on each arm, though she goes without a fight. As she walks, the Punisher holds up his whip, clearly enjoying his moment. The crowd roars, the men fiercely drowning out their female companions.

The woman is no more than twenty. She is dark-skinned. As soon as people see what she looks like, they yell even louder. I want to throw up. I know she is here to satisfy a bloodthirsty crowd. This isn't to scare young women, it's to satiate riled up men. Part of me thinks her name might have been written in a Tamburo here or in another Parish just because of her skin color. And then I think that maybe it wasn't written in a Tamburo at all. Maybe she was picked up by an Officer who didn't like the look of her, or thought she wasn't being respectful enough to him. How would we ever know the difference? And how many would even care?

The Officers rip the woman's dress down to her waist and her face twists in anguished shame. The women in the crowd are mostly silent, but the men are at a near frenzy. Flags are raised, the black bolts of lightning flashing underneath the blue sky. The Officers lead her up the steps to the scaffold of the Trinity. The cry of *Sanguidam* begins to rise, but something in the woman's eyes tells me that she is no such thing. She has the dignity of a Nubian queen as she stands in rags. I don't know who put her here, but she does not have the scared, repentant look of a woman who has been caught. She has the defiant look of someone who knows she is right, despite everyone's accusations to the contrary.

The Punisher has the woman expertly tied to the Trinity in under a minute. She does not resist him, and she hangs like a long branch of a weeping willow, her toes just off the base of the tripod. I do not watch her thirty lashes, but I hear them. I have to bite back my own cries that mirror hers.

Somehow, the woman does not collapse when cut down. She staggers but manages to stand, and she reaches to her waist to pull her dress over herself, crying out as it touches her back. She drops the material and crosses her arms over her bare chest instead. She scans the crowd, likely looking for a comforting face to accompany her to the clinic. No one comes forward.

I find her searching face more painful than the whipping she just endured, and I don't fight my overwhelming instinct to flee. I shove through the crowd without looking back. The last thing I hear as I reach the street is Preacher Pote, his voice full of reverent wonder, calling out, "The *Sanguidam* is repentant and shall be saved. God is good, my brothers and sisters. God is so, so good."

XXI

THE NEWSPAPER DOES NOT PROVIDE DETAILS about the woman's supposed crime; nothing like the last girl, the fourteen-year-old girl named Isabel who handled her own Removal and suffered from complications that ultimately gave away her secret. This woman, not even named in the article, had simply been accused. Anonymously, of course. And since no proof was needed to back up the accusation, she was held in the Parish jail for two weeks before the Punishment was carried out.

It's apparent that we have somehow crossed into new, murkier waters. Will false accusations become a ruthless way to punish women for a multitude of transgressions? For forsaking a lover, or rejecting an advance? Can anyone be labeled a *Sanguidam* just to be whipped in public? Could it become the newest way to maintain the male hierarchy that has existed here for so long? For forever, really.

Has Pote thought of any of this? I think I see him for what he truly is. A zealot. Misguided in his righteousness. A Believer. He wants *Sanguidam* to pay. He wants them to be an example to others, so that never again is an Unborn denied the chance to live. I know his Punishments won't stop such a thing, but he truly believes they will. But would he want women to be falsely accused? I don't think so. And I wonder if maybe I can whisper these thoughts of mine, these silly musings of a woman who lives alone at the edge of the swamp, directly into his ear. I wonder if I can convince him to abandon his Tamburo, before it is too late.

* * *

There are flowers in a Mason jar on the windowsill in my room at the orphanage. I don't see them right away. I'm too busy saying good morning to the girls and herding them into the hall so they aren't late for breakfast. On her way out, Mishael leans into me, her angular jaw set in a rare smile.

"I didn't know you had a *boy*friend," she says, and waggles her fingers at the flowers on the sill. I know who they're from without reading the note. I haven't seen the preacher since the Punishment, when I fixated on the top of his black hat, which barely quivered as he watched with what I can only assume was rapture. I want to speak with him soon about my concerns with false accusations, and I know the only way to speak to him is to entertain his attention on me. But when I see the spray of wildflowers in a jelly jar, purple asters and tiny bluets mixed together with bright yellow marigolds, I don't feel like it's an invitation to speak openly to him. I feel like it's a bouquet of poison ivy. And I don't like how he knew these are exactly the flowers I'd wish for someone to give me, rather than a perfectly manicured arrangement of pink roses shot through with baby's breath, or long-stem tulips. Those flowers are a symbol of wealth since they're so difficult to bring to the Southerly State, and I don't want a sign of prosperity from anyone. I want the wildness and beauty of flowers grown in our own fields. I like the shades of periwinkle and lemony yellow. I like the Mason jar, just like the one Ophelia always used to mix her sweet tea. I don't want to like anything about this. I hate that he knew what to give me.

There's an envelope propped against the jar. It's a tithing envelope, and when I pick it up I see it's *my* tithing envelope, carefully opened and taped shut again. My name is printed on the front. Just my name, no others beside it. He is reminding me how alone I am.

You left the square too quickly for me to find you. I had hoped we could join together afterwards for a prayer and a quiet word. I'm sorry if what you saw upset you, but know this: The Wicked shall be damned in this life and the next, and Justice was truly served. May this deter a thousand other women like her. We are on the side of the righteous. I am humbled to serve our God like this, and I am invigorated with our cause. Yours in Christ, William

William. I must have known that was his name, must have seen it written somewhere inside the *Word of Our Father* church, but he was always simply 'the Preacher,' to me, or 'Pote.' His note sounded almost apologetic. I didn't think he would have intuited that I was upset. Was he trying to convince me that the actions of the Punisher were justified? Or could it be that he himself needs convincing?

I sniff the flowers without meaning to. They do brighten up the room and the girls will enjoy them. If I got rid of them Mishael would notice they were gone the moment she came back. And so I leave them on the sill, but I take his note, wrapped in my lonely envelope, and slip it into the pocket of my skirt. Maybe there is an opening there, in between the lines of perfectly shaped letters, for me to voice my own thoughts on the matter. I don't know exactly how yet, but I think it is surely there, if I just look hard enough.

* * *

It's too hot to go outside after schoolwork, and so the girls flop onto their beds and fan themselves with their new history booklets. The old air conditioner is no match for the swelter of this Southern afternoon. I brush and then braid Serah's hair and comment on how long and thick it is. She flushes with pride.

"Did you bring a new book?" she asks, her tiny face filled with expectation. She always sat as close as possible to Kamon as she read *Little Women* to the girls.

"I did," I tell her. "Would you like a little sneak peek?" She nods and her hair shimmers in the florescent light.

I cross the room and pull out the book from my canvas bag. The cover is innocuous, just a few branches of a tree pressed against a dark red background. I run a finger over the author's name. Harper Lee. This book is banned at Xavier. It's banned in the entire Southerly State. But that's precisely why I brought it.

Maybe I'm not afraid of Rachel anymore, after everything that's happened. Maybe I feel like she would have the good sense to know that this book has nothing wrong in it, it's got no mention of Unborns or Removals or Sinners or Punishers. It's a book about humanity, and how can I be wrong in showing that to my charges? But maybe I think that there's a good chance she just won't find out about it.

Serah grasps the book and holds it close to her for just a moment. It is always that way with me, too. Just that little bit of time to hold a new book and feel it and keep the words a delicious secret. I love that Serah feels it as well.

I wish I could give her this copy for herself, to read alone, curled up on her bed, sneaking pages by flashlight at night. But it isn't fair because there's no copy for anyone else, and so I tell her to go and surprise Kamon with it. She jumps off the bed with nothing but agility and grace and runs across the room to the older girl.

Kamon smiles when she sees the book, but her face is drawn and her hair sticks to her forehead, plastered there with perspiration. While it's hot in here, nobody else looks quite so uncomfortable. I walk over to her and lean down, brushing my fingertips against her forehead.

"Headache?" I ask. "You don't have to read now if you're not feeling well."

"No," she says. "I'm just tired."

I nod and back away. This time is for her, to read to the girls. She loves it and so do they. But as I'm turning away, I swear I see her swallow a gag. She's clearly more than just tired. I've been telling myself she's exhausted and giving herself stress headaches, but now I'm not so sure. Dark circles under her eyes have shadowed her face for weeks. She's been vomiting and fighting nausea. Maybe it's more than migraines. Maybe it's more than the trauma she's gone through and the demons she's fighting. Maybe it's some other unspeakable thing. But he can't have done that to her, after everything else. She's thirteen years old and she's a little girl and he can't have done that to her. Still, the thought is like a ball of sinew in my chest. I push it away but it's strong and demands attention. I look at Kamon's face and I see what I refused to acknowledge before. What I wouldn't allow myself to see.

Benjamin Pierre has left his mark.

XXII

For the rest of the day, I am completely numb. Or maybe numb isn't the right word, because if I were truly numb, nothing would hurt. And everything hurts. My throat aches and my chest is so tight I feel like I can't take a breath deep enough to let air into my lungs, and there's a fierce pounding behind my eyes. But I am numb to everything else around me.

I try to talk myself out of what I see. Maybe she has a virus or the flu. Maybe she's just tired from the nightmares that keep her up at night. Maybe she's overheated. But I know the signs. I see it in her queasy smile and in the exhaustion coursing through her as her body becomes a host. The most tragic part of the whole thing is that I'm certain Kamon doesn't know what's happening to her. How could she? None of this is part of their State-mandated curriculum. We do not speak of such things to girls at this age because there's no need. Or so we assumed. And so I am wrecked with the knowledge that this young girl is too vulnerable and naïve to know what has happened to her. I think of Ophelia and what she must have felt when she saw her young daughter burdened with too heavy a load for both her body and her mind. If I ever had a shadow of doubt about why Ophelia turned into a covert sorceress of reverse midwifery, it is vanished now. I feel blessed relief that I know how to help this girl, and I know that's all my grandmother would have wanted. It is what I am meant to do. And I must protect her at all costs, so that nobody will ever know.

Despite my relief, there is no measure of peace that comes with this knowledge. There is only anger that this has been wrought upon her in the first place, inside the walls that were supposed to protect her. I was supposed to protect her. And now there is this other layer added to her trauma. What if I listened more closely when she asked me to spend the night? What if I told Rachel to fuck off, I was staying, and that was that? Could this have been prevented? Any last vestige of youth and innocence will be stolen away with what has to be done to save her. The weight of the remedy is heavy to bear for a child. But the burden of pregnancy and birth on someone her age is even more dangerous. Damaging, potentially deadly, and completely traumatic for someone who was violently forced into the situation to begin with.

I failed her. We all failed her. It's almost more than I can take. I watched her crack open the binding of *To Kill A Mockingbird* earlier today and read to the girls. Her body shifted as she read through the first few pages, sitting up straighter and leaning into the book. This one will make her think. She's so smart. The book will ignite her. That's what she should be doing; feeding her mind and growing and learning. Not held hostage because her own body betrayed her after everyone else did too. I'm struck dumb by the unfairness of it.

And then, from a place inside me that I didn't even know existed, comes a single thought. They were words I'd already said to myself. *Nobody will ever know.* That's the only way to protect her, to make certain she doesn't become labeled a *Sanguidam*. There can be no complication, no evidence, nothing. I would give my own life before I allowed anyone to find out. The words root themselves inside me. I allow myself to think them, and then think about them, and then think that yes, that is exactly right. Nobody will ever know.

Not even Kamon.

XXIII

Pote is waiting outside Xavier at the end of my shift. He barely registers, I'm so consumed with the other thoughts running through me. It looks like it's going to rain and I wish it would, just to cool down the air for a few minutes. When I see him standing at the bottom of the steps, his hat in both hands, a look of self-satisfaction playing across his face, I remember the flowers from this morning. It seems like weeks ago that Mishael was playfully pointing them out to me. And I know why he looks pleased with himself. He is waiting for my effusive thanks.

This is what I wanted—to have his ear. To offer up a polite thank you and then slip in my thoughts and concerns about the Tamburo, all in a genteel and questioning manner, of course. Just the merest hint of a suggestion, something for him to think about later. But that was my plan in the lifetime before I realized what was happening to Kamon. Now there is this more pressing thing consuming me, and I don't want to speak with him, at least not now. All of that can wait for a few weeks. Surely I have some time before someone else is accused.

"Thank you for the flowers," I say as I come down to street level. I know that's what he's waiting for. I won't go any further than this though. Tonight I will not leave Xavier without Emilie. I have to work through my thoughts with someone, and telling her will be as safe as not telling anyone.

"I thought you'd like wildflowers best, with all of them growing right around you," he says. He's nodding, his pride evident. "I thought you might bring them home?"

“The girls liked them so much, I left them by the window where I found them.”

“Ah, I wondered where your supervisor would leave them for you.” He nods his approval. I hate that Rachel was the go-between.

“And you read the note, I trust?” When I nod, he continues. “It’s natural to have a reaction like I imagine you did. When I turned to find you at the square, I just saw your skirt flyin’ behind you as you ran.” His voice sounds soothing, nothing like the voice that pours gasoline on his matchstick followers each Sunday. “You just have to know that she sinned, and paid her price.”

I glance at the doors, but Emilie isn’t here yet.

“How do you know for certain that she…did what you say?” I didn’t mean to get into all this now. But here it is.

“Nobody has a reason to make up such a terrible thing, ma’am,” he says, squeezing his hat together. And I think he believes it, or wants to.

“It’s a frightening thought that one can be Punished without direct evidence, by an anonymous source,” I say, looking into his surprised eyes. Clearly, this is not the conversation he imagined.

“There was evidence along with her name. You didn’t see it, nobody from the public did, but it was there.”

“But because something is written doesn’t make it true,” I say.

“*Sanguidam* are murderesses, killing the most innocent among us. It’s a grave charge and nobody would make up such a thing. That would be a sin you’d have on your conscience from now until the end of all time.”

“But you’re satisfied with baseless accusations?”

“She will have her trial when she comes face-to-face with God. And I have no doubt that she will roast in Hell when she does.” He puts on his hat and his pale eyes grow darker under its shadow. “I didn’t come here to debate with you about that which you don’t understand. I came here to see if you liked the flowers.”

"Someone probably hated her for the color of her skin," I say. "Or because she didn't want their attention. Or because she was trying to better herself and rise above where they thought she should be. It's too easy to write down a name on a piece of paper."

"I'd watch my mouth if I were you." His tone is suddenly cool. "You are accusing someone of making a false accusation and that's no better than what you're railing against right now."

The doors above us open and Emilie is standing at the top of the steps. She looks surprised at how sticky it is out here, and how threatening the sky is. When she sees us, she's even more surprised.

"I'll look for you in the congregation on Sunday," Pote says, so low that Emilie won't hear his words. "Enjoy your flowers." He takes my hand and squeezes it, tips his hat to Emilie, and much to my relief, walks away. She looks at me, eyebrows raised, and I shake my head. There's much to tell her, but it isn't about the preacher. I let out a shaky breath. It begins to rain.

XXIV

"WHY IS HE BOTHERING YOU?" Emilie asks as we walk beneath a light spray of rain. The mist on my face feels good. If it stays like this, it'll be a lovely walk home.

"He brought me flowers," I say. "He gave them to Rachel."

Emilie rolls her eyes. "I'm sure you don't need her involved."

"I don't need him involved either."

"He's definitely…interested in you? Because it doesn't seem like a preacher should be pursuing women."

"He's not a priest." There are no priests in the Parish at all, and I don't think there are many left in the entire Southerly State.

"Still," she says, shaking her head. Droplets of water nestle into her long hair. "It just seems like he should be focused on God. Or something."

"I don't know. But I can't worry about him right now. Em. Something happened."

I don't look at her. I don't want to see her face as I tell her about Kamon. She barely knows the girl, but she will feel for her. That's just how Emilie is.

If I had a choice, I wouldn't tell Emilie. Not because I don't trust her, but because I don't want to implicate her in anything. It's better for her own protection if she doesn't know about any of this. And I fear it will make her think about her own anguished time. I hate to do that to her.

But I need a sounding board. I have to hear my plan out loud and I need someone to help me work out the details. It's too important to overlook anything and Emilie is smart and she's a thinker. If

I've miscalculated something, she will point it out to me. I cannot make a mistake.

Of course she asks what I keep asking myself: "Are you positive?"

"Yes," I say. "I can see it. The queasiness with a lack of fever, the discomfort. The exhaustion." I can't go by her monthly cycle; it only just started and has been erratic at best.

"But you'll need to have her take a test. To be certain."

"I thought that, at first. But I can't have her do that without explaining it to her. This way is best. If I give her an herbal tea to treat her and she isn't pregnant, it won't do anything bad to her. So I'm not hurting her by treating a problem if it isn't there." After a beat I say, "But it's there."

"You can't do this without telling her," Emilie says. She turns to me and pulls my arm so I stop beside her. Nobody else is on the street; they are already tucked inside their houses. No children want to play in this rain, which is driving down heavier now.

"She's a child, Em. She doesn't even know what's happened to her. All she knows is that she hasn't been feeling well. She's too young, it isn't safe. She doesn't *want* this."

I pull away from her and start walking again. I knew she would find it difficult to get past this part.

"You can't do something like that without telling her, Jane," she says, only she doesn't really say Jane.

"Em. Think about this for a minute. She is too young to birth a baby safely. She had no choice in any of this. It isn't fair."

"And so you're taking her out of another decision. You cannot possibly."

"It's easier for her this way. Think about how agonized you were, having to make that inevitable choice. Think about how much it hurt you. Think of the guilt you still struggle with. And we call it a 'choice,' but you didn't really have a choice, did you? You were out of decent options." I see the beginnings of tears in the corners of Emilie's eyes and they mix with the droplets of rain on her cheeks. "Now imagine being thirteen years old. You've been robbed of the last of your childhood, violated, assaulted. Betrayed. You are so innocent in all of this, you don't even understand what's happened to you. And now someone explains it to you, tells you why you haven't been feeling well. And then there's more agony. More guilt. And the inevitable 'choice'. I don't want to do that to her. I haven't been able to protect her from anything else, but I can protect her from this."

The timbre of my voice has turned into a wheedled strain. I certainly don't need permission from Emilie, but I want her approval. However, I can see I have not convinced her.

"To say nothing of deceiving her, you would be having her partake in a crime. If you want to protect her, how could you even think of doing this?" Emilie asks.

"She won't be a *Sanguidam*. She won't even know. There's no crime she'd be involved in."

Emilie narrows her eyes. "And if she had to go to a clinic because of a complication?"

"It would look like a natural miscarriage. Girls get caught when they damage themselves trying to perform their own Removals. That wouldn't be the case here." There would still be an investigation, I know, but it's still the best option. There won't be a complication, I say to myself. There can't be.

"I think she deserves a choice," Emilie says. We've walked past the Place d'Armes but she didn't veer off where she usually does. Now she'll have to backtrack in the rain. I wonder if she realizes that she's gone too far.

I try to imagine a different time in this place, where we wouldn't be having this conversation. A time where a street musician might have stood under a balcony to stay dry, playing a mournful trumpet riff. Ophelia used to love the street musicians. They aren't allowed to play here now. Sometimes I think that's one of the saddest things that occurred during the Peaceable Separation. My grandmother always told me that when she was a girl, and even a very young adult, this Parish was beautiful. The town she grew up in was the same place she raised me but, in her youth, it was a thriving community on the outskirts of Baton Rouge. It was a good place to raise a family, people said. It was quaint and quiet, and had easy access to the city. Baton Rouge had grit, Ophelia liked to say. Jazz and grime and magnolias and plantations and balconies and petty crime and beignets and tourists. There were celebrations in the streets and people threw back shots of whiskey in dark bars in the middle of the night while musicians played world-class music in the alleys. The fountains flowed with fresh water and the Place d'Armes was filled with lovers and children and visitors. Everything is different now. Jazz has been replaced with zealous hymns, and large social gatherings are reserved for Punishments and church services. Even the landscape is unrecognizable, shrinking every year as the Gulf laps at our heels.

"Emilie, it's better for Kamon this way. I know it with my whole being. I know it like a mother." *Her mother.* "This is the best thing I can do for her. This is how I can protect her. And she is my only concern." I realize I'm getting the exact chance Ophelia did not have with her own daughter. I feel certain that if she could, Ophelia would have given my mother a cup of hot tea during her second pregnancy without telling her what was in it. But I can't think about that. I am only thinking of Kamon and how lucky we both are that I can do this.

"Don't play God," Emilie says. "This isn't for you to decide."

"She's a child," I say. "I'm doing it to protect her. She shouldn't be forced to make an agonizing decision at her age. And there really isn't a decision to make. The end result will be the same. But making a 'choice' will give her more grief and stress than someone her age should have. She's been through enough."

"It's not up to you."

"This is what I would do if I were her mother."

"But you're not," she says. Her words have sharp edges.

"Nobody is," I say. "And so I might as well act like one. She deserves that."

"She doesn't deserve you making such a decision for her."

"I'm protecting her."

Emilie shakes her head. Her cheeks are red and her whole face is pinched.

"Em, she's a baby herself." I don't know why I'm trying to justify this to her. Could it be because I'm trying to convince myself? No. I already know this is right. "It's okay. I promise."

"It's really not," she says. "How can you think I would agree with you about this?"

Her words sting. She's never spoken to me like this before.

"I have to go home," Emilie says, looking at her surroundings and suddenly seeing she's walked blocks out of her way.

"I'm sorry you don't agree with me," I say. We are both soaked through, our skirts clinging to our legs and our black boots shiny with rain water. Strands of her hair stick to the sides of her face and there's a fringe of droplets resting on her eyelashes. "But please trust me. And don't tell her. Please."

"I won't tell her." Then she puts both her hands on my arms. I feel like she might shake me, but she just holds me in place and looks straight into me. "I won't tell her. But I wish to God you hadn't told me."

XXV

WHAT GUTS ME MORE THAN ANYTHING is that Kamon doesn't know what's happening to her. She's tired and sometimes she's nauseated, but she thinks it's a lingering virus. I watched her push Calah away when the girl tried to give her a hug, gently telling her she didn't want to get her sick. She still reads to the girls, and is nearly halfway through *To Kill A Mockingbird*, but she looks drained and almost haggard.

Not only has Kamon not yet been taught anything about human procreation (as the State refers to it) but she knows nothing of Punishments. These girls are almost completely isolated from the outside world. The computers are protected so they don't have access to unauthorized websites, and the Internet doesn't work a lot of times, anyway. The books they read are heavily censored. They don't go to church in the Parish; they receive their religious lessons inside the walls of Xavier, with their booklets and worksheets. And so other than Benjamin's onerous threat to her, Kamon is unaware of the Tamburo or the Trinity. She has the vaguest notion of a box inside a church she's never set foot in, that contains the names of sinners. Anything other than that is in a realm very far away from her.

I think she was scared at first, right after she confessed what the janitor did to her, that he would somehow submit her name and she would be the one to get into trouble. But as the weeks went by and nothing happened to her, the threat slipped further and further away. And as she began to feel more uncomfortable, that overtook any worry she had about being labeled a sinner by Benjamin Pierre. And I want to keep the remainder of her innocence sacred. She has endured too much already.

I did not expect Emilie to push back on me so much. Her reaction definitely gives me pause; she's so sensible. But I am confident that even if Emilie doesn't come around and see my side of things, she won't do anything to hinder my plan. It's Rachel who has me nervous. Rachel, who lives inside Xavier and is constantly observing everything around her. I will need to be meticulous in my care of Kamon. If anything appears to be amiss, Rachel will notice it before anyone else.

She is already unhappy with me. She has never come into my room while Kamon was reading *To Kill A Mockingbird* aloud to the girls. But perhaps one of them spoke of it, and I wouldn't doubt it, since they are enthralled with Scout and Atticus and Boo Radley. Maybe she overheard a discussion in the dining hall. Maybe Belinda heard them speaking at bedtime and reported it to her supervisor, though I don't think so. But something made Rachel do a sweep under the girls' beds and when she found the tattered copy underneath Kamon's mandated worksheets, she confiscated the novel. She's sitting behind her desk now, and I'm sitting across from her; the offending book lays between us.

"This has your name written all over it," she says. I can't help but fixate on her tiny stained teeth set deep inside long, thick gums. Her lips conceal and reveal them with every word. I force myself to look down at the book, rather than raise my eyes up to hers.

"It's my grandmother's name," I say, my voice flat.

"You know what I mean," she says. "What are you thinking, bringing a banned book for the girls? If this thing was laying around during a State inspection, we would be reprimanded severely. Do you know how much funding they'd take away? I can't run this place on a penny less than what we currently have; it's tight enough as it is."

I look up at her when I hear her concern. She hasn't said anything about the nature of the book or that she disagrees with anything inside it. She's worried about being caught. I find that oddly comforting.

"There's no reason this book should be banned, Rachel. It's absurd."

"That isn't for us to argue. We follow the rules here, because when we don't, it's the girls who suffer." She picks up the book with two fingers as if it's contaminated. "I should dispose of this here and now. But I imagine it's meaningful to you, if it belonged to a member of your family. If you want banned books inside your own home, there's nothing I can do about that. But I can make sure you don't bring them here. Don't let me see it again."

Oh, if she knew about the sorts of books I sheltered in my own home. I almost want to laugh at the thought of it. I don't take the book from her. I don't want to take it away from this place. I don't want to take it from the girls.

"They are learning from it." I rest my hands on Rachel's desk. "They learn more from this than their booklets can ever teach them." Rachel sits back, no doubt tired of this conversation. She returns the book to her desk.

"I'm not getting into that with you. You know how I feel. The girls are lucky to be getting the education they are. But that's not our concern right now. I can't have something illegal in here. We haven't had an inspection in a while. When it comes, and it always does, they are extremely thorough. If that book is found, we will all pay. Funding will be cut, including from the food budget. You think it's so wonderful that they're learning? They can't eat words."

I want to stand up for my beliefs but not at that cost.

"I can bring it home with me each night. But let them finish reading it, please. They'll be so disappointed otherwise."

Rachel shakes her head. "An inspection can happen at any moment." Her face is stringent and her voice is cool. "Your stubbornness will only hurt them. I don't think that's what you want." She slides the book toward me. "Put it in your bag and take it with you tonight. Do not bring it here again."

I want to throw the book across the room but it has Ophelia's curling signature inside and she held this, like every other book, so lovingly. After a moment's hesitation, I pick it up and hold it against my chest. When I stand, Rachel stands as well, and she leans toward me, the desk our barrier.

"If you study one chapter a night once you are home, I'm sure you can relay the general story to the girls," she says, barely above a whisper. "So long as they are told not to discuss it outside of your presence."

She takes me by surprise and I can only nod.

"We have to follow the rules here," she says again, louder. "It's for the girls. All of this, all the time, is for these girls."

"I know," I tell her. "Thank you."

"I have no idea what you're talking about." She sits again and picks up a sheet of paper, showing me that it's time to go.

XXVI

OPHELIA'S COPY OF *TO KILL A MOCKINGBIRD* is back on the bookshelf. I re-read the last chapters tonight while eating my leftover stewed vegetables. It stays with you, that book. I cannot wait to get back to the girls tomorrow to tell them how it ends. They'll miss Kamon's voice and it isn't as immersive without Harper Lee's exact words, but it will have to do. I may have written a few phrases onto little slips of paper that will fit nicely inside my skirt pocket, as well. Somehow, if Rachel finds out, I don't think she'll mind.

There's no choice in this wet heat, so the air conditioner is on, but it isn't strong enough. I leave the lights off and ready myself for bed by flashlight, hoping I'm saving enough electricity to avoid tripping a breaker. I don't like the eerie feeling of being in the dark like this, but Miles follows me as I move around and the clicking of his nails on the floor and his quiet panting keep me calm.

I hear a car on the gravel outside just as I finish washing my face. Miles hears it too and his ears stiffen a second before the rest of his body does. His bark cuts through the silence of the house and I shush him. As much as I want him to sound like a guard dog at times, I feel like right now, he should be very quiet.

With dread I realize that Preacher Pote has come back. It's completely dark outside and it's late, much too late for me to open the door for him. But how can I really stop him if he wants to come in? Even if I had a gun, which I have thought at times might be a good idea, though most women don't have one, I can't very well brandish it in front of him like a crazy person. And if he did something that would actually require me to shoot, there would be no getting away with it for me. That one shot would end two lives. So what other choice do I have but to open the door and hope that it's a benign visit?

I keep Miles with me. There will be no locking him away in the bedroom this time. I need his sturdy weight beside me. But when I peer out the small window beside the front door, there is no car. As unlikely as it was for someone to be driving down this desolate road, it seems as though it was just that. A wrong turn, most likely. I let go of Miles' collar and try to stop my knees from trembling. If it wasn't for the shelter of the bayou and the privacy of this place, I would move away from it tomorrow. The very reason that keeps me here is the same reason that instills fear in the dark hours.

Miles isn't placated. He's whining at the front door and his nose twitches. He looks at me and yelps again before pacing back and forth, sniffing wildly. Miles is always right. Someone is out there.

I'm not going to open the door to check, but then I hear a knock, very faint. And when I freeze, utterly unsure if I should call out to the person on the other side or fling open the door or run into my kitchen to grab a knife, I hear a woman's voice. It sounds like she is saying "please."

* * *

I don't know who brought her here. She's so frightened, she doesn't tell me her name. I am scared because nobody told me she was coming. Many times it's Margaret who contacts me, usually with a stolen word after a church service or on my walk to work, where she'll fall into step with me for a brief moment and mutter that a woman in need of help is going to see me. She has made many connections with young women in the Parish. She knows I'm available in the evenings, but she still gets a confirmation from me that it's okay. And so this unexpected visit has nothing to do with Margaret. That worries me.

One of my other former patients must have told her where to go, though it seems unlikely that they'd take such a liberty without letting me know. Still, they have all been sworn to secrecy and I trust their judgement. They are risking themselves each time they offer up information, and that alone is enough to keep them careful.

But I can't badger this woman about any of that, because she is standing in my living room, shaking and crying. I think she is in too much pain to even think of being afraid. And that scares me even more. I know right away that this is serious.

She won't sit down despite my pleadings, and I realize she doesn't want to stain the couch. There's a lot of blood. I am suddenly aware of how completely alone we are. I am wholly unequipped for this. This goes beyond herbal cocktails served up in steaming cups of tea. This is something I have never had to do. Ophelia did, I know. She told me about it, and even showed me her instruments. I've never used them, though, and I don't want to now. But I can already see that the time for herbal remedies has passed, and that this woman is in trouble. However she got here, whoever sent her, I need to help her now.

"You need to sit," I say. I steer her toward the couch but she shakes her head. "Let me bring you into the back." She looks frightened at the words, and I shake my head. "It's just my bedroom. I'll put something on the bed and you can sit. I'll help you."

She wipes her eyes and nods and then takes my offered arm, leaning into me. I see a pool of blood on the floor and push Miles away from it with my foot. He's turned from a guard dog into a detective, sniffing for clues about this mysterious visitor. I need to clean up the mess soon, for several reasons, the least being the dog. But first I need to take care of this woman. She sinks onto my bed as soon as I throw old sheets and towels on it. There is a palpable relief on her face. She trusts me. Someone told her to trust me. She has no idea that I don't know what to do for her. But taking her to a clinic for help would lead to something much worse than this, so I have to do something. I have to try. Someone thought I was her best option.

I don't ask who brought her here. But I want to know her name, just so I can use it to comfort her. I think we will be together for a while.

"Renee," she finally says, her head resting on the pillows I propped up behind her. She's clutching her abdomen and every few minutes her body seizes as a wave of pain crests over her. I can't let her know, but I am terrified. I feel more alone in this house with Renee than I do when there's nobody here. What do I do to help her? And if it doesn't work, if something happens to her? What will I do then?

"Renee, I need you to tell me what happened." I brush my hand over her forehead and wipe aside wet strands of hair. Her skin, every inch of it that I can see, is covered in a sheen of sweat. But she's pale, too pale. Her eyes are fluttering closed and I want to shake her to keep her awake but I don't do anything but say her name.

"Renee?"

She starts to cry again, and this time I think it's the pain and the sadness all at once, all-consuming.

"I know I shouldn't have," she says. And then she doesn't say anything else.

"Renee, listen to me. I don't need a reason why. I just need you to tell me what happened." We are in it now, the both of us together. My night was not supposed to be like this. I was supposed to be planning how to help Kamon. My only thought after washing my face and brushing my teeth was to go through the herbs under the bed and decide how best to mix them for the young girl, and how to administer the tea to her without anyone becoming suspicious. But now I can't even think of Kamon. I am scared that this woman might be dying on my bed.

She's young, maybe twenty-two or twenty-three. I can't tell if she's pretty. She is not pretty right now.

"Tell me what happened," I say again. She nods, just a slight motion of her head, and her lips part. They are chapped and dry and I want to get a wet cloth for them but I don't want to move and stop her from speaking.

"I went for help," she says, and her voice is thready. "There was a mixture I drank, but it didn't work. She…the person who helped me…told me to wait a few hours. But I couldn't wait. I thought I could fix it myself."

"Where were you? What did you do?"

Renee shook her head. "I was at my mother's house, in her bathroom."

"You weren't feeling any effects from the dose of tea?"

"No. Nothing. I got scared it wasn't working. I needed to take care of it." She's crying into her hands, though she doesn't have the energy to sob. It's a muffled, faint cry. It's a hopeless cry.

"Okay, I need you to tell me what you did. Renee? Okay? Tell me what you did."

"I used a bottle," she says into her hands. I don't want to know more but I have to.

"What do you mean, you used a bottle? What bottle?"

"A glass bottle." I wish I could see her eyes but her face is covered, from fear and probably from shame.

"A glass bottle?"

"I smashed the neck on the tile floor."

"Oh, God." Now I know why there's so much blood and I don't know how to fix her. I force myself to breathe. "Did you come here from your mother's house?"

Renee nods, her head still buried in her hands. She pulls her knees up and rolls to her side. I put a hand on her lower back. Her dress is soaked with perspiration.

"My mother called the Jane who helped me, but she got scared. She said she didn't know what to do. She drove me to you."

I should be focused on the woman bleeding out on my bed. I know I don't have a lot of time. But I take just a moment and think about what Renee is telling me. There's a woman out there, doing what I do, and she knows about me but I don't know about her. How is this possible? I obviously know that there are other Removers like me, but we are very careful not to engage with one another. It's safer that way. And most times, just like with Ophelia, the midwifery that we practice is passed down from one generation of a family to the next. We don't need to stray outside our homes for our training, in most cases. So it's disconcerting that a Remover knew so much about me, even where I live. It makes no sense. The only thing I can think for now is that it's okay. This woman obviously doesn't want her identity known. She obviously won't do anything to hurt me. She's trusting me with her patient. Somehow, she has a better opinion of me than she should. I can't think about her right now. I have to do something for this woman.

I tell Renee I'll be right back. I step out onto my porch, gulping in air and swallowing anxious sobs that I can't conceal any longer. I cannot do this. I don't know how to do this. I'm incredibly pissed off that the Southerly State left Renee and me no other choice. Her safety and well-being, probably her *life*, rest solely on me, and I am wholly inadequate. I try to even out my breathing and focus on nothing other than the syncopated rhythm of the bullfrogs calling out from the swamp. I want to run down the steps and away from this house. I've never been so scared in this place, not even when the blackouts come. Not even when Pote was inside. I want someone to tell me what to do. But there is nobody to guide me. And there's a woman inside who will likely die if I don't pull myself together. One more breath, and I turn around and make myself walk back inside.

I wet a washcloth with cool water for Renee's forehead and lips, and wash my hands. I boil a pot of water. I get a hammer. I go back into the room; she's still curled into a ball and crying silent tears. I dab the cloth on her lips and lay it on her head. I put candles on the night table; I don't want to turn on the lights. Renee's crumpled figure, clothed in creamy off-white, lays on top of the blood-stained towels. Shadows painted by candlelight flicker on the walls. The scene is macabre.

I back out of the room and into the hallway. I kneel down and pry open a loose floorboard with the hammer. Ophelia's instruments are nestled underneath the board. I have not seen them in so long. I hoped to never have to hold them. She was the one who placed them there, and it feels strange to touch them after her hands did. Maybe some of her will be with me this long night.

I rest the board back in place and leave the hammer against the wall. I go into the kitchen, my flashlight guiding me, and drop the instruments into the boiling water. I wait. My hands are shaking, but I will be no good to Renee unless I am perfectly steady. I will collapse later, I promise myself. I will break down and tremble and cry. But not yet. Instead, I pace with Miles, the two of us crossing paths in front of the stove. When it's time, I drain the pot and let the instruments cool. I gather them in a clean towel and wash my hands again. I rummage in the back of a cabinet until I find the bottle of brandy. It's the only anesthetic I have. Then I return to the bedroom and shut the door behind me.

XXVII

THE EVENING TURNED INTO the bewitching hours and then to a smoky dawn. I did what I could through the night. The brandy took away the worst of it, but Renee went in and out of restless sleep. My hands shook the entire time. I had trouble standing after I saw the full scope of what she'd done to herself. I used Ophelia's tools to clean anything that might still remain. The instruments were surgical in reality but medieval in appearance. I worked almost blindly. There was a flexible frame for dilation and an annular blade to curette. The blunted hook was used to extract. I knew this because my grandmother had told me, a long time ago. Up until now, my work with women has been almost genteel. But this, with the moaning and the cool metal in my hands and all the blood...it was raw. It was a reckoning. It was barbaric.

I shouldn't be doing this, I kept thinking to myself. She should be in better care. I wished the Jane who brought Renee to me in the cover of night, sliding away on the gravel after dropping her off, had the courage to stay and show her face, so that she might help me. If this woman died, there would be blood on many, many hands, most especially the iron-clad hand of the Southerly State.

I do what I can, and then I sit with her for hours afterward, after the countless stitches. She is ruined, I'm sure. There will be no children for her. This is the first time I've stitched something that wasn't an orange or a banana, and I remember laughing at my grandmother for having me suture fruit. She didn't smile back. She was preparing me for what she knew would someday come. Tonight is *someday*.

There are too many hours in this night. Too much quiet, too much time to think about what's transpired. Too much time to smell the blood. Miles whimpers in the corner. He is haunted by the smell too. I don't like this new side of things; it's hideous. I think about the preacher's righteous prayers for the Unborn, and I think about how it is this, what I've seen tonight, that so offends some people. And I understand.

I feel the blood on my hands from tonight, even though I did not take a life. But I have taken others. My work is usually neat. The blood comes later and I usually don't see it. All of a sudden I'm finding it hard to breathe. The weight of everything I've done, everything Ophelia told me was right to do, bears down on me. It's a lot, in the middle of the night, to really see yourself for the first time.

* * *

Renee is sleeping. I need to give her something to fight infection. I can cover her external wounds with honey, and feed her garlic and ginger, but I don't know if that will be enough. As the first fingers of light crawl underneath the window shade, I know that I can't leave the woman alone in my bed. I also can't simply not show up at Xavier. I wish I had splurged on a new battery for my phone so I could alert someone that I can't come to work today. I don't want to take the time to walk to the orphanage and back, and there's no guarantee that I'll intersect with Emilie on her walk at just the right moment, since it's already later than I usually start out.

The only solution is to fill Ophelia's truck with gasoline and drive to Xavier. I haven't driven in months; it costs too much. I have a few gallons of gas in a little red can in the garage, sitting beside my grandmother's silver Chevy, a pick-up truck with a tiny cab that fits two people. She loved that old truck. It's in pristine condition because she took good care of it and it wasn't driven a lot. Walking was always much more economical.

I pour half the contents of the can into the truck's tank and it starts up right away. I murmured to Renee not to move, that I'd be right back, but I don't think she heard me. It feels good to drive. It feels like freedom. I even turn on the air conditioner, and it's glorious once the musty smell filters through. I turn the fans toward my face and set it as high as it goes. I don't turn on the radio. I don't want to hear the angry words of the State news programs. I wish there was music. Nothing would be better than air conditioning and jazz.

It only hits me when I'm nearly there that I don't have a good excuse for missing work. I don't look sick. The timing can't be worse either, as I want to monitor Kamon and stay by her side. I don't want anyone else to begin to notice the signs. We are short on time. But I need at least two days at home. I'm hoping Renee will be strong enough by then. I can't think about the alternative. That could very well spell the end for me as well. I wonder if her mother has any idea where she is. I'm thinking of all these things, too many things, when I see the clock tower in the distance, and Emilie's slight figure walking toward it. I want to beep the horn but I should be quiet. Instead I drive up beside her.

She quickens her pace and I realize that of course she doesn't know it's me. She must think it's a man who's about to catcall her, or worse. I open the window halfway and say her name. She hears me the second time.

"What are you *doing?*" She laughs and I realize I needed the sight of her open smile more than I knew.

"Get in," I tell her. She walks around the front of the truck and hops into the cab, putting her hands over the fans on her side and letting the freezing air slip through her fingers.

"Nice ride," she says.

"I can't go to work today," I say. Her face falls in an instant. "It's important. I need to go back home."

"You have someone there?"

I nod.

"Did something happen?" She knows my two occupations rarely cross.

"She should be okay. But she was in bad shape when she came to me. I need to stay with her. Can you tell Rachel? Tell her I'm sick. She's going to have to cover my room for me until she gets a replacement. Have her see if Belinda can come early."

"She knows what to do to fill in for someone," Emilie says.

"And check in on Kamon for me, please. If you can. And tell the girls I'm not feeling well but I'm thinking of them and I'll be back soon. Two days, I think."

"It can't be more than that. You'll be in trouble. You're supposed to visit the infirmary if you're sick. Veronica should be the one to take care of you."

"Tell her I couldn't make it in. Tell her I'm throwing up. Tell her I could barely drive."

Emilie nods. "I'll get out here and walk the rest of the way. You don't want anyone to see you. You really do look tired, though."

"It was a long night."

"Maybe it's time to just take care of the children," she says, her hair blowing around her face in small tufts.

"I had that thought last night, or maybe it was this morning. But these women will always need help."

"Then maybe it's time for someone else to help them," she says.

"Thank you for worrying about me. I appreciate it more than you know. I'll think about it," I say, but she knows I won't. It's a calling of sorts, passed down through my blood. I wish she would remember what she felt like once, when she was desperate.

"I need to go hold the babies," she says. I stop the truck so she can hop down. "Good luck."

I watch her until she's inside Xavier. Then I back up so I don't pass the building, and turn around the truck. I'm afraid to see what's waiting for me at home.

XXVIII

Renee sleeps most of the day. She's cool to the touch, but I don't check her wounds. If she isn't showing signs of infection, I think it's best to leave everything alone and allow her to heal. Every decision I make is nothing more than a guess. I'm calmer than I should be though, and I think maybe Ophelia is somewhere nearby, guiding me.

By afternoon, I give her a few sips of the brandy and leave a cool washcloth on her head. My room is dark, with the shades pulled down low and the door closed. I have a fan aimed at the bed until the power chokes and cuts off. Heat swells into the room almost immediately. We sit for hours, me tending to and watching her. She hasn't eaten yet, and I try to ration my own food since I know I won't get paid for these two days off and my budget will be tight for the week.

She's sitting up by the afternoon of the second day, and her color is pink. She is pretty, I can see. She's tired but I think she's going to be okay. She's in a lot of pain though, and I can't send her home just yet.

"Will your mama be worried?" I ask as she sips water from a cup I hold to her lips. She shakes her head and rests it back on the pillow.

"She knows I'm bein' takin' care of," she says.

"But she doesn't know where you are."

"It's okay," she says, sleep in her voice. "The Jane wouldn't have told her where she took me." She seems very sure of this.

"Can you tell me who she was? The woman you first went to?"

"I promised I wouldn't, and I know how serious of a promise it is." She closes her eyes and I can't press her, because she's right, and I would want her to do this exact thing for me. And so I nod even though she can't see me, and I set down the cup on the night table and leave her to sleep. I nearly trip over the slightly raised floorboard in front of the door on my way out.

* * *

By a miracle or the grace of God or just incredible good luck, Renee did not develop an infection. I'm able to leave her alone on her third day and return to work. It's pouring and I'm soaked through completely, but I have no choice but to walk. I can't use the rest of the gasoline, just in case. Rachel asks how I'm feeling but doesn't say anything else about my absence. I'm sure I look bedraggled enough to convince anyone that I was out of sorts for a few days. Which, let's face it, I was. The girls are in good spirits and happy to see me. Kamon looks flushed and healthy. I wondered if perhaps there's nothing to worry about after all, but then I notice that her breasts are swollen under her nightshirt. I want to wrap her up in my arms and make everything go away, but I tell myself to be patient. In another day or two, I will.

By that evening, I tell Renee that she is well enough to go home. She's limping and every move she makes is in slow motion, but she assures me there's no one else in her house except her mama and she can hide away for a few days without anyone else seeing her. I wonder how she doesn't have to get to a job, but I don't want to inquire and maybe it's better if I don't know.

There's no way she can walk home, and it's still pouring, so for the second time in several days, I climb into the silver Chevy. Renee sits beside me after needing help getting up into it. She directs me to her mama's house, but I tell her I'll stop the street before. I hate to make her walk even that short way, especially in the rain, but I can't risk dropping her off right at the door. The streets are empty and not even the bullfrogs are calling out, but I still need to be careful. We drive in silence, the truck moving underneath the Spanish moss that hangs down over the road.

"Thank you." It's the first time she's said it. "I think I would have died otherwise."

"That's what I'm here for," I say, and I wonder if Emilie would agree with that.

"I gave you a run for your money," she says, and for the first time, I see her smile.

We are at the corner of the street that leads to her block. I slow down the truck. The headlights cast long yellow beams on the road and I see glistening worms twisting and curling on the ground.

"Just take care of yourself," I say. "You'll need the stitches removed in about a week. You can come back to me in the evenings, after seven. I'll be there."

"Thank you," she says again. Then she's sliding down from the seat, wincing as she does. She makes her way slowly down the cracked and broken sidewalk. The houses are close together but well-cared for. Their gardens would be lovely in the sunlight. I wait until Renee turns the corner and then I keep driving, but not toward my house. I find myself heading toward Xavier. I can't go in. The girls are all asleep anyway, or they should be. But I sit outside for a few minutes, just being close to them. To her. The rain streams down the window in sheets and everything outside is blurry. But if I squint through the droplets, I can just see Preacher Pote's bouquet sitting on the sill of the window in my room. The heads of the flowers are bent over their stems. I never found the time to throw them away while at work. But if I'm being honest with myself, I think I rather liked watching them die.

XXIX

I DON'T SEE EMILIE ON THE WAY to work in the morning for several days. It's a lonely walk, and the past week has been so draining, I would have liked her beside me to help buoy my spirits. At least, that's how it would have been, before I confided in her. We haven't really spoken since she covered for me while I tended to Renee. Everything was fine that morning, I remind myself. We shared a few smiles, even. We will be okay. We are always okay.

For the second day in a row, Emilie doesn't show up to the break room for lunch. I couldn't have had a private conversation with her there, not with Rachel and Veronica and several other workers sitting at the table, but I was hoping to sit beside her, even if it was just to kick her ankle under the table when Rachel said something particularly grating. I try to convince myself that she isn't avoiding me, but it's starting to feel otherwise. Just as Rachel is folding her uneaten sandwich into its neat little wrapper, I scoot out five minutes early and head to the infant room. Emilie is hovering over someone sitting in the lone rocker by the window. She turns when she hears me, and as her body shifts, I see who's sitting in the chair. It's Kamon. She's holding a baby, looking down at it with an expression of happiness I haven't seen on her in so long.

"What's going on?" I ask. I wonder if Kamon hears the edge in my voice.

"Damaris is teething. She hasn't wanted to be put down all morning." Emilie says. She smiles down at the baby and then at me. "I thought maybe Kamon could hold her for a few minutes while I fed some of the others."

"You took Kamon out of lunch so she could hold her?"

"She said she would be glad to help. Isn't that right?"

Kamon nods, her gaze still on the baby.

"I'm surprised you didn't ask one of the older girls to help," I say.

"Kamon is a natural," Emilie says.

"Kay," I say. "It's sweet of you to help. But I need you to get back to our room. The girls will be returning from lunch in a minute and we're going to start our lessons."

Kamon rolls her eyes. "Can I stay just a little longer? She really likes me. And she's so cute."

"I don't know. How are you feeling?"

"A little better," she says.

"You ate your lunch?"

Kamon shrugs and Emilie gives her head a slight shake in my direction. The poor girl hasn't been able to eat much of anything.

"A few minutes," I say. "But Rachel will not want you to miss your lessons." Kamon leans into the baby and sniffs her head. "You can come back, if Emilie would like more help," I say, because she's being so sweet and I don't want to ruin the nicest five minutes she's had in months.

I step back from the rocker and lead Emilie to a table filled with bottles. I grab one just as she does, and we both pick up a mewling bundle to feed. Our heads are close together.

"What are you doing?" I ask.

"I needed help," Emilie says.

"Em. Seriously. What are you trying to prove?"

She looks at me over her suckling baby. "I'm not trying to prove anything. But do you see how good she is?"

"She's one step up from playing with a doll. You cannot possibly think this comes close to a thirteen-year-old birthing a baby. Besides, baby-sitting for five minutes is not the same as becoming a mother."

"I know that," she says. "Hell, I baby-sit all day, every day, and I'm not a mother. And neither are you."

I take a step back when she says that and the nipple falls from the baby's mouth. I pop it back before she begins to wail.

"I wasn't trying to tell you that Kamon should have the baby," Emilie says. "I was trying to tell you that I think she deserves a say in her own life. I know you are coming at it from a very different angle. I don't know what you'll decide, and I don't think I want to know. But I'm not the one you should be talking to; you need to tell Belinda. You aren't allowed to spend the night. If Kamon was…going through something…the night worker would need to be informed."

I look over at Kamon, still enraptured with Damaris. It feels like Emilie is giving me a blessing of sorts. I want to finish this conversation tonight on our walk home, but I have a feeling she will slip out before me, or wait until I am gone before she leaves.

XXX

If Pote were a woman, he would be labeled a hysterical, shrieking harpy. But because he is a man, he is merely impassioned. He rants from his pulpit, raving and raging like the coming storm he warns of. The hurricane, a monster, as Pote refers to it, is a surprise to me. I don't listen to the State-mandated radio or TV, and I don't have access to the Internet at home. I never go online at work, when the Internet is actually working. I avoid the vitriol that spews from those things as much as possible. Rachel hasn't mentioned a storm to us, and I wonder if she knew about it before today. It's brewing in the Atlantic, Pote tells us. It's gaining in size and intensity and it's headed straight for us. Not just the Southerly State in general, but right toward our Parish. He uses words like "catastrophic" and "deadly." I almost think he's enjoying the impending excitement of it. And then he ramps his rhetoric to fevered heights. He says it's coming right for us because God is steering it this way.

"God is angry." Pote spits and bangs his fist on the pulpit. His eyes, usually that cool, watery blue, flash with flecks of heat. "And how can he not be, brothers and sisters? Are these gathering storms not warnings? Have we been taking heed? No. No!" His fist slams again, harder. He turns to the men's side of the room. "We have men in this Parish who don't lead their families with the strength of masculinity. They allow their wives to coddle their baby boys until they become homosexuals. They might hide their sexuality from us but they cannot hide it from God." He swivels his body to look at us. "Worse, we have women who think it's acceptable to take the life of an Unborn. We will never be all right in this life or the next so long as there's even one Unborn who is denied the right to live. There are people among us who do not pledge undying allegiance to the Southerly State. They do not kiss our God-given flag with love and devotion. There are still people among us who do not put God above all else, and the Southerly State right after Him. And we will never stop being punished by Him until every one of us repents and is saved."

The entire congregation is still. It stinks of sweaty bodies and hot breath and fear. I see Emilie and her sister and mother several rows ahead of me. They're too close to the front again. But even though I'm farther back, I won't slip out unnoticed after the service today. I want to speak to Pote. If I must have his attention on me, it's his ears that I want.

A hymn starts and bounces off the white walls of this building that is so much more institution than holy space. The hymn is a battle cry, rising in tempo and dynamic. There is nothing spiritual within it. Pote has doused his rabid matchsticks with yet another splash of gasoline, and they are ignited. I sit there with the growing rumble all around me, watching God's house burn.

* * *

I slide out the side entrance and walk to the front of the church, waiting while the men file out. I wait for Pote at the bottom of the steps. The church melds with the sky, everything a nearly identical color of dirty gray. Looking at this sky, it doesn't seem like a hurricane is headed for us. It's drizzling slightly but the air is so still, the leaves on the sycamore trees aren't even quivering. There's no indication of a gathering storm, and perhaps that's what makes it feel all the more ominous.

Pote sees me, but he's talking with parishioners. They sidle up to him and sneak in a few words, one woman looking up at him adoringly as he grazes his hand over her shoulder. I don't like waiting for him, but if I can get him to listen to me, it will be worth it.

Finally, he excuses himself from the small throng around him and makes his way over to me. He's looking at me like he knew I would wait for him. It's in his eyes and the set of his mouth.

"Preacher," I say before he can speak. "I was hoping you've had time to give some thought to what we talked about."

"About how alone you are out on the bayou?" He smiles, his satisfaction with himself crawling all over his face.

"No, sir. About the Tamburo. About the problem with not having proof for an accusation?"

"I don't know why you would worry yourself about such things," he says, and he takes one finger and glides it down my cheek. I don't know how the woman at the top of the stairs fawned over his touch; it cuts into my bones like dry ice, searing heat and freezing cold at the same time. I can barely stand it. "You're an entirely different kind of person than any of those sinners could ever hope to be. You keep your nose clean and I know you always will. Don't concern yourself with them."

"Unless they aren't really sinners," I say. "Shouldn't we be sure?"

"We?" He laughs. "None of this concerns you. There is no 'we.' At least, not about such dismal affairs."

"If you visit me and bring me flowers, it would be nice if you would also listen to me," I say. Although I'm afraid this will just encourage more attention from him, shouldn't I at least try to use it to my advantage? But I can already see that he doesn't want my opinions or my advice. You don't seek those things from someone you wish to own.

Instead of deigning to acknowledge what I've said, he points to the clouds hanging over us.

"Were you listenin' in there?" He leans close to me. I see the individual blonde hairs that make up the stubble on his face. "We are all being punished. The storms and the floods get worse every single year. It's God's wrath upon us. God is so angry; we are all being punished for the sins of the few."

Again, I'm struck with the thought that he truly believes this. For him, it's the only explanation for an Earth that has been in crisis for so long. I wonder what reason he'd have for the storms if all sins really were eradicated from the world, but that's unlikely to happen, and the religious leaders might just conjure up new transgressions if that were the case. There will always be something to hate, something to rail against.

I have the sudden thought that perhaps Pote's God really is angry. But what if He is angry with how the Southerly State treats people? Wouldn't it be ironic if the storms were indeed a manifestation of God's wrath? Wrath at the maltreatment of women and people of color and homosexuals and anyone who does not look like a strong, tall, white male? I very nearly say this out loud, but Pote's anger would likely conjure up a whole other kind of storm, and I decide it's best to deal with one force of nature at a time.

XXXI

We have a meeting Monday afternoon in the break room while we eat lunch. Rachel is adamant that all workers be prepared to spend the night beginning on Wednesday at 6:00 p.m. We are to be in place with several changes of clothes and all personal care items. This is just one more reason why only unwed women are hired for this line of work. How could anyone leave their families to come and live here for days on end? And yet these girls are our families, and this old building will provide more shelter than any of our homes will, so nobody grumbles when Rachel states her demands. We are used to it by now, anyway. It seems like each summer has been more and more relentless in its intensity of storms. This is why Pote warns of an angry God. It certainly does feel like there is a rising anger raging all around us. Is it any different for him to blame God than it was for ancient Greeks to think the sun was a wheel on Apollo's golden chariot as he raced it across the sky?

I can't leave Miles at home alone, not for days on end, and not during a storm, where the surge from the surrounding swamps and rivers and lakes will crest over and threaten to put the entire area under water. It's happened too many times before to think it won't happen now. Rachel waves off my concerns before I even voice them out loud. "I know there are pets that will need to be looked after. I do find that their presence is comforting to the girls as well. The animals can serve as therapy pets for the days when we're sheltering downstairs. Just so long as you bring adequate food for them, obviously."

I know Miles will love this. He's sheltered here before, and I remember him sprawled on his back, legs splayed in every direction, tongue lolled out, happy little snorts emanating from him as groups of girls pet and rubbed and loved all over him. The hurricane will not be a hardship for my dog.

It begins to rain Tuesday morning. It starts as a drizzle but by lunch it's a downpour. At 5:00 p.m. Emilie comes into my room.

"I think I'm going to stay," she says. "I can't imagine walking home in this and it'll probably be the same for the walk back tomorrow. I don't imagine it'll let up much before the worst of the storm hits. I don't have extra clothes with me, but at least these are dry."

It makes sense, what she's planning. I'm dreading the walk home myself. Maybe I'll drive back tomorrow morning. I'm sure the truck can withstand the storm, so long as I don't park it underneath any trees. That will be much easier with Miles, and it will keep my belongings dry.

"I can't stay tonight," I say. "I wish I could, but I need to get Miles." She nods but I know she thinks it's unwise.

"You might want to go home and bring him back tonight instead of waiting for the morning," she says. "Doesn't this seem like the beginning of the storm already?" She looks out the window and my eyes trail hers. There are dark shapes and shadows outside, long black branches of the sycamore tree scraping across the window, sheets of rain. And there's wind. How had I not noticed the fierce wind?

"You're right. No sense waiting."

"Driving?"

"I guess so. Miles isn't going to do too well walking in this. Neither will I."

"You'll probably be back in a few hours if you're driving, so I'll be up."

"I'll just throw some things together and head back. I guess we'll start moving down to the basement in the morning," I say. It takes hours to move all the mattresses. The frames of the cots stay where they are. The girls are responsible for carrying their own pillows and blankets downstairs. Emilie will need a lot of help with the small folding bassinets. I wonder if that's another reason she's eager for me to return.

Emilie is staring out the window. She doesn't pay attention to the girls in the room who are as animated as I've ever seen them. Even something potentially catastrophic is exciting in its imminence. There's a buzz of anticipation that the darkening sky lends credence to. It feels like something is about to happen.

When Emilie goes back to her own room, I sweep through the rows of cots, telling the girls that I'm returning later in the evening, maybe before they're asleep. I tell them that Miles will be with me, and there's a collective squeal of joy. Calah's eyes are wide; she remembers Miles from last summer, when he spent a good amount of time curled up at her feet while she stroked his ears with infinite patience.

"I'll see you tonight," I tell Kamon. She's standing by the window, listening to the pounding rain.

"You can't walk home in this," she says. "You'll never make it."

"I don't have a choice. But I'm going to drive back."

"I don't want you to."

"I'll return soon, I promise. With the dog. And I'll be here to stay, until the storm is over."

She turns from the window and hugs me, burying her face in my neck. She's just a touch shorter than I am these days.

"Be careful," she whispers. "Please."

* * *

I actually catch myself looking for Preacher Pote when I get outside. If he's sitting in his car waiting to offer me a ride, I'll take it. That's how drenching the rain is. But he isn't here, and I'm soaked the second the doors slam behind me. The only encouraging thing is that once you're soaking wet, you can't get any wetter. I tell myself there's a hot shower waiting for me at home, and a Chevy pickup truck with enough gas to bring me back to Xavier. That makes the walk home bearable. My umbrella blows inside out so many times it bends and breaks, and I stuff it into a garbage can on the street, already overflowing with refuse.

Men hammer wooden boards over windows and drag tables and chairs inside from their balconies. "This shit's gettin' old," one of them calls to me, but the rest are silent, their heads bowed against the driving elements just as my head is. As I get closer to home, my feet squelch down into the mud and I feel myself sinking, not just into the ground, but in general. I'm tired beyond any usual level of exhaustion. I'm drained from the walk and from being so thoroughly wet. I am, in every sense of the word, spent.

Miles sniffs at me and yowls, immediately sensing my distress. I barely have energy to rub his back and give him his bowl of dinner before leaving a pile of sopping wet clothes on the floor and stepping into the shower. Ironically, it feels wonderful to stand under the water after walking through a deluge. I let it pour down my back and over my hair. I stand there until the water turns cold, and even then I'm slow to turn it off.

As I'm combing tangles out of my hair, the lights flicker and plunge everything into darkness. In the total silence of the house, I hear just how heavy the rain is. I'm sure this blackout will last for the duration of the storm, and maybe a week or two afterwards. I light a taper candle to illuminate my bedroom and begin to pack one small canvas bag. We haven't had plastic bags for years, one of the few things the Southerly State has gotten right, but I could use one now to help keep everything dry. I nearly brush by my bed without stopping, but then I get on my knees and fumble for Ophelia's tins. If I don't take any herbs to the orphanage, I'm cementing a decision not to help Kamon during a time that might be my best chance. The next few days are my only opportunity to be with her overnight. I don't have to use the herbs just yet, I remind myself, though I won't have too much longer. But shouldn't I keep my options open? I wrap them carefully and set them inside the bag.

Clutching the bag and Miles' leash in one hand and the candle in the other, I go into the garage. But of course the automatic door doesn't open without power. I drop the bag and leash and Miles turns in quick circles, sniffing the concrete floor. I struggle for a few minutes with the door's manual lift but I need both hands and I don't have any place to stand the taper so it will stay upright. There's barely room for me to stand between the back of the Chevy and the garage door. I can't get the lever on the door to budge. I scream at it for a minute, not even words, just one long furious sound. I have the sudden realization that coming back here was a necessary but dangerous decision, and I don't know if I've ever felt so powerless and defeated. I pull on the lever with all the strength I have but it isn't enough. Then all the fight goes out of me and I rest my head on the bed of the truck and finally let myself cry.

XXXII

I HAD TO STAY THE NIGHT AT HOME. Miles and I weren't walking to Xavier in the dark, with pouring rain and increasing winds. It was easier to go back inside the house and collapse on my bed, blowing out the candle and plunging myself into the darkness. But now as I wake up and see only a hazy gray coming through the window, I see the mistake I made in waiting. The storm has arrived. The winds aren't as wild as they were last night, but the rain is torrential, and I think it may be even worse than anyone anticipated. Hurricanes bring their own deadly force, but a tropical storm that carries less wind but more rain is absolutely catastrophic for such a low-lying area. Rushing water is already flowing over the ground. It's everywhere, running down the street that leads to the house and gushing into the swamp, churning up the waters of the bayou. There will be no driving the Chevy to Xavier now even if I could get the garage door open; the floods are here and I've seen this too many times; streets that turn into rivers, sweeping away vehicles and people. Now I'm trapped inside Ophelia's old house, and Miles and I will have to ride out the storm together.

Only I can't do that. I have to report to work. I know Rachel would likely understand if I can't make it in, but they need me there. Surely there are other workers who will be trapped at home, having also been caught off guard with the storm's early arrival. Rachel will need as many workers as possible to tend to the girls and keep them calm and safe. I dress quickly, resigned to the fact that I'm going to have to navigate over flooded streets in the little wooden boat, sitting under a torrent of rain as I do. I know I won't be the only one;

people always take to their watercraft during these raging storms. They aren't supposed to, but sometimes it's the only way.

The Mississippi River swells to overflowing nearly every year. In the past one hundred years, there have been many attempts at installing levees to contain these waters. But the storms have become bigger and fiercer and more monstrous with time, though our government does not admit to the growing intensity. No matter what the Southerly State attempts to do about flooding, the water always wins. It swallowed New Orleans and one day it will overtake us. Most failed attempts in the past have been because the levees have been knocked over due to the relentless pounding of encroaching waves. But the last time, a surge of water burst through underneath the levees. Many parishes were under water for days. It was labeled a catastrophic failure, and the levees were not repaired. They were deemed futile in the never-ending onslaught of storms. I'm sure there was no money for another project like it, anyway. And so we have grown used to this during the summers. Relentless heat shot through with damning floods. It's just a way of life in this particular section of the Southerly State.

The pirogue is bobbing upside down in the rising water, tied to the thick trunk of a cypress. I drag a very reluctant Miles outside with me. The full force of the rain is astounding. It's pelting us both with a million sharp shards. I don't know how I'm going to row the pirogue, but I have to try. I look back at the house. I haven't boarded up the windows; there wasn't time. Suddenly I want to escape this place with a driving urgency. I can't untie the boat and begin paddling fast enough. How strange, I think, to sit across from an anxious wet dog in the teeming rain, rowing through streets streaming with water.

There's only about a foot of water so far, but it will get much worse, maybe up to four feet in a few hours. I'm lucky, though it's hard to feel lucky, that I woke so early and caught it before things get even worse. Miles lays down in the boat, his front paws covering his snout. He is the very definition of miserable, and I wish I could lay down and put my arms over my head as well. But I paddle, fighting through a current that feels like it wants to sweep me in the opposite direction. The edge of the bayou and the little house retreat into the distance, and I don't want to think about what either will look like upon my return.

As I paddle closer to the Place d'Armes, I see a man and a little boy sitting atop a black raft. The boy is crying. The man looks too scared to cry. He's paddling his craft against the rushing current and not going anywhere. The little boy calls to him. He doesn't answer. Maybe the man is trying to carry his son from their flooded home. But where can they go?

I reach out to them but the water flushes me right past their raft. The boy stretches an arm to me but I'm swept by too quickly. In another minute I glide by the Place d'Armes and see the Trinity. I wonder if it will withstand the flooding and the wind. It has endured before.

As I come out on the other side of the square, I can tell the water is already deeper. It's churning angrily. My little wooden boat tips and sways and almost gets caught in a vortex of water, a tiny whirlpool that nearly upends me. I'm surprised to see that I've dropped the paddle in the boat and I'm gripping the sides of the pirogue with petrified fingers. My canvas bag is between my feet. I can't lose it. I'm sure everything inside is soaked through.

The water spins us around and I have the sensation of spiraling out of control. The boat is getting pulled into the wrong direction now. I'm moving away from Xavier. The paddle, back in the water, is useless. I'm not strong enough to fight the current. I don't think I can navigate myself back home, either. I'm passing by the square again, the Trinity looking on impassively as I struggle. I'm fairly certain I'm not going to make it.

I hear a motor boat from behind, first the loud rumble and then the softer, slower purr as it sidles up to me. Two men stand in it, one at the wheel, the other leaning over the side, his legs braced against the rocking. He's stretching out his hand. I can barely see him through the rain and my tears.

"C'mon miss, we can get you and yer dog outta here, but you gotta hurry." He's shouting over the motor and the gushing water and the wind and rain. They aren't State workers; they aren't wearing a uniform and their boat doesn't bear the Southerly State symbol, though a large flag flaps viciously behind them. I have no choice but to trust them.

I don't want to leave the pirogue. I can get by without it; I can wade around the edge of the swamp to get to my herbs. But it was Ophelia's. It was carved by my grandfather. It's the only thing he left behind, and it was precious to her. But if I don't let it go, I'll be giving up my best chance of safety. My choice is made.

However, if I get out of the pirogue first, I don't know if we'll be able to pull Miles onto the motor boat. So I struggle to him, pitching forward and heaving him up by his front legs. He's quivering all over. He's so heavy, but with a burst of adrenaline and terror, I manage to drag him over to me and then lift him just enough so the man can reach down and pull Miles towards him. They both nearly fall backward into the boat. Then Miles is standing in the motor boat, his front paws resting on the side, barking at me to join him. I grab my bag and somehow stand up and grasp the man's outstretched hand. I almost slip right through his grip, but his other hand shoots out and takes hold of my wrist, and in another moment I'm in the boat.

As soon as my toes are dragged from the pirogue, it's ripped away, floating with the surging waters. It'll get banged up and carried far from here and I'll never see it again. Maybe, I think, someone who really needs it will find it at just the right moment. Maybe it served me as best as it could, and it's time to offer it up for someone else. I hope that's how it will happen, anyway.

"You shouldn'ta been out in this, miss," the man yells into my face, but I can see he isn't angry. His friend at the wheel guns the engine and we're cutting through the current, powering down the street. In a minute I can't even see the pirogue anymore. But Miles and I are safe, and it brought us this far, so I think it's done its job well.

The men must be vigilantes of a sort, doing what they can since they have a boat. The State is hardly this well-equipped. I bet these guys get a rush out of it. They're calling to each other, debating what streets to turn down. Miles looks relaxed for the first time today, sitting up next to me, his head hanging over the side of the boat. I think he might actually be enjoying the ride.

I look for the man and the little boy on their raft, and I try to explain where they might be to the driver of the boat. He careens down the street and into the square, turning with such force that I'm afraid we might tip over. I reach down and feel for my bag, pulling it up and holding it to my chest. The boat makes another sharp turn and I'm pushed into the side, but I see why he turned so quickly. We're coming up to the little raft, but it's empty. We stare down into the water for a long time, making slow loops, but we don't find anything. The raft floats out of sight eventually, but it takes the driver of the boat a long time before he revs his engine and takes us away.

XXXIII

THE MEN BRING ME right to the doors of Xavier. The steps are almost completely under water. I am grateful to them beyond words. As they rev the engine, turning the boat back out into the flooded street, I know they'll keep searching for people. All day, that's what they'll do. Those men are the good ones. The kind I wished would drop into my life so many times. Funny how when they finally do, I don't even ask their names.

Nobody expected that I'd actually make it to the orphanage. Rachel looks like she hasn't slept yet.

"We can't shelter in the basement, it's flooded," she calls to me in greeting. "Everything needs to go upstairs." I join the line of workers and older girls, carrying mattresses and pillows and blankets up to the second level. There are fewer windows on the second floor, and two workers tape large X's over them in the hopes that they won't shatter. Our shoes leave streaks of water on the floor and some of the girls look like they might slip, so Rachel tells them to wait upstairs for the adults. I wish I'd thought to bring a book for them, but that was the last thing on my mind this morning.

Somehow, we still have power, but we know the blackout is coming so we move quickly. The entire orphanage has been relegated to the infirmary and unused storage rooms.

The older girls play tic tac toe and Hangman on scraps of paper. The younger ones color or nap. Emilie's babies barely fuss, some lying listlessly on their backs, blank eyes staring at the ceiling. Calah is intent on watching a spider climb up the wall until Mishael steps up beside her and squashes it with her fist. Calah turns to Mishael with wide eyes, stunned that she would kill a harmless creature. I know she will cry, and I'm already rubbing her back before the first tear falls.

"What?" Mishael shrugs. "It was gross."

I see Belinda across the room and she gives me an understanding smile. I'm surprised to see her but then I realize she stayed over from last night. She already looks tired. Kamon is lying on her mattress, watching everything going on around her. She looks pale and queasy. I walk over and sit at the edge of her mattress. When I put my hand on her forehead, she turns away from me, something she rarely does.

"You don't look so good," I tell the back of her head. I feel her shift but she doesn't answer.

"Do you need anything? Maybe a cup of chamomile tea?"

One shoulder shrugs.

"I can make it for you, if you'd like. It might settle your stomach."

"OK," she says, but she still doesn't look at me.

I curse Benjamin Pierre under my breath for the millionth time and pull myself up from the mattress. I curse him the entire time it takes to steep the tea. When I bring the cup back to her, I have to help her sit up, and she swallows down a gag before she can take a sip. I sit with her and rub her shoulder as she drinks, and I want a minute to just dote on her, but Calah sees what we are doing and sidles over, wanting to be pet and loved on, and she wants her own cup of tea, and so I have to make another cup before she begins to wail. By the time I return, Kamon is finished and she's resting against the pillow.

"Here you go, sweet pea," I tell Calah, and I make a fuss over her and cuddle her while she sips, but my thoughts are far away. "I made Kamon chamomile tea, but I made you your very own Calah-mile tea." She positively beams at this.

"I just love you," Calah says, resting her head on my shoulder. She pats my hand.

"I love you, too," I say, and I'm instantly upset with myself, because I need to give all the girls the same amount of love and attention, and sometimes I forget that. Kamon needs me, but so does this girl, and all the others around me, all for their own specific reasons. I look at Kamon, and she's asleep, looking wan but peaceful.

"Want to play tic tac toe?" I ask Calah. Her face lights up. I'll make sure she wins. I always make sure she wins. They all need things, I tell myself again, but some needs are much simpler than others.

* * *

It's late at night but I'm awake; I'm beyond exhausted, in that place where your body is tired but sleep won't come. I'm lying on a spare cot in the infirmary. The power has been out for hours. It shut off just after dinner, which consisted of bread and cold chicken noodle soup, the liquid congealed into viscous lumps. Everyone retired upstairs early, while there was still a bit of light coming through the narrow windows. But we're in utter blackness now. I think the worst of the storm is probably over; the rain seems to have subsided. I wonder if the waters have receded on the streets, but I won't be able to see anything until morning. Miles sleeps at the foot of my cot. He must be hungry. The meager piece of bread he had for dinner wasn't nearly enough, but in my haste I forgot to bring his food. I arrived here almost completely unprepared.

I hear rustling around outside in the hallway and then the door to the infirmary opens a crack. I didn't think anyone else was awake. I hear my name, a thin little whisper cutting through the silence.

"I'm right here," I whisper back, shooting up in bed. I don't want to wake any of the girls who are sleeping all around me.

"Something's wrong," the voice says. And then I see a face, as a flashlight shines from underneath her chin. It's Belinda.

"There's something wrong with Kamon," Belinda whispers. "Come out into the hall." My heart starts racing immediately and I can't catch my breath. I stumble out of bed and follow the orange glow of the flashlight. Belinda reaches behind me and closes the infirmary door. "She's in the bathroom," she says. "It's bad."

"Oh God," I say. An icy shiver runs through me.

"There's a lot of blood," Belinda says. "It's her period, but it's definitely not normal. She's can't even stand up, she's cramping so badly. I left her in the bathroom, on the floor. We need to get the nurse. I wanted to tell you first so you could sit with her while I find Veronica."

"Don't get Veronica yet," I say. I flash on what Kamon looked like earlier, pale and sick, struggling to keep down even a cup of tea. Belinda nods and grabs me by the wrist. She leads me down the hall to a dingy bathroom across from one of the maintenance closets. I am not prepared for what I see. My girl is curled up on the dirty orange tiles. She's inside a stall, wrapped around the toilet, crying soundlessly. She jumps when she hears us come in, but she looks so relieved to see me standing there, I nearly burst into tears.

"There's something wrong with me," she whimpers, looking up with desperate eyes. She wants me to tell her it's going to be okay. She wants me to fix it. I don't have the luxury to think. I just have to take care of her.

"You're all right," I whisper, squatting beside her. I don't want her to see how scared I am, so I look into her eyes and hold her gaze. Belinda takes a backwards step.

"I need to get Veronica," she says.

"Hold on. Bring us an old towel and a blanket first. Find a clean nightshirt. Come back quickly." I'm not sure how I sound so efficient. I'm even surprising myself. The woman nods and backs away.

"Kay, listen to me, this happens sometimes. You're just getting some really bad cramps. It should stop soon."

"There's too much blood," she says. "Something is wrong."

"I know it doesn't feel right, but this can happen sometimes." It scares me to see her like this. "You're going to be okay," I say over and over, and hope that it's true.

She stays like that, curled into herself, until Belinda returns. She's carrying everything I asked for. I give Kamon the new nightshirt. The cream-colored one she's wearing is heavily stained. The blood is disconcerting, though I can't let Kamon see my worry. I wrap the old nightshirt in the blanket and give Kamon the towel to use underneath her nightclothes. If this continues, I'll probably have to exchange it with another one in a few hours.

"What do you think is going on?" Belinda asks.

"I don't know," I say. "I need to think."

"We should get Veronica now," Belinda says. "I think she's with Emilie and the babies." I shake my head. Kamon is on the floor again, in her fresh clothes. She's sweating. Her back seizes and I can tell she's going to ride another wave of pain.

"Stay here a minute, Belinda. I'll be right back."

I take her flashlight and go to the infirmary. There are several bottles of pills on a shelf near the window. One contains the painkiller Aspirol and I shake out a few pills. A sleeping girl stirs and shifts on her cot. Miles lifts his head. He'll have to come with me. I don't trust him not to whine now that he's seen me. I tap his hind quarters and encourage him to follow me. He jumps off the bed lightly and trots after me down the hall and to the bathroom. He wants to sniff Kamon, but I push him away.

I give her two pills and a sip of water from the sink, cupped in my hands. I tell her to wait a few minutes and see if it starts to help. I rub her back. Miles slides down on the floor and waits with us. Belinda paces by the door.

I tell Kamon that I'm going to step outside to talk to Belinda for a minute. "And then we're going to bring you back to bed, okay?" She nods and leans against the wall of the stall.

"Belinda, I'd like to talk with you for a minute." I gesture toward the door and she follows me outside the bathroom. I've taken control now. I think she's relieved.

"Listen, there's something I need to discuss with you. Something I think might have happened. But I need to trust you completely. Can I?" She nods, looking at me warily. "I know you know what happened with Benjamin Pierre." Belinda's eyes get wide and then they narrow. She doesn't say anything. "I think," I tell her, "that he got her pregnant. And she's experiencing a miscarriage."

Belinda sucks in a breath of wind through her lips and takes a step away from me. I know she'd ward off my words if only she could.

"That's the most logical explanation," I say. "Think about it."

She nods. She looks like she's going to cry. "That bastard," she finally says, her voice low.

"But if we tell Veronica, she'll have to report it. It's the law. She has no choice. She'll report it to Rachel and Rachel will report it to the State. An investigation will take place. We both know it's a natural loss, but there will have to be a standard investigation anyway. And who does that hurt?"

"Kamon," Belinda says.

"Exactly. More tests and prodding for her to go through, and she's already suffering. She's so young. It would be traumatic for her." Belinda nods.

"We shouldn't even put Veronica in the position of knowing. She can't report what she doesn't know, right? It's best for her that way, as well. You see?" Another nod. "So if we just take care of Kamon ourselves, I don't think anyone else will know. Just some soiled laundry that will need to be taken care of. She might need rest for a day or two."

Belinda thinks for a long moment. Finally she says, "I agree, no more trauma for our girl."

"Thank you," I say. "For understanding. It really is the best way."

"Do you think she'll be upset? Or relieved?" Belinda looks toward the bathroom door.

"Actually, I don't think she needs to know." I wait for a torrent of words, but they don't come.

"You don't..." she trails off.

"Think about it. She's so young, she doesn't even understand what's happened to her. She's only gotten her period a few times. She'll think this is nothing more than a bad one. But if she were to find out the truth…it would be a lot for her young heart to take. Don't you think?"

"Wow," Belinda says. "I don't know."

"If she's told she miscarried, it would confuse her. She obviously doesn't know she was ever pregnant. That's a huge burden for such a young girl. She's been through so much already. I hate him for everything he's done to her. If we could preserve a little of her innocence, shouldn't we?"

"Yes," Belinda says, and she's nodding with conviction now. "Yes. He's done enough damage to her already. You're right."

"So we won't tell anyone," I say. "Let's make sure she rests for a day or two, and we'll keep an eye on the laundry. I can wrap anything that gets soiled in the blanket. I'll keep it under my cot for now. We'll make sure she's taken care of."

"Okay," Belinda says. "We'll keep it between us." She pushes open the bathroom door. Miles thumps his tail on the tiles, thrilled that we've returned. Kamon doesn't make a sound. Belinda and I ease her up and she walks between us, slowly but steadily, back to her bed. I make sure she's covered with a clean blanket. I'll check her sheets at the first awakening of dawn.

I stop Belinda just as we reach the end of the hall.

"This was actually a blessing," I say. "Think about it. Think how much worse it might have been."

"Yes," she says, nodding. "It's like God knew to take care of that girl. Because I shudder to think of what she would have been faced with otherwise."

She turns from me and I creep to the infirmary. I ease onto the bed, but I know I will not sleep for the remainder of the night. It's just as well, because I have several hours to calm my breathing and slow my heart, and still my trembling knees.

It's done, I tell myself over and over. *It's done and it worked and nobody knows*. I think about that steaming cup of tea I gave Kamon. The poison was in the dose.

XXXIV

I LIE IN BED AND RUMINATE on what transpired earlier. Everything went as well as could be expected, although I never thought it would be Belinda to come to me in the night. I thought it would be Kamon, scared and unsure of what was happening to her. I had been waiting for her. She hasn't been getting her period for long, but I knew she'd immediately see that this was different, and I assumed she would seek me out. I should have slept right beside her, but Rachel assigned me to the infirmary, and I didn't want to argue with her. Maybe it was for the best. Belinda helped a great deal, and she didn't suspect that anything was amiss. She believed me. I almost believed myself, I was so convincing.

There had been scant little time when I was packing things up in my house. I forgot Miles' food and I forgot to take a change of clothes for myself. But I'm relieved that I took the packet of herbs from under the bed. I also threw in a few old drawstring sachets to use as tea-bags. Both sides of the argument weighed heavily on me, with Emilie's words fresh in my mind. But if I got stuck at Xavier, with each day bringing us closer to the point where an herbal remedy would not be enough, I wanted to be ready.

I had enough room to throw an old towel in the bag as well, though I couldn't use it once Belinda became involved. She would have wondered why I had such a thing. It's funny how quickly plans can unravel sometimes.

I found it ironic that Belinda wound up helping me, after Emilie warned me that I would need her. I hadn't been sure I could trust her, but I'm glad she was there. Of course, she doesn't know the full story. I don't know her well enough to really know just how loyal she would be, if she knew the whole truth.

Somehow, after my ride on the rescue boat, the contents of the packet were nothing more than slightly damp. I put the herbs and the empty sachets in my skirt pocket to dry thoroughly. I was acutely aware of them, though they weighed almost nothing. Still, I didn't know for certain that I would use them. But then I saw Kamon.

When I saw her lying on her mattress, looking weak and so uncomfortable, I knew I would be squandering my best opportunity to help her if I didn't act. The workers were milling around, completely occupied with getting the girls settled. Nobody would pay attention to me taking a moment to comfort one of my charges with a cup of tea. As I put one hand on Kamon's head, my other hand slipped into my pocket and fingered the contents. There would be no time better than this. Kamon's body would not keep the pregnancy a secret for much longer. She deserved to be free of this, I told myself. Unequivocally, I knew it was time. I had to do this for her. Was it easier to make the decision since she was turned away from me?

As I slipped off the bed to heat the water downstairs in the kitchen, I passed Emilie in the hall. I wanted to tell her. I wanted to grasp her arms and pull her into a quiet corner and whisper to her that I knew it was the right decision and that it would all be done in a few minutes, but she knows me too well. She must have seen something in my expression; she knew what I was about to do. She gave me the slightest shake of her head and looked away, and I knew she didn't want to hear the words out loud. I reached for her hand and she pulled me to her and gave me a hug. It lasted just a moment but was nearly frantic in its intensity.

I wanted to explain to her that this storm was my salvation, and Kamon's as well. A chance like this would not come again. It felt almost ordained by the universe. But I didn't say any of that. I didn't say anything at all. As I turned away from her, I told myself that although there would be suffering, after that, Kamon would finally be blessedly free.

XXXV

THE STORM WATER TAKES THREE DAYS TO RECEDE, leaving behind a sludge of sewage and debris. People were killed, but no rescue organization within the Southerly State is competent enough to know an exact number. Many more are missing. I think of the little boy on his raft, his hand outstretched to me as I was swept by. I wonder if he made it. And I think of my grandfather's old pirogue, bruised and battered and abandoned. It's hard for me to lose something of Ophelia's like that. More and more of her keeps slipping through my fingers.

In those three days it takes for the water to retreat, Belinda and I watch over Kamon tirelessly. Between the two of us, we take care of Kamon's dirty laundry. I wrap everything up in the old blanket and stuff it under my cot. On that third day, washing day, I carry the load down into the basement to the industrial washing machine and run it through twice. The crimson stains turn to a rusted brown, but they're still too noticeable, so Belinda stores them in the back of a utility closet until we find time to secret them away.

Kamon's cramps were gone by late afternoon after that first awful night. She lost a lot of blood but not a dangerous amount. Everything progressed as it should. She was so good about it, too. She never complained. She just rested quietly and kept to herself as much as she could in the tight surroundings. Every once in a while she'd catch my eye and almost smile, like she was sharing in the secret suffering of womanhood with me. My whole chest swelled with a love for her that was nearly overpowering. My God, I thought. Motherhood must knock you right down, leave you breathless, absolutely annihilate you.

When everything calms down and I have a moment to breathe and to think, I start to worry that I've stolen that all-encompassing love from her. I try to convince myself that she will have her chance, when her body and her mind are truly ready. Still, nagging little thoughts creep in when I least expect them.

In the frenzy of the storm, there had been no ambiguity. But as the flood waters recede, so too does my certainty, and I'm left with my own wreckage. For years, women in the Southerly State have bemoaned the fact that they aren't allowed to make decisions involving their own bodies. Have I done the same to Kamon, albeit in the absolute reverse? Am I no better than the bastards who run this miserable State?

* * *

Emilie did not assist Belinda and me during those days, but I saw her go over to Kamon on several occasions and brush her hair away from her eyes or rub her back. She did not take out what she considered to be my failings on the girl, and that made me love Emilie in a new and powerful way.

After three nights, Rachel clears us to return to our regular shifts. By then I feel ready to leave Kamon. She's doing well and I know Belinda will continue to care for her at night. I need to get home and check on the house, although I dread what's awaiting me. The walk home is eerie, even though Miles trots beside me, eager to return to his home and his ample supply of dog food. He thrived on all the attention from the girls, but the meager scraps they fed him weren't nearly enough. The two of us sidestep fallen trees that block the roads and trash that's strewn everywhere, left behind when the rushing waters receded. Roofs are missing, windows are smashed, there are water marks climbing up the sides of houses. People sweep and clear branches and cart away refuse. Some just stand outside their homes and stare up at the damage. My own house didn't fare too badly. No trees are down. No windows are broken. There is water damage, though. There are still pools of water on the floor, warping the wood. The water hadn't reached the second shelf of the bookcase, but everything on the lower shelf is ruined. *To Kill A Mockingbird* is stained and sopping wet. It seems fitting somehow; yet another ending.

I asked Emilie to walk back with me, but when she told me she wanted to go home and check on her parents and sister, I understood. Still, it's lonely to return to this place by myself. The power is still out and it will be for days. There will be deep, dark nights ahead of me.

The herbs under my bed are dry, though the tins sit in brown puddles. I have to check on the herbs growing outside, to see if anything can be salvaged. Without the small boat, I walk the outskirt of the swamp, which is swollen and mucky. At times the sludge is up to my shins, and I sink deeper with each step. Egrets and blue herons take off from the tips of the cypress trees, surveying their landscape. The smell of rot and dank dampness is overpowering. When I finally get to the spot where the clay pots are usually buried in the earth, I want to cry. They've been ripped from the ground and carried away. Gone. The herbs that were rooted in the ground are completely swamped and I know they're destroyed. And so the dried herbs in my tins are the only remedy I have left, and they won't last long. I don't know how I can obtain more and I'm relieved I was able to take care of Kamon in time.

I expect Pote to show up under the guise of checking on me, but he doesn't. I wonder if maybe he's done with me, if he's decided I'm not worth the effort. I hope so. But I also think maybe he's occupied with making a show of being a community leader out in the Parish. Is he praying over the devastation? Is he reminding people that God wrought this upon them, and will continue to do so, as long as there are sinners among us?

The days go quickly, the nights are endless, and soon the storm is several weeks behind us. The power hums back on at home and at Xavier. Kamon has no remaining effects of the treatment I gave her. Emilie smiles at me more easily, though we don't have time to speak much. Belinda and I don't do more than pass on the steps outside the orphanage, always with a nod and a long glance. Rachel oversees the organization inside, and the female maintenance workers clear the devastation on the grounds. Everything feels like it's returning to normal.

Until one morning, about three weeks after the storm. The sky is a brilliant orange etched through with pink streaks. There's just enough air flow to be able to really breathe in the magnolias. The walk to work is lovely, and I'm finding a rare beauty in this place.

I see a woman hurrying toward me, wearing the familiar cream skirt that is the Xavier uniform. But it's not Emilie. It's Belinda. She's left work early if she's already this far into her walk. She calls out to me from her end of the street and picks up to a run.

"What is it?" I call out, running toward her. "What happened?"

She's been crying. She nearly collides with me, grabbing me by both arms and digging her fingers into my flesh.

"Belinda. What is it?" I know it can't be Kamon. It can't be her because she's absolutely fine. She's completely back to normal. "What is it? What happened?"

"It's Kamon," she says, and I shake my head, because she's wrong. But she keeps talking, hideous words coming out of her mouth under this glorious creamsicle and cotton candy sky. "It's Kamon," she says again, twisted words from a twisted mouth. "They took her away."

"No!" Why is she saying this thing to me, this thing that can't possibly be right? I want to hit her for lying about something so serious. "Stop it."

"They took her," she says again, and then again after that. "The Officers of the State. They took her away."

"Why?" I whisper, all of a sudden believing every awful word she's saying. The sun rises above us and cloaks us in harsh white light. It hurts to see and it hurts to breathe.

"They said her name was in the Tamburo," Belinda says, and I shove her away from me. "She's been charged as a *Sanguidam*."

XXXVI

Somehow, my legs bring me to Xavier. Belinda is on my heels; we are both teary and breathless, tripping up the steps and running blindly to Rachel's office. She is waiting for me, of course.

"It was still dark out when they came," she says, standing in front of her desk. "They had the papers, there was nothing I could do to stop them."

"Who? How many? Who were they?" I'm desperate, still clinging to some faint notion that it's a mistake.

"Two Officers of the State. They had the official paperwork. They demanded to be taken to her. And they took her with them."

I feel a scream ripping through me but it doesn't make its way past my lips. Instead of leaving my body it just keeps reverberating around underneath the surface of my skin.

"They were gentle with her," Rachel says, but that's no comfort. Belinda puts her hand on my arm and through a very faraway tunnel I hear her ask, "So what do we do now?"

Rachel shakes her head. "They said she'd been named a *Sanguidam* in the Tamburo. She didn't even understand what they were saying. She was terrified, but she cooperated. I told her we would come for her soon."

"And will we?"

"I don't know," Rachel says. "I don't know what happens next. But I don't understand how this happened. She obviously did nothing wrong, so who would have falsely named her? Who, outside of these walls, even knows she exists?"

And that's the part that takes away my breath. Who would want to hurt her? She's a child. I look at Rachel, her face a collage of disbelief and confusion, and I know it wasn't her. Her shock, anger and fear are genuine. I know she's religious and she believes Punishments for actual offenders are just. But she's so perplexed. It's clear she has no idea what's transpired with Kamon, and even if she had somehow found out, I'm certain she wouldn't throw her to the wolves. She's as fearful and horrified as I am. Emilie crosses my mind for the briefest moment, and I hate myself for it. She would never. She was upset with me, yes, but she would keep my secret. And she would most certainly not cause harm to an innocent child. Could it have been Veronica? As an acting nurse, she is more attuned to seeing things than perhaps I gave her credit for. Did she notice something and make a guess? I can't believe she would do that. Not after some of the things I've heard her say. Not after I've seen how she cares about these girls. Could it have been an older girl, one from the upper teen room? Had they seen something? But how would they get to church to submit Kamon's name? How would they even know the Tamburo exists? My God, I think, Kamon should be the only girl who knows about the Tamburo, because she was told about it by her attacker and abuser. Could he be her accuser now as well?

Was it Benjamin Pierre? Could he have been so angered by my threats and his forced removal that he bided his time at his new job and then slipped his victim's name into the Tamburo? Was he punishing her for telling, just as he threatened he would? He would know that by submitting her name, he's punishing me as well. I had promised him that I would write his own name down as a homosexual if I were languishing in a jail, should he accuse me of anything. But he hadn't accused me, he accused Kamon. Would I even be able to speak on her behalf? Or would her Punishment be executed swiftly without even the pretense of a trial, as most Punishments are?

I sway where I stand when I actually think about Kamon being Punished. My thoughts hadn't gone there until this moment. I was so sick about her being taken away, about feeling like she'd been kidnapped from me, that I hadn't thought of her hanging by her wrists, her flimsy shift bunched at her waist as a bulky, bulging man whipped her back; each vertebrae, linked together like a delicate strand of pearls, drenched in blood.

It was Benjamin Pierre. It had to be. It's the only explanation that makes sense. But could he actually have known what happened? That she was pregnant? There's no way. And so I think it must be the strangest, cruelest twist of fate that he accused her of something that actually did happen, albeit without her knowledge or consent, while he thought it was a false accusation just to get back at her for exposing him.

I wonder where she is right now. In a jail somewhere in the Parish? Has she already been treated harshly? I know what she's thinking, that it's her own fault for telling me what happened to her. That the man who covered her mouth with his hand and hurt her in so many ways was making good on his promise to put her name in the Tamburo if she told anyone about him. She thought she was free of him. But he had full control over her still. He was reminding her of that now.

I can barely see straight, but there is a singular thought that somehow forms in my brain. Preacher Pote. Might he be willing to help me? I have pushed him away and watched his flowers shrivel and dry and die, but could he help me now? I will do anything he wants. Anything.

As I rush out of Rachel's office, she and Belinda call after me but I don't turn around. I also don't tell them where I'm going. I don't do anything but stumble out the doors and down the steps and then, until I think my chest will burst, I run directly for the *Word of Our Father* church and the inflammatory preacher who may be the only one who can save us.

XXXVII

I'VE NEVER BEEN INSIDE THE CHURCH on any day other than Sunday. I've never gone in the front entrance either, but I try the doors now. They're bolted shut; I'm surprised the handles don't come off in my fists when I try to yank them open. The side door is unlocked though, and I slip inside the stark space. The church is completely empty, with only the sound of my heavy breathing filling the air. There are no windows, and the white glow of two emergency exit signs are the only sources of light. The door shuts behind me and I'm engulfed in the blackness of this room that's always so austere and white. I see the shadowy outline of the Tamburo. I was stupid to come. Pote isn't here; I should not be either.

I think of old photographs from Ophelia's youthful travels to Europe. Had I found myself in a Gothic cathedral on the other side of the ocean, I probably would have fallen to my knees, dropped my head into my hands, and prayed. I might not have been certain who, if anyone, was actually listening, but I imagine that standing in a vaulted knave like my grandmother once did, with prismatic light from a Rose window shimmering over ancient stone, might at least inspire me to try. But there is nothing spiritual about this place. Here, in this hollow, soulless space, all I can do is stand stock still and listen to the nothingness. This church was not built as a glorious link between Heaven and Earth. If there is a God, He is not inside here, and He never has been. The devil though…he may have passed through.

I need to know where Kamon is. Is she sitting in a dark room like this? Are there bars on the windows? Is she alone? I feel disoriented; this isn't what I was expecting. When I ran over, I envisioned throwing open the doors and demanding that the preacher help me. Begging him, even. But like God, he's nowhere inside this vacuous place. I have nowhere left to go and nobody else to ask for help. And that is what does bring me to my knees inside this unfeeling, unholy space.

The cry I let myself have is utterly depleting. It's hard to even scrape myself up off the floor when I'm finished. My breath comes in shaky shudders; I am spent. My face hurts and my eyes are swollen.

When I hear the door open behind me, letting in a dingy shaft of light for just a moment, I turn around to see the silhouette of a black-clad man standing in the doorway. A hat, boots, legs spread apart. As he steps through the door, it slams behind him and I'm alone with the preacher inside his domain. I'm not scared. I've done this to myself.

My eyes are better adjusted to the dark. He knows it's a woman in here and not an intruder. There has been no shouting, no threatening to shoot, no combativeness. Just a tentative step forward, squinted eyes, head cocked. I can't move toward him. Neither can I back away. I find myself waiting for him to come to me.

He walks with a hand out, as if feeling his way through a moonless night. Another two steps and he knows who I am. He says my name twice. The first is a question, the second is not. His voice holds just a note of quiet wonder, almost as if he's a hunter who's discovered that his prey has come right to him.

"You were looking for me," Pote says into the dark. He isn't asking.

"I need your help," I say. He's almost to me now. "Please."

"Ah." Here he is, right in front of me. He reaches out a hand and I see him standing in my living room, the snake held tight in his fist. He puts that hand on me now, right on the spot where my shoulder and neck meet in a little hollow dip.

"The Lord is far from the wicked, but he hears the prayer of the righteous," he whispers. "Kneel with me, and we will pray."

He pushes me down, his hand firm on my shoulder, and for the second time I'm on the cold concrete floor. He kneels beside me, his side pressed against mine. He takes my hand and I force myself not to pull away.

"What are we praying for, Miss Dupre?"

"I think you know, Preacher."

"The Lord is far from the wicked," he says again. "The wicked do not deserve our prayers."

"I'm not praying for the wicked. I'm praying for an innocent young girl."

I hear him suck in a sharp breath.

"I don't know why you're concerning yourself with these young girls so much," he says. "They've only got what's comin' to them."

"No. This girl has done nothing wrong. You have to believe me. Please."

"Her name was in the Tamburo. Not her legal name, of course. Only the nickname given to her. Kamon of Xavier Orphanage. If her accuser had left off that last part, I would have had a terrible time finding her. It took a while to trace it back to SC0708. Now why would anyone go and make up such a thing?"

"Because there's a lot of evil in this world, Preacher."

This is why I've come. Something inside my head is screaming at me to keep quiet, but it's my last chance. It's Kamon's last chance. What is Pote always preaching from the Bible? The truth shall set you free.

"She was raped." I whisper it, but the words bounce off the walls. Nothing has ever sounded so loud. "She was raped by a worker and she fell pregnant. Nobody knew, until she started to miscarry. And even then, she was too young to understand what was happening. And so we, I, didn't explain it to her. She'd been through enough already. I wanted to preserve what little was left of her youth. She is not a *Sanguidam*. I believe her attacker has accused her of being one, as retribution for being let go from the orphanage."

I remember Belinda's face softening when I suggested we keep Kamon in the dark about what was happening to her. Why wouldn't this man understand that same rationale? Any feeling person would understand. Of course, I'm braver now than I was right after everything first happened. By now, all traces of herbs are long gone from Kamon's system. Even if Pote demanded an investigation, nothing would show up in her bloodstream. For a single moment I'm relieved that I've said it. But then I see Pote's face, and I know that my words haven't made a difference.

"There's a very good chance she was asking for it, Miss Dupre. A girl her age, flaunting her new body? You can't tell me she was a victim in all this. Girls flirt. They play games. And then they cry innocent after leading on the young men. Her Punishment will set a fine example for the good people of our Parish. Perhaps it will remind young ladies to keep their knees closed."

I want to smash him. Somehow, I do not. He isn't even saying anything new. They all talk like this. I should have known better. I can feel my control of the situation, if I ever actually had any, slip away. I've probably made everything worse. I hate myself for what I do next. But I am out of options. I think about the flowers on my windowsill, and the visits to my home and workplace. I know what Pote wants, what he's been angling for this whole while. Isn't it what they all want? This desperation is the only thing that could ever make me relent to him. I will sacrifice myself if I can save the girl. I have hardly anything to give, but I will give what I have. This is how I love her.

"William." I surprise myself when I say his name.

He stiffens and I know I've caught him off guard.

"Maybe," I say, "there is something besides prayer that I can do. I feel like in this instance, speaking directly to you will be more effective than speaking to God."

As a holy man, he should be shocked that I've blasphemed like this. But I can actually see the pride swell up inside him. I am hit with the urgency of the situation, with the thought that every moment I sit here and lavish praise on him is another minute that Kamon sits in jail. There is little time for this.

I barely know what I'm doing as I crawl in front of him. His face is several inches above mine, and I straighten up as much as I can. My knees ache. The leather smell of him makes a gag rise in my throat and I have to swallow it down. His Adam's apple bobs once, twice. He shaved this morning. I lean in so close to him that my forehead rests against the brim of his hat. He hasn't removed it inside the church. It's stiffer than it looks.

"What can I do to convince you?" He has a crooked smirk on his face. I wonder if my desperation excites him.

I put my palms on his chest. I'm taking a chance, but I don't think he'll pull away. I want him to know I'll do anything. Anything. That's how frantic I am. His right hand shoots up and grasps my left wrist, but he doesn't move any other part of his body. He encircles my wrist with his thumb and middle finger. As soon as I feel him around me, I want to pull away, but I know it's too late.

"Just what is it you're trying to do?" His voice is hoarse, almost guttural.

I have so little experience with men. But with the heat of his breath on my face and his hand around mine, I force myself to look into his eyes. They are nothing but shadows in the dark.

"I'll do whatever you want, if you'll help her," I hear myself say.

Something innate inside of me compels me to lean into him and push my lips against his. There's a wave of revulsion, but I can pay this price. It's fitting that we're in a church devoid of life and spirit. I am devoid of that right now as well.

He doesn't move his mouth. He allows me to press against him, but his body is rigid. His fingers tighten around my wrist. I can tell he isn't breathing. I wonder if I misread him. Maybe he cannot be bought like this. And yet I have nothing else to give.

"William," I say again, my mouth still on his. "Please."

There's a strange look in his eyes.

He pushes me down so quickly I don't see it coming. He grabs my other wrist and pins my arms over my head. My back presses into the cold concrete floor and every instinct I have screams at me to push and kick and try to wriggle my hands free so I can scratch and claw at him, but I instigated this and I need something from him so I don't do a thing. How many other women have paid with this currency? I feel hot tears seeping out of the corners of my eyes. I don't want him to taste them, but I can't swipe them away.

He grinds his mouth onto mine with such force, the back of my head hurts as it presses against the floor. The weight of him is almost more than I can bear. Suddenly he's holding my two hands in one fist and I feel his other hand reaching for my skirt. A knee presses into my thigh. Could swinging from the Trinity actually be worse than this? In this moment, I'm not sure.

Pote grunts something, his mouth still on mine. My skirt is bunched up near my waist. It's going to get so much worse, I know it is. I squeeze my eyes shut. Tears slide down the sides of my face and nestle in my hair. I wonder if the floor is wet. His knee digs into me so hard, I barely feel anything else, just that intense pressure radiating on my leg. I turn my head away from him. I have to have room to breathe. I'm suffocating under him and I need air.

In the middle of a gulping breath, I realize that there's a chance I could get pregnant. The baby's father would be a man full of vitriol and grotesque convictions. Pote would have rights to the child and to me. But then I think that a baby conceived today would be conceived out of great love, my love for another child, and I know that I could never drink birthwort and pennyroyal and be rid of it. And then I cry harder, because I'm helpless and hopeful all at once, and it's overpowering.

Just as I resign myself to the inevitable, Pote pulls away from me. Even in the dark, I see alarm in his eyes. He pushes himself up and grabs my arm, bringing me back to my knees. My clothes are twisted around me. His grasp is unrelenting.

"My God, you're like some kind of bewitching Jezebel," he says, his breath coming out in short huffs. "You're tempting a man of God, Miss Dupre. You have no idea what you've just done to me. But it can't be here, like this."

Everything inside me sinks. I've lost any power I had over him just a moment ago.

"Why not?" I ask, desperation bolstering my nerve. "Why can't it be here?"

"Because I was starting to give up hope that you'd have me. And now here you are, kneeling before me. Begging. How do I know you're not just bartering with me?"

"I'm sorry," I say. "I do want your help." I force myself to look straight into his eyes. "But that's not the only reason I kissed you."

"Then perhaps I should call on you at home again. Since you seem open to finally taking our relationship to the next level. As tempting as it is, we cannot engage in a sacred act between man and woman in a house of God."

"I'd like that," I say. I wish he hadn't stopped himself a minute ago. It would be better to have gotten it over and done with already. And despite everything I've somehow just committed to, he's given no indication that he will help Kamon. He's made no promise. I think it would be foolish for me to bring it up again just now. How much longer will she have to wait?

He leans into me and presses his nose into my neck. I feel him breathe in as if he were smelling a flower. A moment later his hot exhale spreads over my skin. "We will see one another soon," he says. He means it as a promise, but it feels like a prison sentence. "You'd best be heading out for now," he says, but it's he who backs away from me. He leaves the room first, his boots echoing on the floor, right on the spot where we lay moments ago. Then he pushes through the doors and I am alone in the dark again.

XXXVIII

For three evenings, I wait for him to come to me. It's unnerving, anticipating such a visit. Sometimes I sit on the couch, Miles panting beside me, but usually I pace back and forth, trying to discern the tapping of black boots on my porch from the other sounds of the bayou. But the preacher stays away. I think I find his silence nearly as disconcerting as I would find his sudden appearance.

I worry that a woman will appear without warning, just as Renee did. What would I possibly do if I were with a woman and Pote knocked on the door?

On the fourth night, I hear a car crunch over the gravel driveway and I freeze as headlights shine through my front window. I move the curtain aside just enough to see the preacher step out of his sedan. Miles is at the door immediately. My first thought is to lock him in my bedroom, but is that where I will eventually wind up with Pote? The thought makes my chest tighten. Miles snaps at the door as the porch steps creak under the preacher's weight. I grab his collar and hold him against my leg. I waited for Pote's knock for days, but I don't want to hear it now, and I open the door before he can officially announce his arrival.

"Evenin', Miss Dupre," he says. He doesn't look down at my dog, even though Miles is sniffing wildly at his boots. There's a small rectangular package wrapped in brown paper in his hands. He thrusts it at me awkwardly and I have to let go of Miles to open it. I slide my finger under the tape and uncover a framed image. It's a biblical scene, of course; a print of a long-haired man resting his head in the lap of a voluptuous woman. Pote is looking at me eagerly, waiting for recognition, but I have no idea who they are.

"Thank you," I say, hoping he doesn't want to discuss it. "It's lovely."

"I couldn't help but notice that you don't have any artwork on your walls," he says. He points at the frame in my hands. "Samson and Delilah. He was quite taken with her, as I'm sure you recall from your studies. Just as I am quite taken with you."

He's given me State-approved art for my home. I can't think of a gift I'd want less, but I manage a smile.

"You can hang it up later," he says.

"I'll be sure to find the perfect spot," I say, thinking that the bottom of the swamp would be about right. Of course he'll look for it the next time he comes, and I can barely stand the thought that there will be a next time. He walks toward me so I have to take several steps backwards, and suddenly we are both standing inside my living room. I put the print face down on the bookcase.

"Can I offer you a drink, Preacher?" My own throat is burning. "Perhaps a brandy?"

He looks at me with raised eyebrows. "I didn't take you for the drinkin' kind," he says. "I don't imbibe, myself. But a glass of water would surely hit the spot."

I drag Miles into the kitchen with me. Then I kneel down and sink my face into the dog's furry neck and try to steady my breathing. He wriggles gleefully with this sudden affection, his tail thumping against a cabinet. "Oh God," I whisper to him. "What am I doing?"

But however much I am suffering, Kamon is suffering more. She's sitting in a godforsaken jail somewhere, alone and afraid. And if I can't get this man to help her, she will be trotted out in front of a crowd and whipped; she will be marked forever. I know that I will get through this night in order to spare her. When she is back at Xavier with me, and she looks into my eyes and squeezes my hand three times, I will squeeze back four, and know unequivocally that she was worth whatever sacrifice I have to make tonight.

I'm angry with myself for asking about the brandy. I only use it as a sedative for women. I shouldn't have even mentioned it. Still, I think perhaps a sip or two might calm me, and as I bang around the kitchen, filling his glass with water, I sneak a sip of brandy from an unlabeled bottle. It warms up my belly but does nothing for my nerves.

The preacher smiles when I return from the kitchen. Miles gives him one more cursory sniff and then decides to trust my judgement. He curls up in the corner and watches us curiously. I stop a few feet in front of Pote. He takes a step toward me. My fingernails dig into my palms. When I hand the preacher his glass, he cocks his head at me, and I wonder if he smells the alcohol on my breath.

He tips back his head and takes long pulls of the water. I watch it slide over his throat. He bends down and sets the empty glass on the table, and then he takes my hand and leads me to the couch. In another moment his nose is in my hair again, just as it was inside the church, and then he puts two fingers on my chin and turns my face to his and kisses me. It's much more gentle than last time, but somehow it feels even more invasive, and I have to fight not to pull away. I close my eyes because I'm sure that's what he wants, and because I can't stand to see him this close to me.

His hand moves to the back of my head and he pulls me even closer, which doesn't seem possible since his lips are already pressed to mine. My hands reflexively fly up to his chest, wanting to push him away, but he reads this as an invitation and turns his body so he's in front of me, and then he's pushing me back and I feel the familiar pressure of his knee on my leg. I peek through my eyelids. I can't help it. And my eyes meet his heron blue ones, staring down at me. He's looking at me like he owns me, and I suppose he does.

"You taste like alcohol," he says, his lips buzzing over mine. "Did you have to numb yourself for this encounter?"

"No," I say. "Maybe I was a bit nervous."

"Don't be scared of me," he says, his fingers entwined in my hair.

I have a sudden image of him tossing away the speckled king snake from the top of my porch. I squirm under him.

"I prayed you would open your heart to me," he says, touching his lips to my neck. "I knew you just needed a little time." I nod and the stubble on his face brushes up and down over my skin.

His hand slides over my thigh. I hope he doesn't feel me shudder. "You took me by surprise when you showed up at my church," he says. "I haven't been able to think of anything else. I would have come here that same night, or the day after, but I didn't want to seem too eager." He stares down at me and for a second he looks like an insecure boy. But then I hear his voice in the square, proclaiming God's goodness immediately following a Punishment. There is nothing boyish about him.

"I have a confession," he says into my ear. "I was also worried that perhaps you really do only want me because of the girl. Because you thought I would help her. You seemed so desperate in church." I was already stiff and unmoving underneath him, but when he says this, I freeze entirely.

"But I told myself that can't possibly be right," he says. His hand is making small circles on my leg, and he kisses my jawline between words. He's taking his time. He thinks I'm actually enjoying his teasing mouth and fluttering touches. I feel absolutely vile.

"A woman like you would never do that, though" he says, almost more to himself than to me. "You would never sell yourself like that." Is he still trying to convince himself, while he's pinned on top of me, that I am attracted to him?

"I do want you to help her, William," I say.

"But that's not why you're here with me now."

I turn my head away from him so his lips fall away from my neck. "Why are you asking me that?"

"Because you're very hard to read, Miss Dupre. And I want to read you very, very well."

"Yes," I say, a half-whisper. "I would be here either way. But you can help her, yes? She's innocent. It's the right thing to do."

"You have a strange obsession with the accused, I must say. It's unseemly." His hand moves down to my knee and then up under my skirt. I want to push him away but I don't move.

"William?" His hand stops moving. I see his jaw tighten. "Please?"

"I'd rather not think of such things right now," he says. His hand moves again. I reach down and grab it.

"I want to think about it," I say.

Pote's fist punches the couch cushion next to my ear. I flinch and snap back my head to look at him. He pushes up onto his elbows. His forearms are on either side of my head.

"I've been rather patient with you, you know. Waiting and waiting. And now I have you here, and it's apparent that you've been leading me on because of this ridiculous crusade of yours. It's not just with this girl, either. You've been needling me about the Tamburo since the beginning. You're interested in these disgusting girls. You are not interested in me."

"You have the power to help them," I say. I realize my mistake too late.

"Ah. And you've had power over me, making me follow you around like an idiot," he says. He sits up. "That's why you wait for me after my services and humor me about the gifts I give you and put your hands all over me in my own church. I've been wasting all this time chasing after you, and you are not attracted to anything but this power you think I have."

"No." I reach for him but he pulls away.

"Please," he says. "I've already made a fool of myself. And you know what? I don't have the power you think I have. I only do what is right. I do what I must to honor God. If someone is guilty, I have no power to change that. I only carry out what justice they deserve. If you really want to help the girl, say a prayer for her."

"She has a name," I tell him.

"No, Miss Dupre, she actually doesn't."

He stands up and straightens out his shirt. I stand up to face him. I hated his hands and mouth on me but I'm desperate to pull him to me again. But I can see it's no use; I've completely lost him.

He walks over to the door and I follow. I've done something far worse than falling short of convincing him to help Kamon. I've insulted him. Why would he help her now? He will probably relish watching her swing just to hurt me.

He grabs the doorknob but spins around to face me before he pulls open the door.

"I should have taken you right there on the floor when I had the chance," he says. "That's exactly what you deserved." And then he walks out of my house and I hear gravel fly as he screeches out of the driveway. My legs are shaking as I realize that I've made everything infinitely worse, and because of that, I just watched Kamon's chance at absolution walk right out my door.

* * *

One Sunday passes and there's no Punishment, but I'm terrified of what next Sunday might bring. Emilie has been agitated since the storm. I know she hasn't forgiven me for the choice I made without Kamon's knowledge, and the girl's arrest has intensified her worry. I don't think she knows what to say to me, so she avoids me entirely, coming to work early each morning so that she doesn't meet up with me on our walk to Xavier. I don't dare go to church, and William Pote has gone silent once more. I spend each day at work in a fog, going through the motions of being with the other girls, but not feeling a thing other than heartache over the one girl who is missing.

And then Rachel pokes her head into my room one afternoon after lunch.

"I need to speak with you," she says. "Now."

We step into her office. Her mouth is set in a tight line. She's going to tell me that a Punishment date has been set. Which Sunday will it be? I can't possibly go, but how can I stay away? It might well be me who will be there for her at the end of it, waiting near her stretcher to accompany her to the clinic. I feel like my knees might give out.

"Kamon was released from the jail last night. Preacher Pote visited the Officers and said there was a mistake in the accusation. He was here only an hour ago, to tell me himself. He asked me to pass the message on to you."

I grasp the back of the chair in front of me. She's saying that everything is okay. Perhaps my bumbling stupidity didn't dissuade him from doing what was right after all.

"Is she back yet? I need to see her." I'm already taking steps away from Rachel, ready to bolt down the hallway. Of course Kamon is back. That's why Pote was here; to deliver her.

"She's not here," Rachel says. The look on her face, the way she shakes her head, I know I don't want to hear any more. But her mouth opens again, and I see the straight line of tiny teeth, and I hear her say, "She's gone."

"What?"

"She isn't here. I'm so sorry. She's been transferred to another orphanage in a different Parish. A less crowded one. Pote said that was best for her. I guess they have a bigger budget and more space. I told him she needed to be here, with all of us, but he said it was already done. He said he acted in what he thought was her best interest." Rachel is fighting back tears, and I know she's crying for Kamon and for me.

"Where?"

"I don't know. It's confidential. He was clear on that." She shakes her head and looks at me with wet, round eyes.

I can't say anything. There's a white heat at the back of my throat and it lights on fire every word I might say. It singes my words with acid and chokes them with black smoke. He's taken her away from me. One thought screams at me through the haze of my rage. It's the most awful, self-serving thing I have ever thought, and if I weren't so desperate to get the girl back, I would be disgusted with myself for even entertaining the notion. But right now, I actually wish Kamon had been sentenced to a Punishment. Had she been whipped on the Trinity, she probably would have been returned to us in a few days. But Pote has seen to it that she is gone from me forever.

XXXIX

A CRUSHING DESPONDENCY FALLS OVER ME. What if I never see Kamon again? Rachel and Belinda and Veronica keep telling me not to give up hope, but she's probably so far away that I won't be able to get to her even if I find out where she is. I wonder if this is the price I am fated to pay for everything I've done to her. I was the one who angered Benjamin Pierre. I know Kamon would still be with me had I not threatened him and forced him out. It was vengeance that made him write down her name. It was his need to have the final say—and he did.

And then somewhere in the middle of the maelstrom that churns in my mind, a bolt of clarity cuts through everything else and absolutely slays me. If I hadn't given Kamon the herbal remedy, she would have been pregnant when she was arrested for being a *Sanguidam*. Benjamin wrote down her name to punish her and me, but what a surprise it would have been for him to learn she was actually pregnant. I could have told Pote that the accusation against her couldn't possibly be true, and could be proved with an examination. Trials and evidence are basically non-existent, but if Pote thought there was even a chance that a whipping would harm the Unborn, he would make sure she was properly examined at a clinic. When it was proven that she was pregnant, Benjamin Pierre would have been the one in serious trouble, for providing a false accusation and for the near Punishment of a pregnant girl. Of course, he could have turned around and claimed parental rights to the Unborn, but I think the rape, coupled with the false accusation, could have been enough to deny him.

But I stole that from her and, as a result, we are all paying dearly. Even the other girls in my room feel her absence terribly. Mishael is quiet but when she answers a question her words are biting. Calah cries constantly and with little provocation. I know the girls all miss how Kamon read to them and sometimes helped them with their school booklets. Serah misses how Kamon used to brush her hair. And me, I long for every single thing about her. I'd give anything to feel those three pulses from her hand as it squeezes mine. I have taken Unborns from their mothers, and now my child has been taken from me. Somewhere through the heavy blanket of despair, I tell myself that maybe I deserve this.

I haven't had a nightly visitor in weeks, but I know someone will need my assistance soon, and my stock of herbs is almost entirely depleted due to damage from the storm. I've thought of Renee a lot lately. I have flashbacks of her laying on my bed, blood everywhere. And I remember dropping her off near her house and telling her to come to me in one week to get her stitches removed. Then the storm hit and she never came. I wonder if she made her way to me when it was over, only to find my house empty. I don't think I can safely contact her. I can't appear at her door; it would be too easy for the wrong person to answer it. I can only hope that she is all right. Maybe she tugged and cut out the stitches herself when they became itchy and she had nobody to help her. After everything else she'd done to herself, that would be the very least of it.

And so, as I sit on the bed that she bled on, staring at the purple shadows of dusk crawling across the wall, Miles snuffling at my feet, I think that the sudden knock on the door might be Renee. She would be weeks late, but she's the only one I can think of in my muddled mind. Margaret hasn't told me to expect anyone and it can't be Pote, not now.

I'm slow to pull myself off the bed. For days I've felt like I'm swimming in the swamp, my face under the water, sucking in the muck and decay. I want to crawl in bed and hide, but maybe it's good to have a visitor just now. I'm sinking so fast, perhaps someone else can pull me to the surface.

There's another knock. Miles is furious as I close the door before he can follow me out of the bedroom. The knock is heavy and insistent. It's not Renee. It's not a woman at all, I'm sure of it.

Then a deep male voice calls my name and there's another knock, a fist on the door. I don't want to open it but the voice keeps saying my name, over and over, and then a flashlight is shining through the front window and I'm standing right there, a terrified animal caught in the glare, and my hand reaches for the knob even though my whole body screams for me not to. I'm twisting the knob and pulling open the door when the beam of the flashlight swings down to the floor and a tall man in all black takes a step forward. There's another man behind him, dressed exactly the same, and he has a sleek black gun in his hands. I see the tiny flag of the Southerly State patched on their right arms. Officers of the State.

Miles barks and snarls from the bedroom. He sounds like he'll rip out their throats, even though I know he never would, but the Officer in my doorway looks toward the ferocious sound and puts his other hand on his holstered gun. The Officer behind him grips his weapon. God. Guns. Freedom. I look out at the flag I so reluctantly fly, because there's no freedom not to. Ophelia would be quick to point out the irony. I should ask them why they're here. I should tell them it's okay, the dog doesn't need to be silenced by them. I have to cooperate. I have no other alternative. But I don't have a chance to say anything.

The Officer closest to me grabs my wrist. He doesn't hurt me but I know he can. The other Officer steps forward. He points the gun at my chest. There's no need for them to handcuff me. I'm not moving.

"You're under arrest for violating the sacred law of the Southerly State. You've been accused of being a Remover of the Unborn."

I want to scream at them that it's a lie. But they have their orders and my words don't mean anything. And it's not a lie. I am exactly what they say. It's all caught up to me now. The gun is aimed at my chest and two large men are staring me down. Miles is apoplectic but nobody pays him any attention.

"Let's go," the one pointing the gun says, his voice calm and quiet. And I do. I leave my house and my howling dog, and I pass underneath the flag. The Officers raise their fingers to offer up their kisses and they look at me. I cross myself, kiss my fingers and touch the tip of the flag even as I'm silently cursing it. As we step off the porch and they take me away from Ophelia's old house, I think about the very real possibility that I may never see the place again.

XL

I HEAR THE RATS BUT I CAN'T SEE THEM. They're scratching inside the walls. The holding cell is dark and damp. There are bars on one side; the other three walls are made of cement. I don't know where I am. We drove for a long time, me in the backseat of the State car, sitting next to an Officer. After a while he lowered his gun but I was acutely aware of it for the duration of the ride. We are well outside the city. I don't think I've ever been to this part of the Parish. I wonder if this is where they held Kamon. She must have been terrified. I am terrified now.

The other cells on this subterranean level are empty tonight. There is no sound other than the scratching rats. There's a toilet in the corner and a dirty cot pushed against the wall. This is where they hold young girls. This is where they keep them before bringing them out in front of a frothing, angry mob. How has it come to this? And because I don't have anything else to do but think, I sit on the unforgiving floor and wonder why I am still here, in this godforsaken State.

"Why did you not just go north?" I used to ask Ophelia whenever she gave me a quiet history lesson. "Or to the Westerly State?" I always loved hearing about that mythical place stretching along the Pacific Ocean. I tried to imagine growing up with the smell of the ocean instead of the swamp, and the Gulf that threatens to drown us. I imagined what it would be like to be around people who didn't have to kiss a flag and write their names on church envelopes every week and pledge undying allegiance to a place they did not like or understand.

"Because at first my sister told us we should stay and fight," Ophelia said. "And I believed her. I thought if enough of us did, we could make a difference. But we had no power, of course. We were nothing."

"But then after? Why not later on?"

"By then we felt it was too late. It cost a lot of money, and when the Separation occurred, the North got the better end of the deal. Better power grids and better relationships with countries rich with oil. Even gasoline was hard to come by, so we couldn't drive to the next Parish, let alone to another country." In explaining why she stayed, Ophelia often confessed her shame to me. "We weren't being persecuted," she said. "We weren't of a different race or religion or color. Everyone left us alone. I don't think that's a good excuse now, but in the moment, just trying to survive in this new world, it was enough. You'll never know, *Sha,* what it used to be like, before everything crumbled down around us. I hope one day you can get out of here, and then you will see."

But how was I supposed to leave? Ophelia and her husband stayed, and that sealed everything for me. My mother was born under autocratic rule. My grandfather died several years later, in a vicious flood. When my mother was barely grown, she had me and then she died giving birth again, and Ophelia would never leave the Southerly State after that. Even her love of me wasn't enough to take us away from this place. By staying put she could help other women and make sure that what happened to her daughter never happened to anyone else, not as long as she could do something about it.

Ophelia would have been eighty this year, and as much as I love her, I'm angry with her. I'm angry because she got sick and left me, sure. But tonight my rage centers on the fact that she didn't take me away from this place. Instead, she taught me everything she knew to assist women, knowing it could full well get me into the trouble I'm in now. I'm furious because all the little things that were set into motion years before my birth have come crashing down around me tonight and landed me here, in this most hopeless of places.

XLI

THE SPAN OF TIME FROM ACCUSATION to incarceration is swift, but the waiting that follows is interminable. There's a choking scent of mold in the prison. The heat is nearly unbearable. Down the corridor there's an industrial size fan. I think it just might be the only thing keeping me alive at this point. It churns endlessly, an unforgiving sound that cuts through the dank air of this silent place. If not for the noise, I think I would go mad in the heat and the quiet stillness. They took my shoes, and my feet ache with the hardness of the floor.

Three times a day, an Officer comes to the cell and sets down a tray on the floor. These meals are far worse than anything the girls at the orphanage were served. Sometimes there's a slice of grayish meat and hard bread. Sometimes it's a bowl of soup, mostly broth. I never eat it all; I'm not hungry.

The first time the Officer stepped into the cell, he pointed his gun at me. I am nothing but a shrunken woman huddled in a corner of this cement prison, but he pointed a gun at my chest anyway, no doubt to flex his own ego. In that moment I felt like I did when the preacher came to my house: trapped. He could have done anything to me. So far I've been lucky that he chooses not to. But every time he brings in a tray, I have the same feeling of helplessness. I'm at his whim. Maybe the next meal will be the one where he pins me down. Maybe he likes making me wait. Perhaps I amuse him.

I don't know what day it is. I don't know what time it is. Nobody will talk to me, not even the Officer. I am imprisoned in a timeless hole with the skittering rats and the grinding fan. Nobody has spoken to me about my rights or my defense. Obviously. I have no rights. And what I have been accused of is, in the eyes of my captors, indefensible.

Here's the thing: I'm every bit as guilty as they say, but I don't think I've actually done anything wrong. In truth, I've helped innumerable women. But their charge against me is factual. Only… how does anyone know that? Kamon was released and never Punished. I don't think they can accuse me of being her Remover if she was found innocent of her charge. And so it must be someone else I helped? Eliza Pritchard? Renee? Those were my most recent patients. Could it be someone from a long time ago? Could it be a false accusation, the accuser not even knowing how right they actually are?

Through all of this, all the solitary hours and the fear and the trepidation about what's coming, only one thing has made me cry. It's not Kamon. I will mourn her until the day I die and I will ache for her constantly, but I ran myself dry crying for her already. I haven't cried for Ophelia. For the first time, I'm relieved that she's dead, because seeing me dragged to prison would have killed her, especially since I know she would blame herself. I haven't cried for the girls at Xavier, either. They are all right, I know this for a fact. They are well-cared for. Rachel will make sure of that. They miss me, certainly, but there is no tragedy there.

But I cry endlessly for Miles. I don't know where he is. I think of how I left him at home. He might still be there, starving and literally dying of thirst, slumped at the door of my bedroom, waiting for me. He thinks I abandoned him. What if one of the Officers went back for him? They might have shot him for fun. I taste bile in the back of my throat every time I think of it. Then I realize that Emilie would have probably gone to my house when I didn't show up at work. She likely found poor Miles in a frantic state. She would have taken him, I tell myself. She knows what he means to me. Still, I cry for that sweet dog until I'm depleted, laying on the cot unmoving, whispering over and over to myself that Emilie saved him. She had to.

The thoughts that course through me and wrack my body are muddled and sow confusion. I can promise myself that Miles is okay, but I don't know that for certain. I don't know anything for certain. There are no longer any absolutes. Except for one. There is one thought that cuts through everything else. The realization of it has landed me in the darkest of places, making me vacillate between regret and guilt. Not about everything I've done, but about the one thing. The worst thing. I know it with painful clarity now. I didn't allow Kamon to make her own decisions. Everything I did was without her knowledge or consent. I am no better than Benjamin Pierre. No better than the Southerly State. I am one more entity who took away Kamon's rights over her own body. And I am the one she trusted above all others.

My action against Kamon was a different kind of assault, a different kind of betrayal. At the time I thought I was doing it out of love. I told myself I was doing what was right. But everything feels so twisted now. Did she deserve better from me? Even in the thickest haze, I know the answer. I lied to her and stole from her and deceived her. I convinced myself, at the time, that I was taking care of her. But I think I was just taking from her. I not only took away her choice; I didn't even allow her to know there was a choice to make. I have so much time to think and second-guess myself. I have come to believe I'm nothing but a thief and a liar. Will I ever be able to tell her what I did and how very sorry I am? I don't know where she is and I don't know what will happen to me. A part of me is relieved that I don't have to look in her eyes and admit my transgressions. And every time I acknowledge that cowardice, I know I've hit the deepest, darkest recesses of my soul.

XLII

I LANGUISH BETWEEN SLEEPING, forcing myself to eat, pacing, crying, and thinking. Based on the number of meals they've left on the floor of my cell, I think I've been here about a week. I haven't felt the sun on my body in what feels like a lifetime. I keep thinking of my grandfather's pirogue, wrecked somewhere out in the Parish. I remember skimming across the bayou in it, smelling the cypress trees and the wafts of magnolia, breathing in the tendrils of Spanish moss and the sickly sweet scent of decay on the green water. I would give anything, anything, to sit in that little boat again and breathe in the fresh scent of freedom. I even miss the bold colors of my flag of the Southerly State, how they flashed and snapped in the hot breeze. I miss my books, and I wonder if anyone has gone inside the house and looked through them. They are a trove of evidence against me.

There are no books here. There is nothing here. I don't know why they are making me wait so long. *Whip me already*, I want to scream at the silent Officer when he brings my tray. *Beat me. Hang me from the bloody Trinity and be done with it.* Would those moments before I swing be worth it, if I could only turn my face up to the sun? Yes, I think. For a moment of its warmth? Yes.

When I hear footsteps, I think it's time for food again. I'm not hungry. I'm never hungry, even though they must be practically starving me. But this time, the Officer has a woman with him instead of a tray. He walks behind her; she's handcuffed and I see the butt of his gun pressed into her back. He stops in front of the cell across from mine. The woman turns to look at me. She's so young. She's dressed like I am, in a long white, shapeless shift. Her long hair is wildly uncombed and her eyes are wide with fear. Other than her age, it's like looking in a mirror.

The Officer unlocks the cell with his free hand and pushes her inside. She stumbles in and turns to grasp the bars just as they clang shut behind her.

"No, please," she cries at him, even though she just had the cold metal of his gun on her a moment ago. "You can't do this. Please."

He's the same Officer who delivers my meals. But he does something to her that he has never done to me. He speaks to her. I don't think I ever pleaded with him, and maybe that's the difference.

"I don't think you're in a position to be tellin' me what I can and can't do," he says, disdain coating each word. "You filthy *Sanguidam*."

We can't be the only two in the Parish imprisoned. It's impossible. When they brought me here, I was so disoriented I don't remember the walk to the cell. I know there were stairs, lots of stairs, and I feel like we descended for a long time. Are there other prisoners above us? Are we in our own special place in hell, a purgatory of waiting for our Punishments? Is this space reserved only for Removers and *Sanguidam*?

"I haven't done anything wrong," the woman shouts, shaking the bars. When she heard that word on his lips, she knew what would become of her, and the terror took over. The rattling bars echo down the gray corridor. I don't move.

"I have committed no crime!" she shouts in his face, before falling back from the bars. She then grasps at her hair and pulls on it with two fists, as if she wants to yank it from her scalp in her complete desperation.

The Officer looks at her and then he turns to look at me. A smile curls at the edges of his mouth. "You didn't commit no crimes," he drawls, turning back and forth between us. I don't know if it's his actual words or the steely hatred he says them with, but they bring me to my knees.

"You two bitches committed sins."

XLIII

THE YOUNG WOMAN CRIES SO MUCH I can't speak to her. She doesn't hear me over her sobbing. She's the same as all the others who are strung on the Trinity. Young. Trapped. Terrified. It's hours before her cries subside. She lies down on the cold floor, her fingers curled as if she's trying to grasp invisible tree roots with which to anchor herself. Her cheek presses against the concrete and her eyes stare right through the bars of my cell. I don't think she actually sees me though. Hers is the blank stare of the babies at Xavier.

"Hey," I call to her finally. My voice is a whisper-hiss; I don't want an Officer to hear me. They might be watching us on well-hidden cameras anyway, but I take my chances. I don't care if she doesn't answer. It just feels good to speak to someone, anyone. My voice is hoarse from disuse. I gave up screaming in righteous indignation days and days ago.

I don't expect her to answer, and she doesn't. She just keeps staring through my bars and through me, her fingertips searching for something to hold on to, her face stuck to the cement. There is a gravity holding her down; I know this because it pulled me down as well. Its force decreases with time, though the hopelessness does not.

"Hey," I hiss, over and over. "Hey." Sometimes it's meant to call her and sometimes it's meant to comfort her. The only time she acknowledges that she hears me is when she rolls over, putting her curled back to me. I keep hissing, other words too, talking to myself as much as to her. She might well have been my patient at one time. A few years ago she could have been one of my charges at Xavier. A few years from now, she might have become my friend.

I keep whispering to her, even making a silly joke about the food. She doesn't respond. It's only after several trays have been delivered and collected that I finally break through her wall of silence. It's hours after dinner so it must be late evening, maybe even near midnight. Everything else about her is already broken and so the wall was the last thing. Once she starts talking, more into the air than to me, she does not stop. Her words are jumbled and frantic. Her voice is reedy and thin, like she isn't pulling enough air from her lungs to get out the words.

"Why is this happening?" she asks; the first words she's spoken since screaming at the Officer when he brought her to her cell. "I don't understand, I don't understand, I don't understand." She pulls at her hair with two fingers, her body still sprawled on the floor. I see the wild look in her eyes, accentuated by her crazed hair. I see her fingers curl and uncurl. I see each time she swallows.

The ugly greenish lights are always on and so I see her every move, even in these hours that should be midnight black. There is no secrecy in here and there is nothing sacred. I've already used the commode many times since she arrived. I knew she wasn't watching me, but it wouldn't have made a difference; it needed to be done. A few weeks ago I would never have fathomed such a thing. Still, her inattention saved me from white-hot shame that would have flushed through me from having a voyeur, however reluctant.

"Why is this happening?" she asks again, a mantra of despair and disbelief. Her words are laced with a slight twang, and I'm ashamed to admit I find it soothing. She's distraught and confused, but just hearing a voice, a female voice spiced with Cajun, calms me. The actual words she speaks are terrible, but the sounds she makes as she strings together her repeated phrases are sonorous to this lonely, weary prisoner.

Her voice cracks. She pulls herself up to sitting and rests her forehead on the chipped gray bars. I'm sitting with my own forehead pressed against the bars of my cell, and she must look like my reflection.

"The Tamburo," I say, the first words I speak to her while she's actually listening to me. "Someone accused you?"

She moans. Her whole body sinks a little and sags into the bars. She looks like she's melting into them.

"Was your accusation true?" I whisper. I don't know if anyone will hear us, but what does it matter? They have already decided she's guilty.

"Yes," she whispers back to me. The tiny word ricochets off our bars and the walls of our cells and the cement floor of the corridor.

"It's okay," I say. I want to touch her and smooth her hair. Why couldn't they at least imprison us in the same cell? Do *Sanguidam* not deserve even the company of another sinner?

Her fingers crawl up the bars and wrap around them on either side of her face. She looks like she's being held in the stocks, and I know how close that is to the truth. Suddenly she sobs and pulls back her head, still hanging on the bars, suspended in space and time for a moment, her knotted hair hanging down behind her. Then she slams her head forward into the bars. An animal sound comes from her then, more anger than anguish, and I can't do anything but jump up and shake my bars. She pulls back and does it again. I yell at her to stop, of course. I scream for an Officer to come, but nobody does. They're probably watching on a security camera somewhere, laughing. Maybe taking bets on how long it is before she beats herself unconscious, or worse. Blood runs from her hairline to her chin. I want to call out to her. I need her to listen to me, but I don't even know her name.

* * *

The woman is still after a while. I don't know how long it's been. I'm afraid she's dead. She's laying on her side, her face to me, crusted with streaks of blood. If I squint, I think I can see her body rising and falling with shallow breaths, but my mind could easily be playing tricks on me. I don't try to get her attention, because if she is alive, she needs to rest. She's in that blissful place where she's forgotten where she is, and why. I don't want to bring her back to her reality.

She's beaten herself, I think. The lashes on the Trinity can't be much worse. Was she punishing herself? Was she actually trying to kill herself? Was she in a complete rage and out of her mind? Yes, I answer silently. Yes and yes and yes.

When the Officer comes with the trays, she's still unconscious. He unlocks her bars, just enough to slip inside, and leaves the tray at her feet. I watch him kick her, really just a nudge with his toe against the back of her calves, but it makes me want to kill him. We are being treated like animals, by animals.

The offering is breakfast food: a bowl of watery oatmeal and a rotten banana. The banana smells sickeningly sweet and it's mushy inside its black peel. I have heard stories of starving people who have eaten literally anything: the soles of their shoes, paper, even a deceased person. And yet the less I eat, the less I want to eat. The food turns my stomach but so does the woman lying on the floor opposite me. When the Officer walks away from us, his steel-toe boots clinking on the floor, the woman opens her eyes. Her fingers fly to her head and she moans. I can actually watch the realization as it floods over her face.

"Don't move," I call to her. "Leave your head still." From somewhere in the back of my mind I remember Ophelia worrying that I concussed myself after falling off the tire swing she hung from a sycamore tree at the edge of the swamp. She fussed over me for two days, keeping me in her bed. I was her patient, long before I knew she had patients at all. She asked me if my vision was blurry and she told me I needed to stay in the darkened room. I wasn't allowed to read, lest I strained my eyes. But I remember enjoying her doting attention, and how she snuggled down with me and read for hours, reminding me to close my eyes so I wouldn't sneak glances at the fine print. Maybe it was *Little Women*. I can't remember.

Now I tell the woman the same things Ophelia told me, although she can't stay in the dark because the lights are blasting right over her and she has nothing to read anyway, so there's no threat of straining her eyes. Her vision is blurry, she says, cracked words forming over cracked lips. She sees colored spots of light every so often. I tell her to close her eyes, but to try and stay awake. She whimpers in pain and in fear. She looks like she's wearing a crown of thorns, there's so much blood caked to her hair.

Maybe because I can't stand to listen to her anymore, maybe because I want to comfort her, maybe because I want to comfort myself, I do something I haven't done in ages or maybe ever. I start to sing.

I sing a song Ophelia used to sing, a song of Michael rowing his boat ashore. I remember my grandmother's rich alto singing as she worked in the house. I would ask her to sing that song whenever she rowed me in the pirogue. Now, I can almost hear her telling me, "It's a sad song, *Sha.*" A song of enslaved people from so long ago. They needed something to get through this life, the promise of a better life to come." Then she sang in throaty tones of the milk and honey that awaited them on the other side of the River Jordan, if they could only row across.

I shiver as I sing of the deep, wide water. I sing to the nameless woman for a long time. The part about the milk and honey was always my favorite, and I sing that line over and over again, changing the rhythm to draw out the notes. I see the woman's breathing even out after a while, and I think that maybe she's crossed the river in her mind. I hope she stays there for a good long time. I sing into the spaces between the bars, my own vertical music staff, the last word of the song.

"Hallelujah."

XLIV

THE NEXT TIME SHE WAKES, she manages to sit up. I lean forward in my cell, as close to her as I can possibly get. We are two magnets pulling toward one another. She's a mess, but her eyes are calm now.

"Why are you here?" she asks, her voice husky and small.

"I was accused," I say. There are words I don't say: Removal, Unborn, *Sanguidam*. I let her make her own conclusions. I imagine she thinks I took care of myself just as she most certainly did. It seems unlikely that she'd guess I was a Remover.

"Did you do it?" she whispers.

"It doesn't matter. They say I did."

She moans and puts her fingers on her head. The blood is rust colored. Dried flakes and sticky gobs are matted into her hair. I wish I could put a cool cloth on her head. I remember doing that to Renee in my bedroom. And then I flash onto that room, with Ophelia's bed and her tins underneath. And that brings me to Miles, curled at the foot of the bed, and then I feel nauseous and I can't think about it anymore.

She doesn't seem to need my story. She needs to tell her own. She cries as she talks, an endless stream of leaking tears. She tells me everything. I would have assisted her if she'd found her way to me a few weeks ago. But she panicked when she discovered she was pregnant at nineteen years old. Her deeply religious parents would have disowned her, she says, and her boyfriend's mother would never let her move in with them. His mother never liked her, she says. He had no job and no prospects, and she feared she would be out on the streets if she progressed with the pregnancy. She told her boyfriend what she was going to do. It involved her father's letter opener. I don't need to say anything more about that.

Her boyfriend was sick with worry, and he didn't want to lose his Unborn. She feared he would physically try to stop her, so as soon as he left her house that evening, she went upstairs with the letter opener. She would have been all right, she tells me, her fingers clutching the bottom folds of her dress. There was blood everywhere, but her parents were out for the evening and she cleaned everything, even bleached the floor. She hid the soiled clothes under her bed and was going to dispose of them later, when she was in less pain. She slept in her bed, the evidence underneath her.

Her boyfriend came the next morning, begging her not to harm herself or their Unborn. But he soon realized what she'd done. She was getting weaker, losing too much blood. It was impossible to hide. Her mother heard them arguing. It was too much, she remembers now, the fighting and the pain and the blood. She collapsed. She lay in bed, feverish, for several days. She couldn't tell me exactly how long. The day her fever broke, two Officers appeared at her door and dragged her away. I remember exactly what that feels like.

"Was it your boyfriend's mother who told?" I ask. It didn't sound like there was even time for an accusation to be written in the Tamburo. Did someone make a *phone* call? Could you even do that?

"It was my mother," she says.

I don't think I've ever heard anything so tragic. I forget about the fact that I'm imprisoned here too, awaiting my own Punishment. The thought of being betrayed by your mother, to be forsaken like that, guts me. Women betray women here, all the time. But her own mother?

"She followed us out of the house, screaming at me for the shame I brought on the family."

"But she was the one who told," I say. "Nobody would have known."

"It was her duty to God, she said. I deserved to be Punished because of my wicked deeds. And because I robbed her of her Unborn grandchild. But she never would have accepted me being an unwed mother, either. I had no way to win. None."

"And now she will witness your Punishment?" I shouldn't talk about that. I shouldn't even say that word.

"She won't come. Not because she can't bear to see me Punished. But because of the humiliation. My father would come, I know it, but I don't think she'll allow it."

"He would come to watch you swing, or to be there to comfort you after?"

"Both, I think. He will think the Punishment is deserved, but would comfort me after I have paid for my sins." She puts her face in her hands.

"Don't be afraid," I say. "It will be quickly done, and then you will heal."

"I'm not afraid." She pulls her fingers down from her face and looks right at me. "What I did to myself was worse than anything else that can happen, I'm sure. The Punishment will be the end of it; then it will be over."

She's already mutilated herself twice, I think. But I've seen the girls on the Trinity. I don't think she has; I don't think she knows how bad it will be. And the worst of it is surely after: the lifetime of dishonor. I nod at her now, but I wonder if she truly knows how marked she will be. Ostracized. Branded.

"I'm getting out of this place," she says. "I can't do anything about being locked away now, but the Punishment will be freedom for me. After I leave the clinic, I'm running away to the Northerly State. Maybe across the ocean after that. I've heard of people doing it before."

I've thought about it myself so many times, only to be held back by the need to help women who are stuck here. But would I really try to get away? The devil you know is easier to deal with than the one you don't. Isn't that what they say? Or is that what the Southerly State says to keep us here? I don't know anymore. I don't actually understand the logistics of leaving. I know it's not an open border. I know there are fences and guns and walls. Officers are only too happy to shoot you on sight. But that means there's probably also an underground network that the Northerly State has devised to help people escape. I know how dark, underground channels work. I hope there is one to the North, and I hope she gets through. I have my doubts though. I think her reality is that she will live a shunned life right here in the Southerly State, scarred and scared, downtrodden and repressed. But that's only if she makes it through the next few days alive.

XLV

Today is Sunday. I know this because Punishments always occur on Sunday mornings, and they just took the girl away. With her gone, I don't think I've ever in my life felt so scared; not during a blackout in the little house by the bayou, not with Renee, not the night Ophelia died, not even when I found out Kamon was taken away. This is the rawest, most unrelenting kind of lonesome grief. Now that she is gone, I am once again completely isolated in this world of cement and florescent lights and metal bars.

Now that she's gone, I keep replaying the moment they took her. It happened quicker and quieter than you'd think. When I first heard footsteps coming down the hallway, I thought it was the Officer bringing our breakfast trays. But there were two sets of footsteps, one slightly quicker than the other. I saw them both a moment later. The usual Officer, the one who kicked the girl like a dog, was accompanied by an Officer I'd never seen before. This new Officer filled out his uniform much more than his partner did. He was taller too, at least by a head, and his hair was shaved so there was a shiny reflection on his head from the ugly lights.

Neither of them had any food. The shorter Officer's hands were empty. The new Officer had his gun pointed out in front of him. They didn't look at me. They went straight to the cell where the girl slept on her cot. She slept a great deal. It's the easiest way to forget where you are. I was groggy myself, having only awakened a few minutes ago. I was in that space and time when reality washes over you, reminding you, as it does every morning, that things are infinitely worse than you thought while you were sleeping. I needed to use the commode, but there was no way I would do that in front of them. I think I would die before I saw the Officers sneering at me while I relieved myself. And so I stayed on my cot and half-closed my eyes and watched. How awful it must sound, that I just watched. But what could I have done? I am helpless in here. Any noise from me would have done nothing but get me a blow to the head or a kick on the spine. A slap with a gun. Maybe worse. How quickly we can be silenced.

I looked on, feeling complicit as hell, as the shorter Officer reached down and grasped her wrist, yanking her awake. Her hair, still caked with blood, hung to one side and her body was limp. And then she snapped her head up to see him standing over her.

"I guess it's your lucky day," he said. I could see the smile on his face. She tried to wriggle away from him, but his grip was strong and the broad, tall Officer was pointing his gun at her chest, so she stopped moving.

"You're the star of the show this morning," the Officer said as she hung from his arm. "Let's go."

The Officer with the gun did not say a word. He didn't have to. He kept his shiny black weapon trained on her as she allowed her captor to drag her off the cot. But as soon as she stood up, her knees gave way and she started to fall. The Officer caught her, one hand still on her wrist and the other fist grabbing her hair. Her head snapped back. I wasn't pretending to be asleep anymore. I was sitting up with my fist pressed against my mouth. I wanted to call out but I didn't. I thought it might make things worse for her. Or maybe, I thought, it might make things worse for me. I couldn't really breathe.

She stood on her own then, but I could see her legs shaking. Her teeth started chattering. She looked right at me, but she didn't scream or whisper or beg me for help. She knew I had none to give. I looked away. I hate myself for doing that, but I did. I try to pretend that I'm this brave woman with Cajun blood in my veins, a rogue renegade fighter for women, but I couldn't even look a nineteen-year-old girl in the eye as she was being led to the Trinity. I will never forgive myself for that.

Maybe all the fight in her was gone. The wild ravaging she did to herself the other night must have sucked away any remaining defiance. Two bullish men, shielded with buttons and buckles and holsters and weapons and patches and badges, led away a frail, bruised girl, naked under her thin shift. I know this because I am naked underneath mine. I know this because hers will be bunched around her waist soon, in front of throngs of people, and there will be nothing under it.

I remembered that she told me she was not afraid. How her Punishment was not an ending, but a beginning. How she would be free after it, free to escape this repressive place and the mother who betrayed her. I hope she is successful. She won't be, I know it deep in my bones, but I hope so anyway.

But she is afraid, when the moment comes. I watched her walk away; I was crying so hard as she turned from me that my entire body shook. I saw her wet herself, a silent leaking so like her tears. It slid down her leg and between her bare feet and dribbled onto the floor. If there is a God, he must look and act just like one of the Officers, because no other God would allow this travesty. But I prayed to Him anyway, that they please not notice her humiliation. And somehow, I didn't think they did. I'm sure it had less to do with God and more with their shiny black steel-toe boots, but it was something.

In another thirty seconds, she was gone.

* * *

I'm sitting in my cell feeling the abject emptiness, wondering why my turn hasn't come. Why am I still here, when she was brought in after me? Why am I waiting like this? I've been accused of being a Remover, a crime far worse than a *Sanguidam.* Is that why? Will my fate be even worse? I've never seen a Remover on the Trinity before. I have no idea what's waiting for me.

Has whoever accused me showed actual proof somehow, of what I really am? How could the Southerly State do terrible things to me without any proof of such a grave, and rare, charge? I know, I have committed every heinous thing they say. One person's salvation is another person's sin. But wouldn't they need something, some proof, before Punishing me? After all, I don't know if a Remover has even actually been Punished before. We don't leave traces like the young girls who wield weapons against themselves. We are infinitely harder to find. But we are more evil, in their eyes. We are murderers many times over.

I sit on the cold, hard floor all morning. My breakfast never comes, and I imagine the Officer was so giddy with excitement, my nourishment slipped his mind. He must be in the Square now, jeering with the crowd. I rock back and forth, my calloused feet tucked under me, and think about nothing but the girl and the wooden tripod. Is it done? I ask myself over and over. What about now? Now?

I wonder if they cleaned the blood from her self-inflicted injuries and combed her hair. I wonder if they gave her a clean white shift to wear. She looked far more beaten and bedraggled than any other receiver of a Punishment I'd previously witnessed. Would they want her to appear as though she'd been abused in jail? Then again, would anyone care? They would probably think she got what she deserved.

I know that the Punishment is over when a tray arrives with gray egg salad and a package of crumbled saltine crackers. I'm still sitting on the floor, still rocking. A dingy orange tray juts out from the Officer's hand. He stands a little taller and his chest puffs out a bit more than usual. He's smirking. His breathing is quick, and I bet his heart is still racing from the excitement and probably even some twisted arousal. I remember how he called us bitches and told us that we were far worse than criminals; we were sinners. But there is nothing pious about him. I can't imagine that someone as cruel as he actually cares about the lives of the Unborn. What he cares about is punishing women. He cares about being loyal to the Southerly State. He believes what he is told to believe. He's like every other rabid member of the crowd that surrounded the Trinity this morning.

He breaks his rule of not speaking to me when he delivers my meal. This time he comes close to me and leans down so that his mouth grazes my ear.

"Your friend pissed herself, she was so scared." His words buzz over me. "And she was right to. You should see what she looks like now." He laughs, a snuffled snort that he's too excited to suppress. I picture the God I prayed to, his uniform identical to the one hovering over me, a matching sneer.

"I guess you're next," he whispers with dramatic breathiness. He's finding this encounter a delicious ending to his morning.

I imagine myself turning my head and spitting in his face. The satisfaction would be almost worth the beating that would surely follow. Almost. But I'm as timid as I was when I looked away from that girl urinating all over herself. I just sit and stare straight ahead, waiting until he finally straightens up and walks away. Only then do I allow myself to breathe.

XLVI

At first I think I'm imagining it when I see Rachel walking toward me. She looks so familiar, with her long skirt and loose-fitting blouse, and her hair pulled into a tight bun. Her mouth is twisted into a lopsided pucker, like she's gnawing the inside of her cheek. I tell myself I'm asleep, dreaming of my days in Xavier, which already feel hazy and incredibly far away. But then she comes to stand in front of my bars and I see the Officer at her side, the tall one who pointed his gun at the girl this morning. Was that really only a few hours ago? And why is my supervisor here? Why is her face contorted into that screwed up grimace?

"Five minutes," the Officer says to her. He isn't smiling, and I think he probably didn't smile at the Punishment either. He does not look as though he takes pleasure in suffering, as his partner clearly does. Still, I know he will lead me to the Trinity when he is told to, completely at peace, just following his orders.

"Rachel?" I ask stupidly.

Her mouth untwists and she tries to smile at me, but you can't really smile at a filthy, barefoot woman behind bars and so she settles for a quick nod.

"I don't have a lot of time." She gestures toward the Officer, who is pacing at the other end of the corridor. "They weren't going to let me in, but I said I needed to speak with you in regards to your job. In order to inform your replacement."

She did not say substitute, and we both catch her misnomer at the same time. I feel myself sway. Does she think I won't ever return to the orphanage? I think about the girl who was led away.

She saw her Punishment as a release; the start of her new life. It feels like it will be the end of mine.

Rachel, always so stiff and standoffish, takes a step forward and presses her face against the bars. She slides her hands through the narrow slits, palms up. Her fingers curl toward her chest, beckoning me. I don't think I have ever touched her before, but the sight of those smooth round fingertips is so inviting, I step closer and rest my fingers on hers. They are soft and warm. It makes me want to cry.

"Hey," the Officer calls, and strides in our direction.

"Please," Rachel says, never taking her eyes off me. "Might we have a moment to pray together?"

He nods and resumes pacing. The other Officer would have laughed and wondered what a sinning bitch like myself needed to pray about. I'm grateful he's not here.

I don't want to pray, but I don't want to lift my fingers from hers either.

"Lean in," she says, and we are so close I smell her soap. I'm suddenly horrified about what I smell like, but her expression does not show the disgust she must feel. I haven't washed since I've been here. I'm sick with shame at the thought of it.

Rachel glances down the corridor. The Officer is all the way at the other end. She slips one hand away from me to cross herself and nods, indicating that she wants me to do the same. An intimate moment that might once have felt awkward now feels more comforting than I can describe. I don't think her prayers will work; I don't think there is any hope for me. But I want to stand here in the warmth of another person, with soft hands and a soft voice. Her voice has never been soft before, at least not toward me.

She slips her hand through the bars again and my fingers find hers immediately.

"Three minutes," the guard yells. Rachel stiffens. She begins to whisper to me, but her words are anything but a prayer.

"I have Miles," she says. "I went to your house as soon as I was notified of what happened to you. I had to break the back window to get in. But I knew you would want me to take him. He's at the orphanage. The girls love him so much. They miss you, you know. He has brought them so much comfort."

I can barely stand, I'm so relieved. I can't believe she thought to do that.

"Thank you, thank you so much," I say. "Did Emilie ask you to do it?"

She shakes her head. "I only have a few minutes, and there's a lot I need to say."

"Okay." I'm not focusing on her words. I'm weak and exhausted and completely drained from this morning, and now I'm shaking with relief. I have little space in my head for anything else she might tell me.

"Listen to me," she says. "Please. I know what you did. What you used to do."

I shake my head. I can't have this conversation. She's very quiet but I'm always wondering about hidden cameras. She must sense my nervousness, because she drops her voice even lower, until I have to watch her mouth move to understand her barely-there whispers. I'm sure she's trying to be kind, and she probably wants to pray over me to absolve me of my sins, but I can't admit to anything, not even in a whisper. I will not. Maybe she's working for the Southerly State, sent in to get my confession before they destroy me. I start to pull away my hands but she grasps my wrists.

"I knew Ophelia Dupre," she says to me. "I knew her very, very well."

It was my grandmother who suggested I apply to be a worker at Xavier, so I'm not entirely surprised that Rachel knew her. Perhaps that was why I got hired in such a difficult position to obtain. Ophelia must have slipped in a good word for me. But it's the way Rachel is looking at me. The way she says she knew her very,

very well. She's staring at me, waiting. I blink. I will not betray my grandmother, in her death or my own.

"I know what Ophelia was." She lowers her head and keeps her lips very still. I strain to hear, since I can no longer read her lips. "I know how she helped women. I know what she taught you. I know this because I'm a Jane, too."

XLVII

I FEEL LIKE I'M FREEFALLING through the sky, only the sky is a narrow black tunnel with a rushing wind.

"Time's just about up," the Officer says. He sounds bored.

"We've just finished praying, and I'll only be a minute with my questions," Rachel says in an entirely different voice than she was using with me. "Thank you so much for understanding. It's for the young girls of Xavier. If you would please be so kind?"

"A minute," he says, but I think he will give us a long minute. What's it to him, really?

I don't understand what she's just told me about my grandmother. She's talking but I can't hear anything over that rush of wind in my ears. If her hands weren't gripping my wrists, I think I'd fall to the ground.

"Don't say such things." I want her to leave. She isn't going to get any admissions out of me, not about myself or my grandmother. "Go away. Please."

"You need to listen to me. We don't have time. I've written a request to Pote and to the Office of the Southerly State on your behalf, attesting to your innocence. But I don't know if it will do any good." The look on her face tells me she's certain it will not. "You can return to Xavier when you have recuperated. Take all the time you need. But that's not why I'm here. I wanted to see you and tell you that you saved a patient of mine not long ago. You have saved many women. None of it has been in vain, no matter what they tell you. No matter what they do to you." She gives my hands a squeeze. "And you will get through it. You will."

"You aren't a Jane," I say. It infuriates me that she uttered such a thing. "You were always very quick to say that Punishments were fair. You pray all the time."

"And you proudly fly the flag of the Southerly State on your porch. We all do what we must. I feel an obligation now to make sure you're all right. I hate that it's taken me this long to figure out how to come and speak with you. Ophelia helped my sister many years ago. I showed up on that porch in total desperation, and she took us both in and did what was necessary. My sister would have died otherwise. And I went back to the porch a few weeks later, alone, and told your grandmother that I wanted to do what she did. I wanted to save women, too."

"You really need to wrap up, Ma'am," the Officer calls.

Her words have a vertiginous effect on me. I pull my hands away and grasp the metal bars to steady myself.

"I understand," Rachel says to the Officer, before she leans closer. "You were ten years old," she says. "I never saw you, you were always sound asleep in your room when I visited. She told me that one day she was going to teach you everything she knew. But I was long gone by then. Once I was skilled enough on my own, I couldn't see Ophelia anymore. Sometimes we would pass one another in church, but we never spoke. It would have been too dangerous to be seen together. It would have been be so beneficial to have a network, but that network would also tie everyone together, and make it that much easier to bring everyone down. And so the only time I ever talked to her again was when she came to Xavier and asked me to find your application and make sure you were hired. She was worried about you. She knew she was sick by then and she wanted to make sure you could sustain yourself. She made me promise not to say anything to you about what we did. Still, I wanted to several times. I very nearly did. But she was right; it's too dangerous. You became close with some of the other workers. If you'd confided in one of them, believing you could fully trust them, they could have turned on either one of us. Especially if someone had a grievance against a supervisor they didn't like. Besides, you didn't need my help. You were fine on your own."

"Oh my God." I stare at her pink gums and yellow teeth. I imagine us as colleagues in a clinic in a very different place. There were so many times when I needed to talk to someone. When I needed someone's help.

"You saved Renee," Rachel says. We both turn at the sound of the Officer's boots. He's done warning us and he's striding down the hall. "I didn't have the skill set required for her injuries. I didn't know if you did, but I knew your grandmother did, and I didn't know what else to do. And so I found myself driving to Ophelia's once again."

I'm in a state of complete disbelief. I know I will have hours alone to go over what she's telling me, but I want her to say the words again and again until I understand them.

"So if she died, it would be on my hands?"

"I didn't think she would die, if you were anything like your grandmother. It was her best chance at survival."

"You couldn't have done anything like what you're saying while working at Xavier," I say. I don't believe a word of it. Maybe Rachel found out about Renee somehow and is actually my accuser. My mind is muddled but I think I've said too much. I think I've confessed to something.

"I'm available when someone needs help. They know how to send for me," she says. "I have never had anyone come to me. There are too many people at Xavier. But I can go to them, late at night."

"I don't believe you," I say. "But I need to know—did you really take Miles?"

The footsteps are mere feet away. We have run out of time.

"He's with the girls. I promise."

"You need to come with me, Ma'am," the Officer says. His chest bulges against his uniform. His gun is tucked in its holster but he wouldn't need anything more than his own strength to deal with either of us. Rachel looks up at him, Puritan in face and hair and dress, and crosses herself. And then, as she allows him to lead her away, she looks back at me. "I will pray for your soul," she says. "You will be all right, *Sha.*"

When I hear that word, my whole body feels like it cracks in two, and I know that she told me the truth. It makes me feel the weight of loneliness even more. There was someone like me so close, all that time, but for both our safety, she didn't allow herself to enter my orbit. And yet with that word, I also feel Ophelia standing in the cell with me. I hear her shushing, '*Sha, Sha, Sha,*' with every footfall as Rachel disappears.

XLVIII

If I'm suddenly allowed visitors, why didn't the poor girl in the other cell have any? Was she not allowed? Or did nobody want to come for her? She must be in a clinic by now, probably slick with glistening ointment on her bare and bloodied back. Is someone sitting by her bedside? Is a nurse changing her bandages a little too roughly, administering a bit more punishment? Is she lying there with closed eyes, starting to plan her trip north? Has she been beaten into submissiveness? I will never know the answers. I'm sure it's better that way.

I don't want to think about Miles either, though I'm so relieved he's all right. The girls at the orphanage will lavish him with attention. I wonder if he looks for me. I'm sure he's picked up my scent in my room and down the hallway. I don't know if I'll manage to escape a Punishment, or if I'll escape a Punishment alive, so there's a good chance he won't see me again. I think of Rachel's face, trying to mask her fear for me. I remember her promise that my job is waiting for me. We both knew she didn't really believe what she was saying.

Seeing them take away the girl, seeing her wet herself in abject fear, brings a new level of terror to me. There's nothing to do but think. I still barely believe what Rachel told me, even though I know she was telling the truth. It's unfathomable. How I wish I had someone to talk it all over with. I don't understand why Emilie hasn't come. Did she not have a good enough excuse to give the Officers? Couldn't she have accompanied Rachel, pretending she was there at the behest of her supervisor? But I think

I understand why I haven't seen her. She can't face me in here, locked away and waiting. She knows my fear of the Trinity. She warned me too many times. And she knows too much about me. Of course she needs to stay away—for both our sakes.

Maybe a Remover gets more time to languish in jail because it's agony to wait. This is a punishment in and of itself. They don't even have to do anything to me; I torment myself with the wondering and the guessing. A beating at this point would almost be welcome.

I don't know what my saturation point is. Every time I think I've reached it, another wave of swampy water washes over me and pollutes my thoughts with more flotsam. They must know what they're doing to me. Leaving me here would be a far worse fate than taking me outside in the glorious sunshine and whipping me. Maybe they'll just hold me here until I go mad. I think I'm halfway there already.

Every time I hear someone coming, I'm actually hopeful that the time for my Punishment has arrived. It's psychotic, how they make you actually want it, hope for it, crave it. But it's never that time. And I should know better, because it's not Sunday anymore. Sunday is six days away, and then five. The footsteps are never anything other than a delivery of food. For two days, six trays worth, I listen to those footsteps. And then on the third day, which my muddled mind thinks must be Wednesday, it's not the breakfast tray that arrives. It's Preacher Pote.

* * *

I remember the way he looked as he left my house: rebuffed and embarrassed. Now his demeanor is the complete opposite. His face is pulled tight and his fists are clenched at his sides. He is in complete control of himself. Of course I am different too, and nothing but a filthy husk of the woman he once found so alluring.

He crouches down in front of my cell so that he's looking up at me. I'm on my cot, hugging my knees to my chest. I didn't move when I saw him approach. I think that surprised him. I didn't say a word. But my eyes haven't left him.

"You should come closer so we can talk properly," he says. He holds out one hand, the other touching the floor with three fingertips to keep his balance. "Please."

I don't know if it's desperation to be near any living person, or because he gave me a directive and I'm too broken to resist, but I walk over to him and sink down to the floor, with only the bars between us. I stare at the exposed metal beneath the chipped paint. His face is fuzzy behind the bars. I don't want to focus on him.

He says my name. There is no affection in his voice.

"It might go easier for you if you confess," he says. "If you tell me what you know, if you lead us to others like you, we might even be able to make your Punishment go away." He makes no mention of our time together. I think of the flowers he brought me, the framed artwork, his unwanted kisses. It's like none of it ever happened. And how interesting, I think, that despite his earlier protestations, he does indeed consider himself powerful enough to make Punishments disappear.

"I don't know anything," I say. It's almost true, too. A few days ago, I didn't know anything about anyone. And now they would have to actually rip me from limb to limb before I give away Rachel. What is it that he thinks I know?

"What happened?" I ask him. My voice cracks. I never wanted his attention on me, but I think I was safer when I had it.

He laughs, a terrible sound that pings off the metal bars.

"You know exactly what happened," he says. "I'm the fool who had no idea what you really are. You played me completely, Miss Dupre. I thank God I found out the truth before it was too late."

"William," I say. He cuts me off with a disgusted snort.

"Do not," he says, "even think to say my name." He hardens his eyes on me. "You need to confess," the preacher says. "What you have done is heinous. A sin greater than all other sins. But telling the truth will set you free."

"I have nothing to confess," I say.

"You're lyin' to me," he says. He takes off his hat and sets it on the floor.

He says my name again. I hate how it sounds in his mouth.

"Maybe you should go," I say. "I have nothing to confess, but I think I'm beyond saving anyway."

Pote's eyes slide around inside their sockets. He doesn't blink for a long time, and then when he does, it's a slow blink, as if he has to remind himself to open his eyelids again.

"I see you're going to do this the hard way," he says. "I was hoping it didn't have to be like this." He narrows his eyes and looks straight into me. Through me. "I don't need your confession. I know everything I need to know about you. I just need the information about the others."

"I don't know what you're talking about." But the way he's looking at me, I suddenly think that maybe he's not bluffing. He knows something.

"Cut the shit," he says. And then he invokes the same spirit Rachel did, only he does it in the cruelest way possible. "I know about Ophelia," he says. I can't help it—I gasp. "She's burnin' in hell right this very moment for the many sins of her life. And you'll follow her, unless you cooperate with me. I heard all about your plants and what you have hiding in your house. It sickens me that I set foot in there. I was horrified when I found out what you did to that poor innocent girl in the orphanage. Thank God I had her sent far away from you. You can't hurt her anymore. Now don't you want to try to redeem yourself? Don't you want to save whatever shred of your soul you can? Tell me who the other Removers are, and help yourself."

I feel all the blood in my body turn to liquid ice. I know I've given away the truth with my stunned expression, but it doesn't matter, does it? He already knows the whole truth. And there's no way he could. Nobody knew all of those things, about my grandmother and what I had hidden in the house and about what I did for Kamon. To her, I correct myself. What I did *to* her. Nobody knew those things except for my closest friend in the world.

Emilie.

XLIX

I SAY HER NAME OUT LOUD without even realizing it. Emilie. My voices raises up in a question. I know it's her, that's not the question. The question is *why.*

I'm not crouched down anymore. I stood up as I said her name, and Pote rose with me. He looks surprised. He's said more than he wanted to and given away his source. But again, what does it matter?

"She came to me to confess her own sins," he says. I can't focus on his words. I keep seeing her face, with the golden freckles under her eyes and her crooked smile. I see her turning around to wave at me in church. I see her pinching a crayfish and sucking the juice from its curled tail. I see her walking beside me on our way to Xavier. I see her begging me to be careful. "They will destroy you," I hear her say. Was it more than a warning? Was it a threat? And then I see her stepping into the hallway of the orphanage with a baby on her hip, and I understand everything. It wounds me more than the Trinity ever could.

"Her sins were eatin' at her soul," Pote says. I can't breathe but I stay with his words. I need to hear this. All of it. "She came to me to confess the Unborn she had removed, years ago. The guilt was tearing her apart. She wanted to pray with me. She said she had nobody else to talk to. Her family didn't know. The Unborn's father is long gone. And her dear friend would never understand. At first I didn't know she was talking about you. Imagine my disgust when I learned what you really are."

I try to regulate my breathing, but it's suddenly impossible. I grip onto the bars and watch his mouth. He's left his hat on the floor and I have an urge to slip my bare foot through the bars and crush it.

"Emilie was so conflicted. She wants to be a mother, you know. She feels robbed. She made a mistake. But the more she thought about it, the more she realized that she'd been pressured by you. She thought if she'd had more time to think about it, she would have come to a different decision. But you were insistent, she said. You told her what was best for her. She saw that with clarity as she prayed about it."

I'm shaking my head. I remember comforting Emilie at the time. I carefully explained her options. I told her that she didn't have much time, since she was already well past the optimal five-week mark for the herbs to be their most potent. But one thing was always certain: she didn't want the baby. But that was years ago, and she's been surrounded by babies for so long. I'm crying, for her and for me. Pote keeps talking. Apparently, my tears don't bother him as much as hers did.

"She was sick about it," he says. "She hated herself for allowin' such a thing to happen. It tore at her. And then she told me about the girl. SC0708. How the same person who assisted her so long ago took it upon herself to induce a miscarriage on that poor girl— Pote raises his voice like he's preaching to his congregation— *without even consulting her*." Satisfied with his delivery, he lowers his voice and shakes his head. "The sin of it was too great to keep to herself. It was breakin' her, she said, carrying the weight of it around. It was consuming her."

Oh God. I obviously knew it was bothering her but I didn't know how much. Did I misread her sad resignation about what I wanted to do as acceptance? I didn't know the thought of it was bending and breaking her. Fuck. I hate myself for telling her. I hate myself for putting her in that position. I hate myself, period. I have failed…failed everyone.

"Emilie saw the decisions that you made for SC0708, and she felt that perhaps you'd persuaded her to do something while she was not quite in her right mind during her own...situation. That's what sent her to me." Pote looks at me very carefully. "I do think she transferred what happened with the orphan to her own situation from years ago. It triggered something in her, brought her back to her own grief." He looks at me like he is almost confessing to me. "I hated hearing it. I really did. But what she told me was illegal and beyond being a crime, it is a sin. Sins upon sins, really. I had no choice but to accuse you. It's my God-given duty to do so." His blue eyes narrow.

"She didn't say your name," he says. "But I knew it was you, when she talked about the orphanage. You begged me to help the girl, but you didn't tell me the truth. You tried to seduce a man of God, when you'd done the worst thing you can do in God's eyes." His hands are still stuck through the bars. I look down at them. They're pale and smooth. His fingernails are bitten down to little nubs. There's a crescent-shaped scar on his thumb.

"She offered herself up for Punishment, you know. She said she deserved it. But I could see that she'd already suffered so much. She's repented and has been saved. A Punishment would be unnecessary.

"I told her I knew who she was talking about. You should see how she cried. She begged me not to do anything. She said she thought it was a private confession, but I told her she was doing God's work. I told her there was a reason the truth came out. It set her free, just like it will do for you. Such transgressions cannot be kept in confidence. I told Emilie that I'd have you arrested and just let you sit in jail and think over everything. Give you a chance to atone. Give you a chance to cooperate with me."

The same Officer who hurried Rachel paces at the end of the hall. He hasn't called out to the preacher to tell him to rush. I suppose a man of God gets all the time he needs.

"So," Pote says, leaning in to me, "if you tell me the names of other Removers, there might be somethin' I can do for you."

"I don't know what you're talking about," I say.

Preacher William Pote twists his lips into a sneer and leans in close to me. "How do you have the nerve to lie to me now, after everything you're already done? Who did you think you were, to come into my church and invite me to your home, tryin' to use me to get what you want? Lyin' to my face while you sinned behind my back? You played the part of a seductress well, and I'm just thankful I was strong enough to resist you. Little did I know how perfect my choice of artwork was for you. Delilah was a traitorous woman, and all Samson did was love and trust her." He looks ready to spit at me. "I don't even think you were worried about the girl. I think you were tryin' to save yourself."

He's already changing the narrative of our encounters. When he says these words with such contempt in his voice, I understand that it wouldn't matter if I did give him names. What really matters is that I tried to manipulate him and, by doing so, I insulted his ego. I emasculated one of the Parish's most influential men, even though nobody knows that but the two of us. He wants me to pay for what I have done, not to Kamon and all those other women, but to him.

"They will destroy you," I hear Emilie say again. And so, it seems, with her help, they shall.

L

When they come for me, I instinctively scuttle away like a Louisiana blue crab trying to outpace a net, but there's nowhere to go. I'm already inside their trap. The shorter Officer grips me underneath my armpits and pulls me off the floor. The taller Officer watches. His gun is aimed at my chest. If I fight back, will he pull the trigger? Would that be an easier end? But no, I don't think he would shoot me. The public is ravenous for the display. And that's how I know, with the Officer's hands pinching the skin under my arms, what day it is. Sunday.

We walk up the steps I remember descending when they brought me into this place. From the stairwell, I hear men on each floor we pass banging on their cell bars, hooting and calling out disgusting profanities. It was quiet when I was brought in. They all know what day it is. They are riled up in anticipation, though they won't see the Punishment. Maybe they know the Officers who patrol their floors will be in a good mood today. Maybe they'll relay the best details.

I trip halfway up the last flight of stairs. The Officer, who's had his hands on me the entire time, shoves me forward instead of grabbing me, and my face hits the edge of the cement stair. Only after I hit it does he yank me back toward him. I taste the blood running from my cheek into the corner of my mouth. A drop falls onto my white shift, blooming outward like a crimson ink stain on paper. *Sanguidam*, I think. But that's not even the word for me. I don't think they have a clever Latin amalgamation of words for the travesty they think I am.

The tall Officer pushes open a metal door and suddenly we are outside. The sunlight that I so badly yearned for sears my eyes and I can't see anything but harsh flashes of light. The other Officer twists my hands behind me and snaps handcuffs on my wrists before I can even use my arms to shield my eyes. There's a van waiting for us. I can't see more than its shadowy outline but I hear it rumbling. A moment later they shove me into the backseat, the Officers flanking me on both sides. I haven't said a word this whole morning. What is there to say?

We drive for an endless amount of time. I can't do anything but stare at the back of the head of our driver. Little gray hairs travel down his neck. His hands are loose on the wheel. He's relaxed, I think. None of this means anything to him.

I still don't have my shoes. Will they be returned to me afterwards? I don't know how I'll even survive the morning, but I can't stop thinking about those shoes. They walked endless miles back and forth between the bayou and Xavier. They walked beside Emilie's matching pair, almost every day, for years. The thought of her makes me wonder what I have to return to after this is over. The friend I valued like a sister betrayed me, even if it was unintentional. The girl I loved like a daughter is gone. There will be no women for me to help, since my secret is out. Rachel promised me my job, but I'll be shunned by society. Surely someone will have me removed from the orphanage. If people find out what happened with Kamon, they'll never let me near a child again. I think of Belinda, who would be so hurt that I lied to her face the entire time we were caring for Kamon. I could never go back there.

We're pulling up to the entrance of the Place d'Armes Square. The van crawls to a stop and they pull me out. My arms are so sore. The driver doesn't look back at me. I wonder if he's going to leave the van and join the throngs of people in the square. I'm strangely relieved when I hear him rev the engine and drive away.

Someone is playing a drum. It's militant in its rhythm. The sun cuts through the thin material of my dress and I know I'm already completely exposed to the jeering crowd. My legs aren't going to hold me for much longer. The Officers drag me along a narrow path that's been roped off to keep it clear from onlookers. I'm not resisting, I just can't walk anymore. The terror of this place and of this day has taken over my body.

A Punisher stands at the base of the tripod. Only his eyes are visible through a narrow slit in his mask. He's waiting for me. I try to run; there's nobody on earth who would see this hulking man and willingly be led to him. But I'm gripped on all sides, by my two Officers and two others who have materialized out of the crowd. My handcuffs are removed but my arms are held straight at my sides as if I'm in a vise. Fingers dig into me on all sides. The anticipation of what's to come is absolutely excruciating. I don't scream, but I'm already hyperventilating.

A whip dangles in my Punisher's casual grip. Through the haze of my fear, I look into his eyes. I know those eyes. Those eyes belong to Benjamin Pierre. This is the new job he's found, the one I forced him to find. He's smiling under his mask. Or is it him? Maybe I only think it is. He's done this to me, to all of us. Does it matter whether he's the one wielding the lash?

I would give anything to hear the smooth notes of a saxophone drifting across this gathering place right now. I would give anything to see people strolling through this square, laughing and chatting under the sycamores and ducking into restaurants. How idyllic it must have once been. And then I realize something so crazy, I almost want to laugh: It wasn't perfect for some people. For some people, today is perfect. The dystopia that my grandparents fearfully saw coming was the dawn of a utopian society for others. They think the Southerly State is exactly as it should be, finally. I don't belong here, and I know unequivocally that after this Sunday morning, I will find a way to leave this place.

I will find a way to get myself to that mythic Northerly State, or perhaps even the glimmering Pacific sea that has lured me with a siren's call for my entire life. I have to.

Of course, there will be one last thing to do here first. I have to get Kamon out of here as well. I'd take every one of my girls if I could, and every other girl in Xavier as well. But I cannot leave here without Kamon. For so long, I've stayed to help countless women. Now I know I need to leave, to help one girl. The women needed me, but Kamon needs me more. I have an unexpected ally now. Rachel will help me; she knows the headmistresses at other orphanages. Surely something can be arranged. I know it won't be easy, but I will do it, because a mother's love can make you do anything.

I have said so much of my story. I think I have said everything. But my God, have I still not said my real name? It's just as well. That woman will not exist beyond today. There is blessed relief in that thought, of shedding this old name and this old life, and breaking through borders and walls to come out the other side. The Punisher takes a step toward me. He looks strong, but you know what? I think I am stronger. No matter what they say, I know I am not an anomaly or a heroine or the devil. I am simply one woman, any woman, every woman. Womb. Man. I send up a prayer to Ophelia and square my shoulders. Best to get on with it.

AUTHOR'S NOTE

Although THE PUNISHINGS is set in the near future, aspects of it are rooted in the past. As I began research for my novel, it became increasingly clear to me that our society is not as far removed from some ideals and practices as one would hope.

The punishments that occur on the Trinity have undertones of the Salem witch burnings. Women's clothing was often ripped away first, stripping them of their dignity and sexualizing them in front of an angry crowd. Quite often, a wooden tripod was employed to string up the victims. Like Jane in the novel, women were often imprisoned in dungeons, with no evidence beyond hearsay, and held indefinitely.

The abortifacients mentioned in the novel were also taken from history. Pills like Farrer's Catholic Pills and Madame Drunette's Lunar Pills were cleverly marketed to women, "warning" them of ill effects on pregnancy. Several herbs, such as pennyroyal and birthwort, were used to make teas that would terminate a pregnancy as well. Today, as clinics are closing and bodily autonomy is threatened, many women are turning to the internet to research alternative methods.

The Tamburo was indeed used in Florence, Italy as an anonymous system to turn in "sodomites" in the thirteenth century. While this novel was written and copyrighted in 2020, I got chills when a year later, the state of Texas passed Senate Bill 8, which is not only a near-complete ban on abortion, but allows vigilantes to sue anyone who they say performs, aids, or abets an abortion. The accuser will be awarded $10,000 if they win the case. Other states are sure to follow. While I used the Tamburo to add dramatic action to a storyline, a year later it seems frighteningly close to a new reality.

While I did not have the protagonist in THE PUNISHINGS reveal her true name, her reason for going by Jane is also based on the past. In the 1960's, floating clinics existed to provide safe abortions. To find one, women were instructed to call a designated phone number and ask for "Jane." I also had the Southerly State revert back to the time in the 1960's in the United States, when only married women were allowed to obtain a prescription for birth control pills.

As for the zealous teachings of Preacher Pote and the governance of the Southerly State, many of their traits fit the list from "Fourteen Ways of Looking at a Blackshirt," by Umberto Eco, an Italian book depicting fascism. Nationalism, machismo, disdain for intellectuals, and intertwining religion and government are all employed tactics.

ACKNOWLEDGMENTS

Thank you to my son for making me smile each and every day, and for being the very best kid anyone could ever ask for.

Endless appreciation for my husband for reading countless drafts, supporting my career change from the very first moment, and believing in all my books.

A tremendous thank you to my parents for being my earliest readers and biggest champions.

I will never be able to express proper thanks to my retired agent who worked with tireless enthusiasm on this novel and shaped it into what it is today.

And thank you to so many friends and family for their excitement and encouragement throughout this entire process. I'm lucky to have each and every one of you in my life.

READING GROUP GUIDE

I grew up with the comfortable understanding that women had control over their bodies. The struggles that women faced throughout history, and the Roe v. Wade ruling of 1973, seemed like events rooted far in the past. I assumed that "forward" was the only direction women would continue to move. With the introduction of severely restrictive abortion bills over the past few years, rights that women once took for granted are now under threat. This frightening realization inspired me to write THE PUNISHINGS.

I began to speculate about a future where two very different sets of ideals caused a fracture in the United States of America. I imagined a woman trapped under the oppressive laws of a dystopian new world that was created in the split. A woman forced to contend with two aspects that arise from a total abortion ban: overcrowded orphanages, and desperate women who put their lives in danger by taking matters into their own hands.

THE PUNISHINGS touches on women's rights, motherhood, the battle between science and religion, and life in a patriarchal society. There are several moral gray areas throughout the novel, some of which I still struggle with, hoping to find a 'right' answer. The questions below are meant to guide you in a thought-provoking discussion as you navigate through your own opinions and beliefs.

1. Though THE PUNISHINGS is set in the future, the world the characters are living in has retreated into the past. Women don't have rights to their own bodies, segregation exists again, and religion trumps science. How does this world compare to the U.S. today?

2. In the novel, the Southerly State has reverted backward in technology. Do you think there will come a day when society has become as technologically advanced as it can be? Think about how inundated we are with our own inventions and the waste they create. Will we have to take a step back to save ourselves and our planet?

3. Did Ophelia Dupre make the right decision to stay in the Southerly State and assist women? Was she right to teach Jane such a controversial and dangerous practice?

4. What keeps Jane in the Southerly State? Does she view her work as upholding a woman's right to choose, or as a necessary evil to save lives?

5. Jane wants to be a mother, but knows the likelihood of that happening is quite small. Is that why she becomes a mother figure to Kamon, or is something else at play? Do you think the loss of her own mother influenced her decisions?

6. Jane is sometimes angry with herself for her lack of action, such as when she handed out the history booklets to the orphans, even though she knew the information was false. Could she/should she have stood up for what she believed?

7. The orphanage lacks resources. Discuss the urgency to protect the rights of the Unborn, as compared to the urgency to properly care for the orphans.

8. The arcane punishments and detrimental medical procedures in the book have all occurred throughout history. Do you think we learn from our mistakes, or is history cyclical?

9. Did Jane do the right thing by not telling Kamon she was pregnant? Did she do the right thing by terminating the pregnancy without Kamon's knowledge or consent? Is there

ever an instance where it would be justified to keep something from a person if you believe you are protecting them?

10. Is Jane any better than the Southerly State since she didn't allow Kamon bodily autonomy?

11. Is Preacher William Pote evil or misguided? If someone believes something is right in their heart, does that justify their actions?

12. How might it have helped Jane if she'd known the truth about Rachel all along? Was Rachel's self-preservation detrimental to them both, or a necessary precaution?

13. Why didn't Emilie turn Jane in as soon as she heard about her plans for Kamon? Do you think she subconsciously wanted Jane to be found out when she confessed her own "sins" to the preacher?

14. Do laws prevent people from doing things? Are there instances where they sometimes just make an inevitable action more dangerous?

15. Do you agree/disagree with Jane's actions? Why? Do you think she got what she deserved?

16. At the end of the book, Jane comes to the startling conclusion that the Southerly State, a place that has been hellish for her, is an ideal society for others. Discuss how we can move forward, when our ideas about an "ideal" society are often so different.

17. Do you think America will heal its divisions, or will there one day be a separation based on differing ideals?

18. Do you think Jane managed to leave the Southerly State?

ABOUT THE AUTHOR

H. R. Bellicosa is a writer, avid traveler and most importantly, a proud mom. She lives with her husband, son, a sweet dog, and a cantankerous cat, all of whom make her laugh every day.